Susan Page h... ...s for God.
Her stories never fa... ...gives spe-
cial atten... ...love, and
I highly reco...

—TRACIE PETERSON, bestselling author of the
Striking a Match series

Susan Pa... ...occupy
a great d... ...er sev-
eral years... ...of her
titles as I... ...ne who
demands... ...te set-
tings, and... ...today's
finest Cl...

—C... ...oks

Susan P... ...g read.
Strong c... ...hat are
complet... ...e top of
my to-b...

—L... ...s
D... ...ard
w...

Susan P... ...a page-
turning...

—L...
2(

I have come to expect exciting plots, g... ...s over-
coming physical and spiritual challenges, and vibrant and his-
torically accurate settings from Susan Page Davis. And she
doesn't disappoint.

—HENRY MCLAUGHLIN, award-winning
author of *Journey to Riverbend*

TEXAS
TRAILS

←— ★ —→

COWGIRL TRAIL

SUSAN PAGE DAVIS

A
MORGAN FAMILY
SERIES

MOODY PUBLISHERS
CHICAGO

©2012 by
SUSAN PAGE DAVIS

Edited by Pam Pugh
Interior design: Ragont Design
Cover design: Gearbox
Cover image: Masterfile (842-03198572)
Author photo: Marion Sprague of Elm City Photo

Library of Congress Cataloging-in-Publication Data

Davis, Susan Page.
  Cowgirl trail / Susan Page Davis.
     p. cm. — (Texas trails : a Morgan Family series)
  ISBN 978-0-8024-0586-9
  1. Cowgirls—Fiction. 2. Cattle drives—Fiction. 3. Families—History—Fiction. 4. Texas—History—19th century—Fiction. I. Title.
PS3604.A976C69 2012
813'.6—dc22

                                                          2011042354

We hope you enjoy this book from River North Fiction by Moody Publishers. Our goal is to provide high-quality, thought-provoking books and products that connect truth to your real needs and challenges. For more information on other books and products written and produced from a biblical perspective, go to www.moodypublishers.com or write to:

River North Fiction
Imprint of Moody Publishers
820 N. LaSalle Boulevard
Chicago, IL 60610

1 3 5 7 9 10 8 6 4 2

Printed in the United States of America

To Vickie and Darlene,
my fellow authors in this series.
Thank you so much for your support
and encouragement all along the trail.

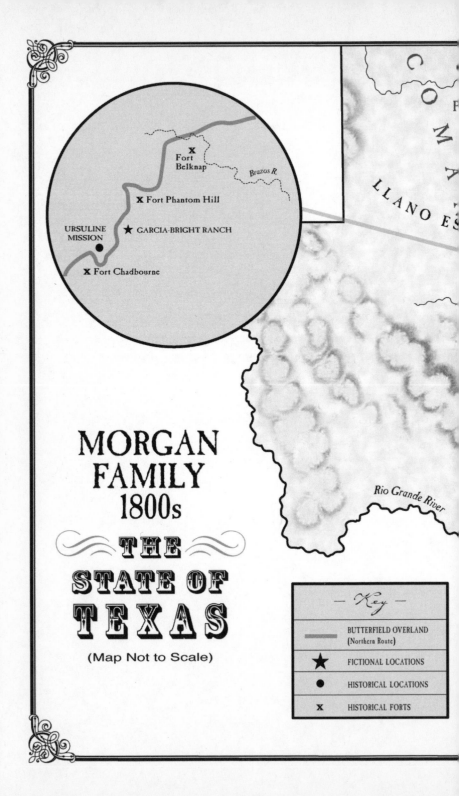

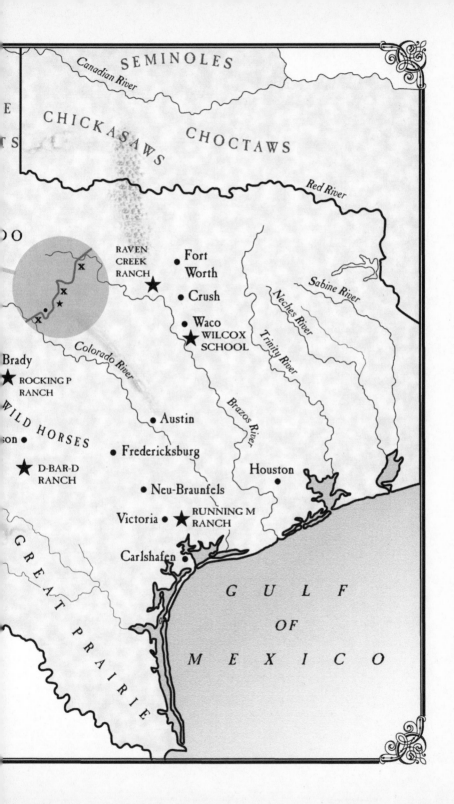

ROCKING P RANCH,
NEAR BRADY, TEXAS, JULY 1877

*T*he *princess* wants to ride this morning. Saddle up her horse." Jack Hubble, the ranch foreman, clapped Alex on the shoulder and walked past him into the barn.

Alex shot a glance toward the house, but the boss's daughter hadn't come out yet. "Uh . . . which horse?"

"Duchess, of course. Come on, I'll show you her gear." Jack strode into the tack room, and Alex hurried after him.

"That's the chestnut mare out back?"

"That's right. Here's Miss Maggie's saddle." Jack laid a hand on the horn of a fancy stock saddle with tooled flowers and scrollwork on the skirts.

"She doesn't ride sidesaddle?"

"Nah. Maggie's been riding like a boy since she was a little kid. Her father lets her get away with it, so don't say anything."

Alex nodded. His own sisters rode astride around the home place, and no one thought a thing about it. Why should he expect the boss's thirteen-year-old daughter to behave differently? But he had. Maggie Porter was a pretty girl, blonde and blue-eyed. She'd looked like a doll on Sunday morning, wearing a pink dress with gloves and a white straw bonnet when the family set out for church in the buckboard.

"Here's Duchess's bridle." Jack placed it in his hand.

"Just saddle the mare and take it out to her?" Alex asked.

"Get your horse ready, too."

Alex stared at him. "*Me?* You mean I'm going with her?" He'd been hired at the Rocking P less than two weeks earlier. Now wasn't the time to argue with his foreman, but it seemed a little strange.

Jack laughed. "You're low man around here. Oh, the fellas don't mind, but it gets kind of boring. It's an easy morning for you. And Maggie's a good kid. Let her go wherever she wants on Rocking P land, but make sure she doesn't do anything dangerous. Where's your gun?"

"In the bunkhouse."

"You'll want it today, just in case."

"In case of what?" Alex's first thought was Comanche, but the tribes were now confined to reservations—his parents had followed the saga of the Numinu with special interest.

"You never know, do you?" Jack said. "Snakes, wild hogs, drifters."

"All right. How long does she ride?"

"As long as she wants, but get her home by noon. Her mother gets fretful if she's late for dinner." Jack looked him up and down. "Oh, there's one other thing."

"What's that?"

"Maggie's young, but she's starting to notice you boys. Don't do anything to give her ideas."

"You mean—"

"I mean, she's a thirteen-year-old girl on an isolated ranch. She's cute, and she's smart. She's getting to the age, if you take my meaning."

"I'm not sure I do, sir."

"It's Jack," the foreman said. "My meaning is this: if you lay a finger on that girl, I'll tear you apart, and then her father will flay your hide. You got it?"

"Yes, sir. Jack."

"Good." Jack ambled out to the corral.

Alex pulled in a deep breath and hefted Maggie's saddle.

— ★ —

Maggie watched the new cowpuncher saddle the horses. He'd sure taken long enough to get the tack out and hitch Duchess and his own mount in the corral. The rest of the hands were long gone, out toward the north range.

She stood outside the fence while he saddled Duchess, then a black-and-white pinto for himself. He never looked her way once while he worked. He wasn't very old—seventeen or eighteen, she guessed. And he was cute. If Carlotta were here, she'd swoon. Maybe sometime she'd ask Papa if the new cowboy could escort her as far as the Herreras' ranch.

Her cheeks heated at the idea. When had she started thinking about boys that way—and showing one off to her best friend? She supposed it was Carlotta's fault. She always chattered about the boys in town and the young men on the various ranches. Carlotta was a year older than Maggie, and her mother was talking of sending her to Mexico City to stay with her aunt for a year or two and finish her education. Maggie hoped she wouldn't go.

The cowboy finished adjusting the straps and then

double-checked Duchess's cinch before he led the horses out of the corral.

"Here you go, Miss Porter."

"It's Maggie. You're Alex, aren't you?"

"That's right. Do you need a boost?"

She scowled at him. "Not since I was seven."

"Oh. Excuse me." He turned away and hid his smile.

It was a very nice smile, not mean or anything. Maggie wished she had let him help her, but she'd gotten to the age where Mama said she mustn't let any of the men boost her into the saddle. Except Papa, of course.

Alex swung onto the pinto's back. By the time Maggie was up and had smoothed her divided skirt and gathered the reins, he looked as though he'd sat there an age, waiting for her.

"Where are we goin'?" he asked.

The wind gusted and caught the brim of the felt hat she wore riding. She reached up and pulled it down over her ears. "I thought we'd head south. There's a pond there, and sometimes there are birds on the water."

"All right. I've never done this before. Do you want to lead the way, or what?"

She flushed again, and her embarrassment was compounded by the realization that he noticed. "You can ride beside me."

He nodded, and she couldn't read the expression in his eyes. Did he think she was too old to need a nursemaid? Or too young to be blushing when a cowboy looked her way?

They walked the horses for a few minutes, until they got off the road and onto the range. The grass was dry and brownish—it hadn't rained in weeks. But the wind never stopped blowing.

Alex didn't say anything, but matched his horse's stride to Duchess's when Maggie picked up a trot.

After a minute, she said, "I'm sorry to keep you from your regular work. I expect you'd rather be with Jack and the others."

He shrugged. "I don't mind riding. Beats sinking fence posts."

Maggie nodded. Some of the men complained about all the new fences they were stringing. Her father said they had to do it, so Jack told the men to put a lid on it—she'd heard him tell Harry and Nevada that.

"Some of the men think riding with kids is a waste of their time," she ventured.

"Well, I can see your pa not wanting you out here alone. It's a big range. My sisters aren't allowed to go far by themselves."

"You have sisters?"

"Two. One's about your age."

"What's her name?"

"Elena."

Maggie thought about that. Elena sounded Spanish, though Alex didn't look Mexican. He had brown hair and eyes, but not too dark, and not the olive-toned skin Carlotta and her family had.

"I wish I had a sister." Sometimes she felt the loneliness sharply. With only her parents and the ranch hands around, some days she thought she'd die of boredom. She'd never been to school—her mother taught her at home. But they did have regular church in Brady, and she saw the Bradleys or the Herreras once a month or so.

They came over a rise and looked down on the pond.

"Now, that's a pretty sight." Alex gazed down at the water and the trails leading over the prairie to it, the two cottonwoods on the far bank, and the waterfowl gliding on the surface.

Maggie smiled and squeezed Duchess a little with her legs. The mare pricked up her ears and tensed. "Race you there." She kicked Duchess, and they tore for the pond. A moment later, Alex and the pinto edged up beside them. He didn't tell her to be careful or to watch out for holes. He just sneaked that pinto past her inch by inch. He reached the pond first and turned to look at her, grinning.

Maggie laughed at the joy of it. Finally, someone to ride with who wouldn't let her win a race and wouldn't scold her or fuss over her. She was almost there when the wind seized her hat and blew it off.

"Whoa!" She pulled Duchess up and wheeled to see where her hat went. The wind buffeted it along like a tumbleweed. Before she could decide how best to fetch it, Alex's horse streaked past her.

At first she thought he'd fallen off—the saddle was empty. Then she saw his boot sticking over the cantle, and one hand clamped on the saddle horn. The next thing she knew, he'd galloped the pinto right up to the hat, reached down while hanging off the horse's side, and snatched it off the ground. Then he bounced up into his saddle, pivoted the horse on his haunches, and bounded back to her.

He halted next to Duchess and dusted off Maggie's hat with his cuff. Smiling, he bowed from the waist and held the Stetson out to her. "Your chapeau, Miss Maggie."

She stared at him, still not believing what she'd seen. "How did you learn to do that? Are you a circus rider?"

He chuckled, obviously pleased that he'd startled her. "My mother used to live with the Comanche, and she learned a lot of their riding tricks."

She eyed the tousle-haired boy keenly—because he seemed more like a boy now than a hired man—and decided he was telling the truth. "That was amazing."

"Thank you, miss. Now where would you like to go?"

Maggie put her hat on and tugged it down. "Guess I need a string on this thing. Let's follow the stream up to the hills. There used to be buffalo bones up there."

Alex grinned. "Let's go. We just have to be back by noon." He glanced up at the sun.

Maggie fumbled inside her collar and pulled out the pendant watch her mother made her wear when she went out. It had a pretty enameled flower design on the back. She wouldn't mind, except that she *had* to wear it. She'd have liked it better if Mama didn't remind her all the time.

"It's not even ten o'clock. We've got ages." She set out gleefully, her heart singing. A friend. She would try not to think of him as a cute boy. But she could hardly wait to tell Carlotta about him.

CHAPTER ONE

ROCKING P RANCH
NEAR BRADY, TEXAS, MAY 1884

Cattle herded easier than cowboys any day. Alex Bright often wondered why he'd agreed to be foreman on the Rocking P, when riding fence and busting broncs was so much easier.

"It ain't right," Leo Eagleton insisted. "You gotta tell the boss, Alex."

"Tell him what?" Alex asked. "You know he's not changing his mind on this."

"Well, we don't have to take it." Nevada Hatch, Alex's righthand man on the ranch, looked as angry as Leo. "Mr. Porter used to let us run our own herds on the range. If he's going to take that away from us, he's got to raise our wages. That's all."

"He won't," Leo said.

"I'm thinking of looking for work at another ranch," Joe Moore, the wrangler, said as he untied the cinch on his saddle.

"We hardly get enough pay here as it is, but if we can't run our own brands—"

"We oughta strike," Nevada said.

Alex stared at him. "Strike?"

"Sure. They did it last year, in the panhandle."

"Yeah, but . . ." Alex shook his head. "That'd be shooting your horse out from under you. This ranch is a good place to work."

"Was," Nevada conceded. "Lately it's not so great."

"That's right," Leo said. "Mr. Porter won't give me time to fix the roof on the cabin. Sela complains about it all the time. Drip, drip, drip—she nags just like the leaky roof when it rains."

The other men laughed, and Joe said, "At least it ain't rained for a while."

"Yeah, be thankful for that," Alex told him. But he knew Leo spoke the truth, and it bothered him. In the last year, the ranch's owner had paid out less and less for maintenance on the buildings. He hadn't given the men who stayed on over the winter the Christmas "extra" he'd always handed out in the past—a few dollars and some new clothes, usually. The lack of a celebration and gifts hadn't sat well with the men.

One of the older men, Harry Jensen, had been on the Rocking P a lot longer than Alex had. "You know, our wages haven't been raised in ten years," he said.

"Prices have gone up, though," Joe said.

Alex let out a deep breath. He was going to have to talk to Mr. Porter, no getting around it. This new edict about the men's herds was the last straw. Being able to brand a few mavericks and sell off a few beeves of their own each year meant a lot to the men, especially married men like Leo.

A couple of the other hands ambled over. Usually when they rode in for the night, the boys couldn't wait to get inside for supper, but this time they lingered as if waiting for him to say more.

"You know Porter's got enough land for every one of us to run a dozen head or so," Nevada said.

"Yeah, but he claims all the mavericks on his range belong to him, and he might have a point," Alex said.

"Then he should up our wages." Harry looked around at the others, and a murmur of agreement supported him.

"But we're starting spring roundup tomorrow," Alex said.

"Exactly." Nevada's bushy eyebrows drew together. "We hit him when it will hurt the most."

Joe spat tobacco juice in the grass. "If we refuse to round up his stock, Porter won't have a herd to sell this spring."

Harry nodded. "I say we strike."

"Hold on," Alex said. "What makes you think Mr. Porter wouldn't go and hire a new crew?"

"We'd have to get the men on the other ranches in on it," Nevada said. "Tell them what we're doing."

"I bet they'd want to strike too," Joe said.

"If not, at least we could tell them not to let any of their men hire on with Porter. I bet they'd do that to back us up." Nevada looked around at the others.

"That didn't work so well in the panhandle," Alex reminded them, hefting his saddle against his hip to carry it into the barn. "They had five ranches striking, but the owners still found more workers and refused to hire back the men who struck. We'd probably do ourselves out of our jobs if we tried it."

"You know we can't live on thirty dollars a month without our maverick herds," Nevada said.

"Yeah, some ranches are paying forty now," Leo put in.

Harry nodded. "That's right, and now Porter's claiming our herds for himself. We own those cattle, even if he doesn't let us keep any from now on."

"Yeah, we should be able to sell them and keep the money," Harry said. "We've been doing it for years."

Alex looked around at them. Mr. Porter had treated him fairly—some might say more than fairly. Alex had been on the Rocking P for seven years now, and Porter had bypassed older men when he promoted Alex to foreman last year. That called for a certain amount of loyalty.

He'd always admired Porter for the way he ran his vast spread. Letting the men keep a few mavericks was standard procedure and allowed the boss to keep wages low. He'd also provided cabins for three of the married men and allowed them to bring their families to live on the ranch.

But lately, the boss was slipping. Alex could see it, and the men could see it. He'd tried to talk to Mr. Porter a couple of times, when it seemed like maintenance was being neglected, and when the supplies for the men's cook had lacked several items the men enjoyed. Mr. Porter had answered him more gruffly than usual—even a bit angrily. Alex had let it go, thinking they'd talk again later, when he caught the boss in a better mood. Surely they could work this out.

And another thing—he'd heard Porter's daughter was coming home soon. If Maggie Porter weren't in the mix, Alex might not have hesitated. The men were right—the boss no longer treated them fairly. But if he sided with them, would he lose his job—and his only chance to make a good impression on Maggie Porter?

He turned to face the men again. "All right, listen to me. I have to go in tonight and settle the details of the roundup with the boss. I'll mention your complaints."

"Grievances," Nevada said quickly. "We're not complainers, Alex. We're hardworking men with grievances."

Alex gritted his teeth. "All right. I'll bring it up."

←—— ★ ——→

Maggie Porter stepped down from the stagecoach in Brady, Texas, scanning the small crowd of onlookers eagerly. Her gaze lit on Shep Rooney, a cowhand who had been with her father's ranch as long as she could remember. She swallowed her disappointment and made her way to him.

"Hi, Shep!"

"Afternoon, Miss Maggie. Good to have you home."

"Where's Papa?" She looked around once more, on the chance he'd stepped into the stage line's office out of the hot sun for a moment.

"He's out to the ranch." Shep's smile for her was the same as it had always been, but his hair had gone mostly gray, and his beard was streaked with white. "You got a trunk?"

"Yes."

"I'll have the stage people put it in the wagon." He spoke to the station agent then came back to her side, limping as he walked. "Your pa woulda liked to have come, but the boys are all out on the roundup, and they'll start the drive in a few days. Lot going on at the ranch."

She nodded and walked to the wagon with him, wondering why Shep wasn't with the other cowboys. The team of bays in harness looked familiar, and she paused to pat their noses. "Is Duchess waiting for me too?"

Shep smiled. "Yup, she can't wait to see you. I see Alex take her out now and then to keep her in shape for you."

Alex. Maggie guarded her expression. She'd have thought her girlish crush would have passed by now, but even the mention of him still brought on a flutter or two. He was the best-looking cowboy she'd ever seen, and not that much older than she was. When she'd left at eighteen with her mother, she'd kept her memories of Alex Bright as a secret treasure she could take out and gaze at now and then, the way she did the Mexican silver dollar her father had given her on her tenth birthday. The memory of Alex was another pleasant keepsake.

Shep fussed with the horses and got her luggage loaded. They started out, and he kept the team trotting steadily. Maggie plied him with questions about the ranch.

"How's the roundup going?"

"The boys just went out yesterday. They'll be at it three or four more days at least. Then they start the drive."

"Lucky cowpokes."

Shep smiled. "You still want to be a cowgirl?"

Maggie smiled. When she was younger, her father had taken her out to the spring roundup for a day. She'd looked forward to it every year, as soon as Christmas had passed. She'd vowed she could ride and rope as well as a cowboy and begged her father to let her stay out with him and the men. He'd always brought her home in the evening, though.

"I don't think I'll ever stop loving the roundup and watching the men start off on the drive. But I've developed a few other interests now, Shep."

"Yeah? Like what?"

She didn't answer right away. During most of her absence she'd attended her mother, whose long illness had worn Maggie down. Seeing her mother fail and die at the sanatorium had taken something out of her that she didn't think she'd ever regain. That's why Papa had sent her to San Francisco after the funeral. Seven months with her cousin Iris had started the healing process. How could anyone stay melancholy around Iris? The young woman lived a life of constant activity.

"Iris helped me learn to love art," she said. "And music, and . . . and lots of things."

"Well now," Shep said. "We don't get much of that on the ranch, and that's for sure."

Almost Maggie regretted not going away to a finishing school like Sarah Bradley and some of the other girls from ranches did. She'd gone to the sanatorium with Mama instead and led a gentle life for a year and half, followed by the whirl with Iris. Perhaps that was education enough. She needed some time at home now; the ranch would complete her restoration.

"How come you're not out on the roundup, Shep?"

He nodded toward his left leg. "It's this bum knee. Did something to it last summer. I can't take more'n half an hour in the saddle these days. But so far, your pa's found plenty for me to do." Shep's face sobered. "Gotta admit, some days I wonder if he'll keep me on."

"Why wouldn't he? You're good at so many things."

"Well, thanks, Miss Maggie. But things aren't the same at the ranch. I putter around and clean out the barn and corrals and mend harness. I drive into town for supplies. But I wonder how long your pa will pay me if I can't get back in the saddle."

His words troubled Maggie. Surely her father would take care of an employee who had served him faithfully for many years.

"I hope they do all right on the drive this year," Shep said.

"Why wouldn't they? It's only to Fort Worth now, not all the way to Kansas. A couple of weeks on the trail. That should be a picnic for Alex and the other men."

Shep shook his head. "They aren't happy, and when people get mad, things can go wrong."

"What do you mean?" Maggie asked. "Has something happened?"

Shep smiled at her, but he seemed to have lost his good humor. "You papa told us we can't run our little herds anymore, or claim mavericks. The boys are angry about that."

"Are you mad too? You have a maverick herd, don't you?"

"I had a dozen steers I hoped to send on the drive this year. But it looks like that won't happen now. There's other things too."

"What other things? Papa's always been a good boss. Every-one says the Rocking P is a good place to work."

"Well, the boys feel different now."

They were almost home, and Maggie would have to save that to think about later. She'd ask Papa about it, because on the surface, it didn't seem fair. She sat on the edge of the wagon seat, holding her hat down with one hand and bracing herself with the other. She couldn't wait to get her working hat on again. This flimsy thing she'd bought at a milliner's shop in San Francisco was all feathers and net—no match for the Texas wind. She ought to have anchored it with an extra hatpin.

As Shep guided the team over the crest of the last rise, she caught her breath. Rocking P land stretched out as far as she could see. She'd longed for the people who loved her—Papa and Dolores, mostly, but she'd also craved this place. This was home. She'd often thought the "P" in Rocking P should stand for "peace," not "Porter."

Maggie reached up and pulled out her long hatpin and whipped the hat off.

Shep looked over in surprise.

She smiled. "Can't stand this thing any longer." She turned around and opened the valise that sat in the wagon bed behind her. She tucked the hat in and dropped the hatpin after it. Reaching up, she loosened her bun and shook out her long hair. She'd missed feeling the Texas wind blow through it, lifting the strands and ruffling her locks.

"Now you look like little Maggie," Shep said. "Guess you'll be out galloping Duchess in the morning."

"I sure will."

He drove into the yard and drew up before the ranch house. Maggie jumped down without waiting for his help. The door flew open as she ran toward it, and she tumbled into Dolores's arms.

"Miss Maggie, we missed you so much!"

Dolores, a cowpuncher's widow, had taken care of the Porter family since Maggie was about five years old—when her mother became too ill to do all the cooking and cleaning herself. Dolores had always been there for Maggie, entrenched in the kitchen but always ready to listen to a girl's woes.

When Mama grew more and more frail, Dolores helped Maggie in ways she'd never realized until now. She'd kept her busy and taught her to think of others. She'd trained Maggie to help keep the house neat and clean, and to cook a passable meal if need be. She'd had the "girl talks" with Maggie that most girls had with their mothers. She'd made Maggie's birthday cakes and dried her tears. And when the time came for Mama to go away in a last, desperate effort to regain her strength, Dolores packed for both Mama and Maggie and helped the girl find the grit that helped her through those last agonizing months with Mama.

As she pulled away from Dolores's embrace, Maggie found her cheeks were wet with tears. She wiped them away quickly.

"Thank you. I've missed you, too."

Across the big parlor, the door to her father's office opened. He stepped toward her, smiling.

Maggie ran to him and hugged him.

"There, now," he said. "Welcome back, sugar."

She clung to him for a moment, knowing things had changed. She'd been home only a few weeks after Mama died, and they hadn't really settled into a routine then. But now she was home for good. Without Mama, they'd have to muddle their way into a new family pattern. She'd never be his little girl again. What was her role now?

She pushed away from him. "Papa, you're so thin! Hasn't Dolores been feeding you?"

He chuckled. "You have to ask? You know her cooking.

No, I'm just . . . a little off my feed, I guess."

Shep came through, carrying her valise. "I'll put this in your room, Miss Maggie, and I'll get one of the boys to help me with the trunk later."

To her surprise, Papa didn't jump in with an offer to help.

An hour later, Maggie and her father ate together at the table to one side of the big parlor. She could hear muted voices from the kitchen and decided that Shep was eating out there with Dolores.

"I was sorry to hear about Shep's injury," she said.

"You and me both."

"It must have happened before—before the funeral, but I didn't realize it then."

"We were both pretty well distracted in September."

"Yes."

Her father didn't seem to be eating much, but Maggie didn't mention it.

"So the other men are out on roundup."

"Yes. I expect they'll bring the first cut in tonight, and Alex will come in to tell me how things look. I hope we'll have a good herd to send to Fort Worth."

"Are you going out to the roundup?" she asked.

"I don't think so. The boys can handle it."

Maggie's disappointment struck hard. She'd hoped they could ride out to the range together and join the fun for a day.

"Papa . . ."

"What?"

She shook her head and reached for the milk pitcher. Everyone seemed too sober. Maybe it was just that the men were gone, and the whole ranch seemed too quiet. Then too, Maggie had only been home once since her mother left—for those three weeks at the time of Mama's funeral. Maybe she just wasn't used to the house without Mama.

"How are the Herreras doing?"

"Good, so far as I know. I haven't seen Juan for a month or so." That wasn't unusual during the busy seasons, with the houses on the large ranches several miles apart. But Carlotta, Señor Herrera's daughter, was Maggie's girlhood friend.

"I'll want to visit Carlotta soon," she said. "She wrote to me a few weeks ago, and I didn't get a chance to answer before I left San Francisco."

"She'll probably be happy to see you," Papa said. "I hear the Riddle boy's been hanging around there some."

Maggie smiled. The neighboring rancher's beautiful daughter had never lacked for suitors. "She mentioned it. I don't think she's sure whether she likes him or not. She said she rides better than he does."

Her father laughed. "That girl always was a handful. Did Iris take you to the opera? You said in your last letter that you were going."

"Yes. You would have loved it, Papa. The costumes were so elegant, and the singing! Every voice was perfect. I could have gone every night for a week and not gotten tired of it."

They continued to chat throughout the meal, and some of Maggie's anxiety quieted. She went to her room after supper and unpacked her valise. When she opened her armoire, she found her old riding clothes hanging inside. She smiled and pulled out the brown serge skirt she had defiantly split and stitched into loose trousers. When she stood still, people couldn't even tell it was divided, but it allowed her to ride astride modestly. She'd try it on in the morning to see if it still fit. If not, she'd have to wear the fancy riding habit she'd bought in San Francisco. Duchess might not like wearing the sidesaddle and letting the heavy skirt hang down her side.

Hoofbeats coming up the lane drew her to the window.

Alex Bright. He rode his leggy red roan to the hitching rail and slid out of the saddle like a man who had worked hard all day but wasn't done yet.

He was even better looking than he had been when she left two years ago. Alex had always sat easy in the saddle and made his dusty hat and worn work clothes look fit for a cattle baron. But Maggie studied him with more mature eyes now. She'd expected to be disappointed when she saw him again. Instead, she knew what she'd felt as a teenager was real.

He walked up the steps to the front door and disappeared from view. With a sigh she turned to her bed to finish unpacking. After hanging up the extra skirt and blouse she'd carried, she transferred the last few things to her dresser. She wondered when she'd get her trunk. She was almost glad Shep hadn't brought it in yet—she was too tired to unpack it. That could wait until morning.

She went to her dressing table, picked up her hairbrush, and ran it through her long golden hair. Though she kept her hands busy, her mind thought of Alex, only yards away. On impulse, she laid down the brush and went out to the parlor, but it was empty. She turned toward her father's office. He kept the small room for business only.

The door was open a few inches, and she could hear Alex talking, his voice deep and rhythmic. Someone had told her once that he was from a musical family—related to a famous composer, unless she'd gotten it wrong. She'd heard him sing at roundups and at church. Maybe that's why she'd fallen so hard for him—his voice was enough to make any girl swoon.

Stepping closer to the door, Maggie wondered if she dared knock quickly and barge in as though she had something to tell her father. If she pretended she didn't know Alex was here . . .

←— ★ —→

"I think three more days will do it," Alex said. "The men are doing a great job, scouring the canyons for strays. We brought in more than five hundred steers tonight. They're in the north pasture now."

"How many calves have you branded?"

"About two hundred. And we've culled out quite a few of Señor Herrera's beeves, and some from the Lazy S. When we're done, I'll send one of the boys over to tell them they can come get them."

"All right. I'll have Shep get your supplies ready for the drive. The morning after you bring the cattle in, you head out for Fort Worth," her father said.

"Sir, there's one other thing I need to talk to you about."

"What?"

"The men aren't happy with the pay situation, like I mentioned a couple of days ago. Since you told them they can't keep their herds or put their own marks on any mavericks this spring, some of them are really upset."

"You know those are Rocking P cattle. I lose money every year when I let the men have some of them."

"I know, sir, but some of the men will really be hurting this year if they don't have their herds to sell. Especially the married men."

"Well, I can't do any better. You tell them the pay is the same as always. I'm not treating them any worse than the other ranchers."

"No disrespect, sir, but some of them think you are."

"Oh, really?" Her father sounded belligerent now. Maggie hoped Alex wouldn't push him too hard.

"Yes, sir. They heard that the Lazy S is paying more. And they say you've let things go. The cabins need repair, and—"

"You tell them if they don't like it, they can go elsewhere."

After a pause, Alex said, "Mr. Porter, they're serious. Some of the ranches are paying forty a month now. The men would like that, if they can't have their herds. It would mean a lot to them if—"

"No! I told you I can't do any better. *Get out of here.* And tomorrow night I want to hear that you've got a thousand head in the pasture."

"Please—"

"Go."

Maggie jumped back, but she was too late. The door swung open and Alex stalked out, his jaw tight.

He saw her almost at once and his steps faltered.

"Maggie."

"Hello, Alex." She tried to smile, but that was a lost cause.

They stood for a long moment looking at each other. Maggie couldn't break the stare. He looked so mature and handsome and . . . sad. The urge to apologize welled up inside her, but she knew it wasn't her place until she knew more about the situation.

The meeting had gone askew from the way she'd planned it, and she was at a disadvantage. He knew she'd heard part of his conversation with her father—how could he not, when she stood here so flustered?

"Welcome home." His voice was flat. He stormed out the front door and was outside before she could catch her breath.

Maggie gazed after Alex, hovering in indecision. If her father didn't hire such handsome cowboys, her life would be a lot easier.

CHAPTER TWO

*A*lex caught Red's reins and was about to mount when the ranch house door opened and Maggie flew out. The rosy glow of the sunset washed over her, and she looked finer than the palomino filly he was training for Mr. Porter.

She must have come home yesterday or today. He was sure he'd have heard about it if she'd arrived before they set out for the roundup. The two years had been kind to her. She walked straighter and more confidently, and she met his gaze directly, without the giggles and blushes she used to try to hide. Her hair spilled over her shoulders, framing her face. She'd always been pretty, but now she was knock-you-breathless beautiful. She wore a tailored gray dress with dark red trim—a grownup woman's dress with pleats, and a bodice so well fitted that no one would mistake her for a kid anymore.

He looked away and busied himself with the reins.

"Alex—"

"Yes?"

"I'm sorry. I didn't mean to overhear—oh, that's not true. I did mean to. But only so I'd know when it was safe to interrupt."

He considered mounting and riding off right then. His head whirled with what Porter had said, and he knew he'd have a hard time keeping the men calm when they heard it.

But Maggie was a distraction he couldn't ignore. He wouldn't dare imagine she had taken a personal interest in him. When he'd come to the ranch, she was thirteen, and she'd only cared about him if he could bring her a horse to ride. True, he'd seen some signs of a crush later, but he'd ignored that and made a point of treating her the same way he always had. And if his own common sense wasn't enough, the old foreman, Jack Hubble, had dropped a warning in his ear—don't mess with the boss's daughter.

Alex respected Jack, and he'd learned a lot from him. Maybe that was why Mr. Porter had chosen him as foreman when Jack retired—Alex listened. But now that trait was putting him in a difficult spot. He listened to the men, but he had to listen to the boss, too. And he couldn't see a way to reconcile the things he was hearing. Obviously, something had gone wrong with the Rocking P's boss. Financial setbacks? That would explain some things, but not all.

"What's up?" he asked Maggie, trying to smile in spite of the way his stomach churned.

"Just thought I'd catch up with you. Last time I was home, Jack was still foreman. Congratulations."

"Thanks." Alex turned toward Red and stuck his fingers under the saddle girth. Loose, as he'd expected. He worked the cinch knot loose and tightened the strap. He'd barely seen Maggie the last time she was home—for her mother's funeral last fall. He'd been busy with ranch work and getting ready to take over from Jack. He'd attended the funeral with the other men, but besides that he'd only seen Maggie a couple of times, from a distance. She'd been preoccupied with her grief and the constant company that came to the ranch.

"How are things going?" Maggie asked.

"Fine."

"So . . . the roundup's going well."

Alex hesitated only a second. "We just started, but yeah, it's going great."

Maggie's troubled expression told him she didn't believe that. She took a step closer, and Alex tensed. What did she really want?

"Alex, we're old friends. I hope you'll be honest with me."

"What about?"

"For starters, my father looks very tired. Has he been overdoing?"

He swung around and stared at her. If anything, Mr. Porter had slacked off. In the past, he'd been right out there with the men, riding fence, bringing in strays, and punching cows on the roundup.

"He . . . uh . . . he's maybe slowed down a little."

Maggie frowned. "I was afraid of that. Funny, isn't it? You don't expect your dad to grow older. I rode the stage all day, imagining his face when he saw me get off. But instead, when I got to Brady, Shep was there. Papa didn't even go into town to meet me. He's not sick, is he?"

Alex swallowed hard. "I, uh . . . not that I know of." He tried not to let his gaze linger on her face.

She nodded. "Shep told me things have been different around here. The men aren't happy. I was sorry to hear that."

Alex didn't know what to say, so he just waited.

"He also seemed concerned that he might not keep his job because of his leg injury. Do you know anything about that?"

"Not really. He twisted his knee last summer, and he was laid up for a few weeks. Since then he hasn't been able to ride much."

"That's too bad. But he's been here for a long time. Papa wouldn't turn him out because he hurt his leg."

Alex didn't want to disillusion her, but he had his doubts. "You know, a lot's changed since you went away. I'm sorry to say it, but it's not all for the better."

She laid a hand on his sleeve. "Alex, please tell me what's going on."

"I don't know. Your pa just doesn't seem to care like he used to. About the men, about the ranch . . . and I'm sorry about that."

"So am I. Maybe he'll talk to me about it. Thanks, Alex." She removed her hand and gave him a businesslike smile. "So. Duchess is ready for me to ride, I hear."

"Yeah. She's in good shape. She's getting older, you know, but she'll still take you where you want to go."

"I can't wait. But I guess you won't be around to ride with me, like in the old days."

He chuckled. "I don't think you've needed an escort since you were about fourteen. You're a big girl now." Immediately he felt he'd crossed a line, and his cheeks burned.

Maggie seemed to appreciate the lighter tone.

"Maybe not, but I'd still enjoy riding with you sometime. I'd hoped Papa and I would come out to the roundup, like in the old days."

Alex shrugged. "I doubt you can get him out there, but it'd probably do him some good if you could."

He swung up into the saddle.

"I'll try to talk to Papa tomorrow. Maybe he'll listen to me."

"That'd be good," Alex said. "You know he's told us we can't have our own herds anymore? He used to let the men claim up to ten mavericks apiece every year at the roundup. Now he's put a stop to it."

She looked at the ground. "Shep said something about that. It surprised me. And I . . . I heard you and Papa speak of it tonight."

More like, she'd heard them arguing.

"I don't think he'll change his mind. And the men don't want to keep working unless he raises their wages or gives back their herds."

"Don't want to keep working? What do you mean?" She stepped up close to Red, peering up at Alex with stormy eyes.

"I'm sorry," he said. "That's the way it is. The word 'strike' was mentioned today. I tried to talk them out of it and promised to talk to the boss. You heard him. He won't give in."

Maggie studied his face for a moment. "I'm sorry. Truly sorry."

"Me too. I didn't tell your pa the way the men are talking, but . . . things can't go on the way they are, that's all." He lifted the reins, and Red perked up, ready for a signal to move.

"Well, good-bye." Maggie's lips twitched, as though she wanted to say more and could barely hold it in. She looked young and vulnerable again.

Alex wished he could tell her things would sort themselves out and the Rocking P would go back to being the happy, prosperous place she remembered. But he couldn't.

He touched his hat brim then turned Red and loped away.

———— ★ ————

When she went inside, Shep was walking toward the door. "Alex gone?" he asked.

"Yes."

Shep's face fell. "I was going to ask him to help me get your trunk in."

"I can help you, Shep."

"No, it's too heavy."

Maggie laughed, though she wasn't feeling playful. "Just because I've been away a couple of years doesn't mean I've gotten puny."

A smile cracked his weathered face. "All right, missy, let's see what we can do."

They got it as far as the kitchen, where Dolores stood at the sink, washing dishes.

"Set it down." Panting, Maggie straightened and put her hands to the small of her back. "What if we leave it here and I take small loads to my room? You can take it out to the barn tomorrow, when it's empty."

"That's a good idea," Dolores said.

"Thank you. I don't think I'll even open it until morning. I'm ready for bed."

"Let me fix you something for a snack." Dolores reached for a dish towel and dried her hands.

"No, thanks. Supper was wonderful, and I don't think I could eat another bite." Maggie gave her a hug and smiled at the old cowboy. "Good night, Shep."

"Sweet dreams, Miss Maggie."

In her room, Maggie quickly changed into her nightgown. She'd looked forward to this day for a long time, but now that she was actually here, she felt let down. Her father had spent a minimum of time with her. Most of the men had gone out on roundup and left the home ranch nearly deserted. Everyone she talked to was glum and told her things had gone downhill.

The one thing that had turned out better than she'd anticipated was Alex. He'd matured into a rugged cowboy. She'd seen appreciation in his eyes when he looked at her, but he'd kept a reserve between them. Maybe he didn't want to start a romance. She'd ask Carlotta Herrera if Alex had a sweetheart. She hoped not. That would be a hard blow to handle. Or maybe something else held him back. Maybe Alex was interested in her but was afraid her father wouldn't approve.

Papa had always liked Alex, though. When she was younger, he'd even teased her occasionally about how much she liked the young man. He'd promoted Alex while she was away. Alex was his foreman now, and that pleased her. Papa must rely on him a lot.

If her father seemed in a better mood tomorrow, she'd sound him out on how he felt about Alex.

She smiled as she blew out the lantern on her bedside table. Maybe it was time she made her feelings clear to Alex, now that she'd established in her own mind that she still cared for him. Let him see her admiration and watch for a response.

The things he'd said about the cowboys bothered her. Papa had always been a bit of a skinflint—he said that's how he built his fortune—but the men deserved to be treated well. And maybe better paid. If the hands weren't happy, the ranch wouldn't run smoothly. Anyone who grew up on a ranch knew that.

She rolled over on her pillow and pulled the quilt her mother had made close beneath her chin. It smelled like home. As she drifted off to sleep, she thought of Alex again. She hoped the pay issue wouldn't stand between them. When she talked to her father tomorrow, maybe she could sway him where Alex couldn't.

The men had already driven all the cattle out of the closest, most easily accessible areas. Alex and most of the twenty men on the roundup set out in the morning to go farther afield. The cook and wrangler would stay in camp, along with two more cowboys who were in charge of branding today. The others rode out soon after sunup, separating to look for scattered bunches of cattle.

Alex took Leo Eagleton and Tommy Drescher with him. Leo had been with the Rocking P for five years, but Tommy was younger and less experienced. He'd only joined the outfit a few months ago, and Alex wanted to keep an eye on him until he was sure Tommy was skilled enough to stay out of trouble.

Nevada and two other men rode with them the first mile, until they spotted a few cattle in a dip in the rolling range.

"You get those," Alex said. "We're heading for Willow Gulch." The small canyon was hidden in a fold of low hills a couple of miles away, and the sparse trees growing there offered a little shade. A few cattle could usually be found there in the heat of the day.

They found almost thirty cattle grazing in the gulch and drove them back toward the camp. Two cows led the bunch. One had a calf. The other was a speckled red cow and bony, probably getting past breeding age. Alex would send her to the stockyards. She wouldn't let the others past her, but swung her head menacingly, with her wide horns pointing toward any that came too close.

As they approached the holding pens, Alex hung back to make sure none of the stragglers went astray. Tommy and Leo rode along the flanks of the bunch, pushing them toward the fence. Joe Moore saw them coming and hurried to open the gate, shooing the cattle inside away from the opening.

At the last instant, the speckled lead cow ducked aside. Leo rode toward her with a whoop, swinging his lariat. The longhorn charged his horse, straight on. Alex spurred his horse, but knew he couldn't get close to Leo in time to help. Even though Leo's horse pivoted, the rogue cow slammed into its shoulder, and Leo went down with his mount.

Alex galloped Red toward Leo, but half a dozen steers followed the leader and veered away from the gate. Alex yelled and headed off the rest. The mama cow trotted into the pen with her calf close behind, and the rest followed. Tommy closed in behind them and seemed to have the remainder of the bunch under control. Alex turned back to Leo and jumped from the saddle.

Leo's horse had pushed himself up off the ground and stood trembling a few yards away. Leo lay sprawled in the trampled grass, his face contorted with pain.

"What hurts?" Alex said, bending close.

"My leg." Leo's right leg lay stretched out, but the left stuck out to the side. "Horse fell right on it. I couldn't push off in time." He grimaced.

"All right, don't try to move. I'll get a couple of the men to help get you over to the wagon."

Tommy and Joe rode over and sat on their horses, looking down at Leo.

"What happened?" Tommy asked.

"That spotted cow in the lead charged me," Leo said between gritted teeth.

Alex pushed his hat back. "Tommy, go get someone to help you bring that bunch in. There's six or eight of 'em that got away. And watch out for that speckled cow. She's mean-er'n a sidewinder. Joe, ride to the chuck wagon and get Leo's bedroll and a couple more men. We'll need to send Leo home."

Leo's face contorted, but he didn't protest. His wife, Sela, would be upset, of course, but she'd take care of him.

Alex wasn't sure whether to straighten the injured leg or not, but they'd have to move Leo. No doctor would come out here. The nearest one lived in Brady, and they'd have to send someone from the ranch to get him, if he'd come as far as the Rocking P ranch house.

Tommy came back with Early and Bronc, two of the men who had been working at the branding fire putting the Rocking P mark on the calves the others brought in. Bronc Tracey was an outgoing man of about thirty, with coffee-colored skin and a woolly beard, and known for his funny stories. He was married and lived in one of the cabins near the home ranch. Early Shaw was a confirmed bachelor—a tough cowpoke who'd seen the backside of forty and couldn't be shocked. He dismounted and knelt beside Leo, on the opposite side from Alex.

"What you thinkin'? Take him back to the ranch?"

Alex nodded. "Thought I'd send you and Stewie in the chuck wagon with him." Stewie was their camp cook, otherwise known as William Stewart, but Bronc had come up with the appropriate nickname a couple of years ago on their spring drive.

"Sela's gonna be mad," Leo said with a moan.

"Aw, she'll likely coddle you like a baby," Alex said.

Early laughed. "You afraid she'll finish you off? I always knew she wore the pants in your family."

Leo's mouth twisted again. "Right now I don't care. Why don't you just knock me out so I don't have to feel this?"

Alex laid a hand on his shoulder. "Take it easy, Leo. You're gonna be all right."

Bronc came over with Leo's bedroll. "You want to use his blankets?"

Alex stood and reached to the bedroll. "Yup. I figure that's the easiest way to lift him into the wagon."

"Stewie's going to drive it over here," Tommy said. "He had to pack up some stuff first."

"All right, let's lay out the blankets and get Leo on them so we're ready when he gets here."

Leo twisted his neck and looked around. "Where's my horse? Is he dead?"

Early scrunched up his weather-beaten face. "Not by a long shot. We'll have Joe look him over, but he's standing yonder gawking at you."

Leo grunted. "It hurts. Kin I yell now?"

"Yell all you want." Alex reckoned Leo would let loose when they moved him. He undid Leo's bedroll and shook out the two blankets. The cowboy's extra shirt and socks fell out on the ground. Alex picked them up and passed them to Tommy. "Put those in the wagon when Stewie gets here."

Early was cautiously feeling all of Leo's limbs. When he got to the bent leg, he touched Leo's knee, and Leo let out a vehement stream of Spanish.

"What'd he say?" Bronc asked.

"Best you don't know," Alex said.

"Yeah, your wife won't want you learning to swear in Spanish, too." Early didn't look up as he spoke, but continued to gently prod Leo's leg.

"Leave me alone," Leo screamed.

Early jumped back. "Man! Did you have to yell in my ear?"

Sweat poured off Leo's brow, trickling down his temples. "Yes! I had to. You touch me again and I'll knock you clear to the Rio Grande."

"Sorry," Early said. "We've got to move you, though."

Leo heaved out a deep breath and clenched his teeth, closing his eyes. "I know."

"Did Sela teach you that kind of language?" Tommy asked.

"I sure hope not," Early muttered.

"Sela wouldn't mouth off like that," Alex said.

"Oh, yeah?" Leo glared up at him. "She would if she hurt as bad as I do right now." He clenched his teeth and closed his eyes.

Alex spotted the cowboy's dusty hat over near his horse and ambled over to collect it. He was glad Early was along. He and Stewie probably had more experience with injuries than the rest of the crew put together. Between the two of them, the older men could decide how best to position Leo. They'd get him onto the blankets, and then they'd all help lift him.

"Here comes the wagon," Tommy called.

Alex stood by while the Early and Stewie debated what to do. Finally Stewie gave Leo a couple of swallows from a whiskey bottle, and they moved him over to the bedroll. Leo screamed and slumped unconscious on the blankets. Early used the opportunity to straighten the broken limb.

Alex's stomach churned as he watched. When Early looked up at him and nodded, four of them took hold of the blanket and carried Leo to the back of the chuck wagon. There was barely enough room to lay him in there among the supplies.

"You'll get him back to the ranch all right?" he asked Stewie.

"Sure. Send one of the boys to ride ahead and let Sela and Mr. Porter know. I'll try to get back here in time to fix supper for you, but I left a crate of canned beans yonder just in case."

"All right," Alex said. Maybe he should go and report to Mr. Porter. He'd planned not to go in tonight, but to wait until tomorrow, when they'd drive another bunch of cattle into the pasture closer to the house.

He decided he'd serve the boss better if he stayed out here and kept the roundup on track. Without Leo, the whole process would take longer, and he'd be without another man for the rest of the day as well, with Early going along to help deliver the patient.

He glanced around. "Early, if the boss wants you to go for the doc, do it."

Early nodded and mounted his horse. Stewie climbed to the driver's seat on the chuck wagon.

"Should we put another man back there with Leo?" Alex called.

"No room," Stewie said.

Alex clenched his jaw. He was glad he wouldn't lose more manpower, but he hoped Leo wouldn't jounce around too badly and wind up with pots and canned goods falling on him. Stewie always battened things down pretty snugly, though. He waved his assent and walked over to where his red gelding waited.

CHAPTER THREE

When she returned from her long ride on Duchess, Maggie let the mare walk the last mile. Duchess was getting old. As much as she loved her childhood mount, it was time to think about riding a different horse—one that could carry her for hours without puffing and gasping.

A sweet palomino filly danced in the corral next to the barn. Maggie had spotted her the morning after she'd come home. When she went out to saddle Duchess, she'd seen the golden horse prancing about, as though she wanted to play. Did Papa have plans for that filly? Maybe she belonged to one of the hired men. When Papa seemed to be in a good mood, she'd ask.

Duchess perked up her ears as they approached the ranch buildings. Maggie peered around and spotted the ranch's buckboard in the distance, headed toward Brady. It was too far away for her to recognize the driver, but somehow his hat and back didn't look like Shep's.

She put Duchess away, giving her a quick brushing, then hurried across to the ranch house and went in through the kitchen door. To her surprise, the room was full of black-haired, dark-eyed little boys, whom Dolores was trying to persuade to sit down and stay put for a handful of raisins and a biscuit apiece. Sela and Leo Eagleton's children, no doubt. The littlest one, Pablo, was crying.

"Well now, what's this?" she asked.

Dolores turned to her with a harassed look. "Oh, Miss Maggie, these poor little fellows! They want their mamacita."

"Where is she?"

"She's gone to take their papa to the doctor."

"What happened?" Maggie asked. "And is that who I just saw heading to town in the buckboard?"

"I expect it was," Dolores said. "Poor Sela. She's got to drive the wagon and mind the baby, too. Leo was hurt on the roundup. Stewie brought him here in the chuck wagon. One of the cowboys who came along offered to ride to town for the doctor, but Mr. Porter wouldn't let him."

Maggie stared at her. "Are you sure?"

"Of course I'm sure. Shep was off on an errand for your father, and the boss told Sela that if she wanted to get Leo to the doctor before nightfall, she'd best take him herself. Of course she had to take little Angelina with her."

The baby was only a few weeks old, so that was understandable. "And you offered to watch the boys," Maggie said.

"Yes. I don't mind doing it, but I'm wondering how I'll manage." As she spoke, Dolores stooped and picked up Pablo. She cradled him against her shoulder and rocked back and forth. "I need to get supper ready soon."

"Let me go and change my clothes," Maggie said. "I'll come back and take the boys out to play catch for a while."

"*Gracias*. That would help so very much." Dolores turned to answer the oldest boy's plea for more raisins.

Although Dolores fed the Eagleton boys their supper in the kitchen, Papa complained all through the meal about the noise he could hear them making. Maggie grew tired of attempting to cajole him into a better mood. After supper, she helped Dolores clean up and wash the dishes. Then they took the three boys to Sela and Leo's cabin and after much wrangling tucked them into bed.

"I will stay out here tonight," Dolores said. "Will you sit with them until I fetch my nightclothes?"

"Of course." Maggie took a seat in Sela's rocker, but in less than three minutes she heard Pablo weeping. When Dolores returned, she was holding him in her lap and singing the few Spanish songs she knew. Pablo's sobs were just beginning to subside.

"Are you sure you'll be all right out here with them?" Maggie asked as she passed him over to Dolores.

"Oh, yes, we will be fine."

With some misgiving, Maggie left them. Dolores and the boys should be safe out here, although all the men were away but Shep. He was in the bunkhouse, and would be the closest one for Dolores to call if she had an emergency. Maggie doubted their cook-maid would get a lot of sleep. Maybe tomorrow night she'd come out here to stay with the boys and give Dolores some respite.

She considered trying to reason with her father again, but when she got to the house, he wasn't in his office or the parlor. His bedroom door was closed. Maggie lifted her hand to knock, but thought better of it. Perhaps it was better to leave him alone and tackle the subject in the morning.

← ★ →

Alex pushed the men hard all afternoon. They brought in hundreds more cattle and sorted them into the holding pens. The ones they wouldn't take on the drive to Fort Worth were let loose. The cattle belonging to other ranches were placed in a separate pen from Porter's. They swapped off at the branding fires. Nobody liked to work that duty very long.

As the sun dipped in the west, Alex rode into camp weary, covered with sweat and caked dust. From a quarter mile away he could see that the chuck wagon hadn't returned.

"I'm heating some of them beans," Joe called from the fireside as Alex slid from the saddle.

"Thanks. Have we got coffee?"

"Uh-huh. One pot full for all of us."

The other men straggled in.

"That all we got?" Nevada kicked the end of a log sticking out of the fire, causing the spider full of beans to wobble precariously.

"Watch it!" Joe glared at him. "If you want to spill your supper, fine, but don't ruin ours, too."

"All right, boys, take it easy," Alex said.

Stewie had left cups and spoons, but had forgotten to leave the tin plates, so they ladled beans into their cups and sat around the fire in disgruntled silence, eating them without any liquid handy. When they'd eaten, they had to rinse out their cups so they'd have something to drink their coffee from.

No one wanted to sit up and tell stories. They all headed for their bedrolls early. Alex was reaching for his blankets when he heard the creaking wheels of the chuck wagon.

"Stewie's back," Tommy yelled.

A couple of minutes later, Early rode up.

"What took you so long?" Nevada asked.

"Had to stop and fix the harness on the way back." Early slid wearily from the saddle.

Stewie brought the chuck wagon in and positioned it in the usual spot. "You boys hungry?"

"We et the beans," Nevada said. "What else ya got?"

"I'll fix you some pan bread real quick, and Dolores set about making gingerbread as soon as she heard what happened. By the time we were ready to come back, she had a triple batch cooked. I'll let you all have one piece while I get the rest ready. Come on, Bronc. Help me set up my kitchen again."

The men cheered and settled down with slabs of the gingerbread while Stewie opened up the back of the chuck wagon and set about fixing the rest of their meal.

"All right, Early," Alex said. "Did the doctor come?"

"Nope. Not when we'd left. Mr. Porter wouldn't let us ride for the doc or take Leo into town."

"You're joshing," Alex said.

"No, I'm not. Instead, he told Sela she could take the buckboard and drive Leo into town herself."

Alex stared at him. How could the boss be so unfeeling? Sela had three small children and a newborn, and now her husband was injured so badly he wouldn't be able to work for weeks, maybe months. "That's not like Mr. Porter at all."

"I'm telling you, Alex, we gotta strike," Nevada said.

Alex frowned. "Quit talking that way. We've got work to do out here."

Nevada tossed the dregs of his coffee into the fire. "It makes me sick, what happened to Leo. If the boss won't take care of his own men, he doesn't deserve our respect. I don't want to work for him anymore."

"Me either," Tommy said.

"Hold on, boys." Alex stood. "Listen to me. I'll send someone tomorrow to find out how Leo's doing and take his gear to Sela. Let's not get all het up about this until we have more information, all right?"

No one said anything audible, but a few of the men muttered to their buddies. Alex poured himself another cup of coffee. "Stewie, you got more gingerbread?"

"Sure do."

Alex walked to the back of the chuck wagon to get it.

"I heard Miss Porter's home." Stewie laid a large slab on Alex's plate.

"Yeah, I saw her last night."

"You did?" The older man frowned. "You didn't tell us."

Alex shrugged. "Was she there when you took Leo in?"

"Naw, didn't see her. Dolores told me. I'll bet if Miss Maggie had been around, she would have made her pa send for the doctor, not make Sela drive poor Leo all the way into town. He was in bad shape by the time we got to the ranch."

Alex sighed. "I don't know what we can do about all this, Stewie. I'm upset too, but it seems to me that if we up and strike, we'll all be without jobs. That won't help anyone."

Stewie nodded. "Reckon you're right. It was hard, though. Downright mean of him. Sela had to take the baby with her in the buckboard. Dolores told her she'd keep the three little boys, but she couldn't handle the baby and watch them and do her work too. That ain't right. The boss shouldn't have made Sela go."

He was right, but Alex still held back. If he started badmouthing the boss, there'd be no turning back. Right now he was walking a tightrope. If he took one false step either way, the men would cut loose. But Mr. Porter was dead wrong.

———— ★ ————

After breakfast the next morning, Maggie took the Eagleton boys out to the corral and gave them rides on Duchess. Leo Junior, the oldest, was already quite a good rider at the age of six. Manuel and Pablo had to be lifted into the saddle. Maggie put them both on the horse at once and led them around the corral while little Leo watched from the top fence rail.

Maggie had always found it amusing that after his first son was properly named for him, Leo had allowed Sela to give the rest of the children Spanish names. That seemed to be the way of things with the cowboy and his bride. Leo had the first word, and Sela had the last. They'd always seemed very happy together. But now Leo was gravely injured. How would Sela cope with the family and their precarious finances? From what Dolores had told her, Maggie surmised that Leo might be laid up for a very long time.

All of the boys had taken two turns on Duchess when a lone cowboy rode in from the range. When he got to the barnyard, Maggie recognized Joe Moore, the outfit's wrangler. He had an affinity for horses. On a roundup, each cowpuncher had at least three horses at his disposal, and often more. Joe's job was to keep them ready to work. He'd been at the Rocking P for a year or so before she went away, but she didn't know him as well as she did the older cowboys.

"Good morning, Joe," she called as he trotted up to the corral.

"Miss Maggie." He touched his hat brim and swept a glance over the boys. "Any news about Leo?"

"No, nothing new. I thought perhaps I'd ride into town later. I have some things Dolores gathered up for Sela and the baby. I understand they left in a hurry yesterday." Maggie shot a sideways look toward the little boys and hoped Joe wouldn't go into too much detail about their father's condition in front of them. If Pablo began to cry again, she wasn't sure what she'd do.

"Yeah." Joe opened his mouth and then closed it. After a moment, he pushed his hat back a little. "I can take a bundle for Sela."

"Thank you." Maggie pulled out a smile and nodded toward the boys. "Let me get these cowpokes down, and I'll go get it."

"Well, uh . . . I could lead them around another turn if you like, while you fetch the stuff."

Maggie hurried to the kitchen. "Dolores, Joe Moore just rode in from the roundup. The men want to know how Leo is doing. Joe says he'll ride into town and find out—and he'll take those things we gathered up for Sela."

"Oh, good." Dolores laid down her paring knife. "Can you run to the cabin for them? I left them on the table. I'll wrap up some food for him to take Sela and Leo."

Maggie doubted Leo was eating solid food today, but she dashed out the back door and down the path toward the Eagletons' cabin. On the table inside, she found the pillowcase Dolores had stuffed with diapers, baby clothes, and a few extra items of Sela and Leo's. She knotted the opening. When she got back to the house, Dolores was out near the corral holding a couple of wrapped items for Joe to put in his saddlebags. The three little boys sat in a row on the fence, watching them like baby robins waiting for the next worm.

"Can you carry this, Joe?" Maggie asked, holding out the pillowcase. "It's mostly clothes."

"Sure, I can tie it on behind the saddle."

While he arranged the items, Dolores gave him several messages for Sela, ending with, "And tell her the boys are being good little gentlemen."

"I'll try to remember all that, but I don't suppose she'll believe that last one." Joe swung up into the saddle and touched his hat brim again. "Ladies. Boys." He nodded to the three solemn children and trotted off toward town.

"I can handle the boys now, Miss Maggie, if you want to pay that visit you were talking about to Miss Carlotta."

"Are you sure?" Maggie looked doubtfully at the boys. Leo

Junior had already climbed down from the fence, and Manuel followed. Pablo tried to swing down and hung whimpering from the top rail by his arms. Maggie lifted him and set him on the ground with a pat on the head, and he toddled off after his brothers toward the barn.

"Here now, young Leo," Dolores called. "Don't go far. I have something special for you in the kitchen."

That brought all three boys back to swarm Dolores.

"Are you sure?" Maggie asked.

"Yes. Go now, before I change my mind."

CHAPTER FOUR

The half-hour ride eased some of Maggie's strain. Just being back in familiar territory and riding her beloved horse over the grasslands unchaperoned boosted her spirits. She'd missed this freedom and the raw honesty of the Texas landscape.

When she cantered up to the low adobe ranch house, a cowboy came from the barn and took her horse.

"I will put him in the shade for you, señorita," he said with a pronounced Mexican accent.

Maggie smiled. "*Gracias*. I expect to be awhile with Señorita Carlotta."

The Herrera house was built around a courtyard, and she found Carlotta and her mother there in the shade, stitching something that could only be a party dress.

Carlotta jumped up, casting her sewing aside.

"Maggie, *querida*! I heard you were back." The dark-haired beauty ran to her across the stone courtyard. "I am so happy to see you!"

Maggie hugged her friend and greeted Señora Herrera.

"I've been dying to see you both."

"How is your father?" Señora Herrera said. "I heard he has been ill."

Maggie eyed her uncertainly. "I'm not sure. He does seem a bit thinner and . . . well, he hasn't discussed it with me, but I assume that if he was sick, he's getting better."

"Ah, that is good." Señora Herrera left to order some refreshments for the girls, and Carlotta drew Maggie to a cushioned settee.

"Come, you must tell me everything about your stay in San Francisco."

"All right, but first tell me what's going on in Brady and at the ranches."

Carlotta pulled a sour face. "Do we have to talk about the ranches? My father says your father is having trouble with his men, and that they are not happy with their wages."

Maggie was surprised the news had traveled so quickly. Had the Rocking P cowboys spread the word to the hired hands at other ranches?

"Tell me, have you heard anything else about our ranch? I'm wondering how things have been while I was away. I get the feeling there's a lot my father hasn't told me."

"Well." Carlotta looked around to check if anyone was near. "My parents say Señor Porter has fallen into melancholy since your mama died. It is very sad."

"Yes," Maggie said, thinking of her father's anger and hopelessness. "I'm trying to cheer him up, but he insists I can't make things better. And he won't listen to the men, even though I can't see that they're asking anything unreasonable."

"I'm so sorry." Carlotta smiled. "Forgive me—I know it is not funny. But it seems as though they think they are factory workers or something. If they leave, then production will stop."

"I know," Maggie said. "But life doesn't stop on a ranch just because someone's not doing his job."

"Oh, these men. They say we're dramatic, but they think they can force people to do what they want with a little threatening. I say ignore them. That's what my father would do. He'd say, 'Stop that idiocy and go back to work.'"

Maggie forced a smile. Her father had tried that and it hadn't worked. "Well, if worse comes to worst, I may be out there rounding up the cattle."

Carlotta laughed. "You could do it. The men, they think we are helpless, as well as emotional. They don't know that we could do most of their work as well as they can."

Maggie could see no reason to bemoan the situation at the Rocking P any further to Carlotta. "So, tell me about our friends. The last time I was home, you said that Peter Riddle had come a-courting. Are you still seeing him?"

"Ah, no, that was a short-lived infatuation, I fear." Carlotta laughed. "As soon as I discovered what a poor horseman Peter is, I lost interest."

Maggie chuckled. "Oh, you are too exacting!"

"No, I don't think so." Carlotta shook her head, sending her waves of glossy black hair bouncing. "He cannot even ride as well as Lupe."

Maggie's laugh became a hoot, since Lupe was Carlotta's four-year-old sister, the youngest of the family's five children. Carlotta joined her, and their laughter echoed off the adobe walls of the courtyard. Maggie hadn't let out such a laugh since long before her mother died. After a minute, she searched her pockets for a handkerchief to catch the tears that had slipped from her eyes.

"Show me what you are sewing," she said. "Is there a party coming up?"

"Not for weeks, but Mamacita and I want to have plenty

of time and not be rushed. I plan to embroider the bodice in gold thread that Papa brought from Dallas."

She held up the partly finished garment, and Maggie exclaimed over it. For a few minutes, she almost felt she'd gone back in time to the days before she accompanied her mother to the sanatorium. But her life would never again be as simple or as carefree as it had then.

Carlotta's mother pressed her to stay to eat dinner with them, and Maggie declined.

"I would love to, but I must get back and help Dolores with the boys." She had told them about Leo's accident. Both the Herrera women knew Sela Eagleton.

"I will stop in at Dr. Vargas's when we go to town," Carlotta said. "I do hope Leo will be all right."

"I haven't given Sela what I made for the baby," Señora Herrera said. "We must be sure to go into Brady soon and see her."

Maggie pushed Duchess on the way home. She hadn't intended to be gone so long. She'd be late for the noon meal, and she could only imagine Dolores trying to keep the boys quiet in the kitchen while she served Papa at the dining table. Maybe Shep would lend his help. She rode cross-country, over the range, so that she would get home as quickly as possible.

When she burst into the kitchen, Dolores was drying the dishes. Tears streamed down her face.

"What is it?" Maggie asked. "What happened?"

"The little boys."

Maggie looked around the empty room. "Where are they?"

"Shep took them into town."

"What for?"

Dolores's face crumpled. "Your papa. He said they cannot stay here. He said I can't watch them and do my work properly."

Maggie put her arms around her and pulled Dolores to her.

"I'm so sorry. I shouldn't have gone off and left you with them."

"It is not your fault."

"Let me talk to him."

Dolores shook her head. "He will not change his mind."

"We'll see about that." Maggie stormed from the kitchen and across the parlor to her father's office. Blood pounded in her temples. She threw the door open without knocking.

"Papa! What's this I hear? You sent the little Eagleton boys away?"

He pushed back his chair and gazed at her. "Don't overset yourself, Maggie. They need to be with their parents."

"You know Sela can't take care of them right now. This is unconscionable!"

"She can find someone in town to watch them."

"What if she can't?"

He shrugged. "It's not my problem. I pay Dolores to keep house and cook for us, and that's plenty. I won't let other people take advantage of her good nature."

"I was helping her with the boys."

"Not this noontime, you weren't."

Maggie stamped her foot. "I went to Carlotta's for a couple of hours. Papa, how could you do this?"

"Very easily when my ranch is at stake."

"Oh, like keeping those poor little boys for a few days is a threat to the ranch." She whirled and hurried back to the kitchen.

"I saved you a plate," Dolores said.

"Give it here, quick. I'm going into Brady."

Dolores blinked her red-rimmed eyes. "You are bringing the boys back?"

Maggie hesitated. "No, I don't think so. But maybe I can find someone in town who will help Sela for a few weeks. If I can find a place for her and the children to board . . ."

"That may be all you can do," Dolores said.

"Well, I've got some spending money left from my trip." New resolve gave Maggie hope, and she lifted her chin. "I should be able to pay for a couple of rooms for them for a few weeks if I can find a place. Anyway, I'm going to try."

— ★ —

The men worked grimly all day. Each time they rode into camp to deliver a bunch of cattle, they asked Stewie if there was any word. Finally, as they gathered at suppertime, Joe Moore stood by the fire, waiting to address them all.

"Leo's leg is broken in three places. The doctor says he may never be able to ride again. I'da been back sooner, but I rode into Brady to get it straight from the doc. Leo looks awful. They've got him doped up because of the pain."

"Oh, man, what's Sela going to do?" Early asked.

Joe winced. "I don't know. The boss said she'd have to take the kids into town with her to stay while she tends to Leo."

"Stands to reason she can't leave them at the ranch," Bronc said.

Nevada glared at him. "Why not? In the old days, the family would have helped her out—maybe found somebody to watch those kids for Sela."

"Well," Joe said, "I was headed back here when I met Shep totin' those kids in the wagon. He said Porter told him to take them to Leo and Sela and not bring them back."

Alex had to bite back the angry words he wanted to say. Several of the other men were not so restrained. The mildest comment was Harry's "That ain't right."

"My Rhonda would take care of 'em if she wasn't working," Bronc said. His wife assisted Dr. Vargas at his office to make extra money for the family, and they had a small house midway between the ranch and Brady.

"Well, Mr. Porter said he can't have them on the ranch without their parents there to supervise them," Joe said. "Don't get mad at me—I'm just telling you what I heard from Shep."

"Has Sela got a place to stay in town?" Alex asked.

"She said she'd been right there at Doc Vargas's since it happened, but she looks plumb wore out."

Alex could understand the men's anger. It wasn't right, and they all knew it. Sela couldn't sit at her husband's bedside and tend to three rambunctious young children and a new baby.

Tommy looked at Alex and Nevada. "Can't we do anything about this?"

"Yeah, we can." Nevada bristled with fury. "This has gone too far. A man gets hurt bad like that, his boss should take care of him, not toss him away like a piece of garbage."

Alex clenched his teeth. His hands curled into fists, and he couldn't hold back any longer.

"All right, boys. Maybe it's time we talk about a strike."

———— ★ ————

The sun had set by the time Alex rode toward the ranch. He'd left the other men at the camp with instructions to keep a night watch on the cattle as usual until he returned. He hoped they wouldn't let their anger boil over.

He galloped the first few miles just to work out some of his fury. Then he reined in the horse and finished the trip at a slower pace. By the time he reached the ranch house, he was calmer.

Lord, You'd better help me, so I don't blow up and say things I shouldn't say.

Alex wasn't sure the prayer even made sense, but he knew he couldn't go back to the roundup camp without either a promise from Porter or the courage to lead the men in walking off the job.

His brisk knock was answered almost at once. Maggie stood just inside the big parlor, wearing a blue dress that matched her eyes and showed off her figure.

"Uh . . ." Alex cleared his throat. "Is your father in?"

"Yes, he's in his study. Come on in, Alex."

He snatched his hat off and followed her inside. She sounded glad to see him, and she was smiling. But he'd thought she and Sela were friends, back before Maggie went away. How could she be so happy if she cared about Sela and Leo?

"How's the roundup going?" she asked.

"Not good." He didn't meet her gaze.

Maggie hesitated. "I'm sorry to hear that."

"You know about Leo?"

"Yes, and I'm sorry he and Sela are going through this. I went in to see Sela this afternoon."

"Is she all right?" Alex asked.

Maggie shrugged. "She has a lot to deal with, as you know. But she's a strong lady." She went over to the study door and knocked, then opened it. "Papa, Alex is here to see you."

"Send him in," came the muffled reply.

Alex walked in and closed the door. He turned to face Mr. Porter and squared his shoulders.

"Alex. What's the news?"

"We're striking."

"What?" Porter's face went deep red. He pushed himself up from his desk. "How dare you come in here and tell me that?"

Alex swallowed hard. "I don't like it either, but we don't know what else to do, sir. The men have some demands. If you're willing to meet them, they'll go on with the roundup just like normal."

"You insolent—Have you forgotten everything I've done for you?"

With difficulty, Alex managed to hold his gaze. "No, sir, I haven't. I've always admired you and appreciated every chance you gave me. But this thing with Leo, well, that was my limit."

"Your limit."

"Yes, sir." When Mr. Porter said nothing, Alex went on. "The men want more pay if they can't have their own herds, and we all want to see Leo get some compensation—not just Leo, but anyone who's injured while he's working for the Rocking P in the future."

By that time, Porter's face was purple. "And you agree with the men on these . . . demands?"

"Yes, sir, I think they're reasonable."

"And if I say no?"

"Then we all walk off the job together."

"In the middle of the roundup?"

"Yes, sir, if need be."

Porter stared at him stonily while he inhaled and exhaled. "All right, Alex. You go ahead and do that."

Alex's stomach dropped. "Sir?"

"You heard me." Porter's voice rose. "Go tell the boys. You can all leave. I'll hire someone else. *Now get out of here!*"

CHAPTER FIVE

The door to her father's study opened and Alex stormed out, his face taut. Maggie didn't think he even saw her. He marched out the front door and closed it firmly behind him, rattling the windows.

She ran and opened it, then flew across the porch and down the steps.

"Alex, wait!"

He turned toward her, his brown eyes hard with anger. "What is it?"

"You've ruined everything!"

"Oh?" He laughed and turned toward his horse.

Maggie stepped closer. "I wasn't here when the men brought Leo in, but as soon as I found out what happened, I tried to get Papa to help him and Sela. But Papa was all out of sorts. Not with Leo. He was angry because the men were making trouble, but after—"

"*We're* making trouble? That's insane."

"His words, not mine. Forgive me. I was going to talk to him tonight. I think I could have gotten him to sympathize—but not now."

Alex shook his head, and Maggie reached to touch his arm.

"Yesterday I thought we could get things back to normal here, but then today we had a setback." She hadn't wanted to tell him about her father's latest breach of conduct, but Alex and the other men would find out anyway when they visited Leo.

"What happened?"

She looked up into his brown eyes. Maybe he would listen, and together they could figure out what to do. "I'd been helping Dolores care for Leo and Sela's children, but I—I went away for a couple of hours. I shouldn't have done that, but I did. And when I came back, Papa had sent Shep to take the boys to Sela in town." She couldn't keep her face from crumpling as tears flooded her eyes. "I really thought I could make him understand, and that after a while he would see your side of it. But I shouldn't have gone away this morning."

"So how does that make it all my fault?"

She sighed. "I'm sorry. That was uncalled for. I still hoped that if I just had another day or two to work on Papa, I might be able to get him to relent. But now you've defied him outright. He'll never forgive you."

Alex glared at her. "I'm not the one who needs forgiveness, Maggie. There's a lot you don't know."

"Please—" Her voice shook, and she hated that. He wanted to play the injured party? She would not cry in front of him.

"I thought you were Sela's friend," he said. "What are Leo and Sela going to do now?"

That hurt a lot. She'd never known Alex to be so stubborn. "I don't know. I've done what I could to help them."

"I'm sure your father thinks *he* has, too." Alex jumped into the saddle and rode away.

Maggie stood watching him until his horse disappeared into the darkness. He never rode in from roundup this late. He should be getting ready to sleep, with the other cowboys. It would be nearly midnight when he got back to the camp. But would it matter, if they truly intended to strike? They might be up all night laying plans.

The breeze stirred, and she felt tears wet on her cheeks. She wiped them away and went back inside. She was exhausted from her long day, but she couldn't leave things as they were.

The study door was still shut. She pulled in a deep breath and marched over to it. Without knocking, she turned the knob and went in.

"Papa, I want to know what's going on, and I want to know now."

He was sitting behind the desk, slumped in his chair, but he straightened when she spoke. His face was gray, and he grimaced as he moved.

"Don't meddle in things you don't understand, Margaret."

Maggie cringed at that. He'd never called her Margaret unless he was displeased with her behavior. It had been years since that had happened. She stepped closer to the desk.

"I want to understand, Papa. Help me to understand, because the way you're acting baffles me. I've never seen you like this before."

"Times have changed."

"Times aren't the only things. *You've* changed. What is it? What happened while I was away to make you like this?"

He met her stare for several seconds and then faltered. "Oh, Maggie, I didn't intend for it to be this way."

She rounded the desk and knelt by his chair, taking his hands in her. "Papa, tell me. What is it?"

He let out a deep sigh, full of remorse. "Your mother's treatment . . . sweetheart, it took a lot of money."

"More than we had put away?"

He nodded. "All of that and the money I'd earmarked for new stock, and more besides. I still owe a lot."

"But . . . you paid for my upkeep, too, while I was with her. I never heard that the bills were late."

"I made sure they weren't. Didn't want you to worry. But the sanatorium . . . that bill got so big I couldn't do it. I just couldn't do it." Tears glistened in his eyes, and he turned his face away from her.

"Oh, Papa. Why didn't you tell me, when I came home for the funeral? I didn't need to go to San Francisco. I could just as well have stayed here with you. I'd have been happy."

He was silent for a long time. At last he said, "Then you'd have known."

She pulled herself up and put her arms around him. "I love you, Papa."

He reached up and squeezed her arm. They didn't move for a long moment. At last Maggie pulled away.

"So that's it? That's why you won't listen to the men?"

"I can't pay them more. I used to let them have their little herds. But every maverick a man puts his own brand on is money out of my wallet. I can't afford that now."

"It meant so much to them," Maggie said. "Not just extra income, but the men took pride in their herds."

"I know." He sighed. "Now they want more money—money I don't have."

"Why don't you just tell them?" Maggie asked.

"I can't do that."

"But Papa, you used to look out for the men. You kept the ranch nice, and you paid them enough for them to live on and tuck away a little for the future. Now they feel as if you don't care about them."

"I've been so tired," her father said. "Since your mother

died—no, before that. Ever since you went away with her, things have been hard. That was a bad year, and we haven't recovered financially since then. The bills and all . . ."

Through the window, she could see the moon rising. She wished they could be outside, enjoying it together.

"Papa, let's ride out to the roundup camp tomorrow." Even as she said it, she knew it was impossible. Even if her father felt up to it, his rift with Alex had ruined every possibility of a successful outing.

"The men are striking."

"Yes, it seems so." She stood there watching his face, not knowing what to say. She had no solutions to offer. "Can't we just tell the men that for now things are tight and you can't raise their pay, but maybe after the drive, if we get a good price for the cattle—"

"They won't listen."

"They will if you talk to them man to man. Assure them that you hear their concerns. Maybe even tell them you'll give them a little bonus after the drive to Fort Worth."

"You haven't heard a word I've said, have you, Maggie? I can't afford a bonus. I can't even afford to pay them." He shook his head. "I can't believe Alex turned on me. I was counting on that boy to keep the men calm until the drive was over."

"He was upset about Leo and Sela. Papa, what happened? I came home from Carlotta's today, and Dolores told me Shep took the children to Sela. I thought Dolores was going to keep them for her while she stayed in town with Leo."

Her father scowled. "Dolores can't do her work and watch three rowdy little boys. I told you that."

"But Sela can't have them with her at the doctor's office."

"That's not my problem."

Even to Maggie, he sounded cold.

"Papa—"

"Where did you go this afternoon? You missed supper."

Maggie sucked in a deep breath. "I went to town to help Sela."

His eyes narrowed. "I didn't expect you to go against me."

"Papa, she couldn't afford lodging, or someone to watch the children. If you wouldn't let her stay here in her own home, I felt I had no choice."

Her father stood and held up both hands. "Let's not say any more about this. I've put everything I could scrape up into the herd, and I'm counting on the money we get when we sell it to finish paying off the bills. Maybe then I can think about painting the bunkhouse and giving the men a bonus."

"Will that take care of everything, Papa?" Maggie looked deep into his eyes. "Because if you think there are enough cattle to sell, and if prices are high this year, well then, that should take care of it, right?"

"We won't know until the end of the drive."

She nodded, her mind racing. Now was not the time to tell him she'd spent what remained of her personal funds to hire a woman to watch the Eagleton children for Sela. "All right. What if you ask the men to continue at the wages you're giving them now, and if the drive goes well, you'll give them extra when it's over?"

"I can't promise them that. What if there's barely enough to pay the hospital bills?"

"Then, we tell them at the sanatorium that we're paying what we can, and we'll pay the rest next year."

"No. No, I can't carry any bills over until next year."

"Why not? If you can't pay it all now, you just can't. That's it. Won't they take what you can give them and wait for the rest? I mean, if you send as much as you can, that will be a sign that you intend to pay it all eventually."

"I said I can't do that."

Maggie winced at his angry tone.

Papa put a hand to his forehead and closed his eyes for a moment. "I'm sorry. I'm going to bed. I'll see you in the morning." He walked out of the room.

Maggie followed, her steps dragging. She felt adrift. Her father had been the one solid thing in her life—Papa and the ranch.

No one had lit the lamps in the parlor, and the room was dark. Light still spilled from the kitchen doorway, and Maggie walked slowly toward it. Dolores was covering a large pottery bowl with a linen towel. She looked up and saw Maggie in the doorway.

"*Buenos noches, chica*. You look so sad. What is wrong?"

Maggie stepped into the kitchen and sat down on a stool near Dolores's worktable. "It's Papa. I don't understand him."

"What do you mean?"

"He doesn't act like himself. I talked to him just now, and he's worried about money. Did you know about that, Dolores? He's afraid he won't be able to pay the bills from the sanatorium. I had no idea Mama's treatment cost so much."

Dolores gave her a sad smile. "They had a new treatment, but it was expensive. He wanted to try it, to give your mama every chance. I know he is worried. But I'm glad he talked to you."

Hot tears burned in Maggie's eyes. "If I'd had any idea, I'd never have let him pay for my trip to San Francisco. But when I was home last fall—when we had the funeral—he didn't say anything about it. He wanted me to go. In fact, I wanted to stay here with him on the ranch, but he insisted. He said it would be good for me."

"Oh, my sweet Maggie." Dolores came to her and gave her a hug. "I am so sorry. After your mama's death, he saw how sad you were, and that made his grief worse. You were a brave girl to stay with her all those months while she got weaker and weaker. I think your papa wanted you to go to a new place and have happy times with your cousin."

"Yes, I expect you're right. He wanted me to forget all the bad times. But I'm glad I could be with Mama then, Dolores. And I'll never regret being with her through those last months of her illness."

"Of course not. But you had some other things to think about in San Francisco, no?"

"Yes. Distractions. That's what he wanted for me, wasn't it?"

"I think so."

Maggie nodded. "But Papa didn't have any distractions. He had to stay here and worry about the money I was spending."

"Oh, do not say that. He wanted you to go, and to have pretty clothes and see the sights. Do not be sorry that you went."

"I *am* sorry. This has made Papa into a different person. He's so . . . so angry. If I'd stayed here, we would have spent less, and maybe I could have helped him stay happy." She shook her head. "Not happy after Mama died. That's not what I mean. But . . . I just don't understand this." The tears spilled over and ran down her cheeks. Dolores handed her a handkerchief.

"There, my dear one. You mustn't cry. Your papa, he doesn't feel well. You cannot blame him for being different than he was when you went away."

"He's been sick?" Maggie stared at her. "I did wonder. He's lost weight, hasn't he? And he doesn't look healthy. I thought it was because he hasn't been out riding the range with the men."

"Maybe it is partly from that, but I think it is more the opposite."

"What—?"

Dolores sighed. "He does not go out riding because he is ill. He is very tired and ill."

"Now you're scaring me. Has he seen a doctor?"

"Oh, yes. The doctor comes every week."

Alarmed, Maggie crumpled the handkerchief. "What is it? What's wrong with him?"

Dolores shook her head. "He does not tell me. Shep either. But I think it is bad, and I am glad you are home now."

Maggie stared at her for a moment then wiped away her fresh tears. "This is not fair. I came home three days ago, and I had no idea any of this was going on. I mean . . . when I was here last fall, we were all preoccupied with Mama's death and the service."

"That is natural."

"Yes, but was Papa sick then? I thought he seemed thinner and sadder, but I figured that was because of Mama dying. I felt sort of that way myself."

"I think he probably wasn't feeling well then. Last summer he seemed not to be so . . . active." Dolores arched her eyebrows in question. "And the money trouble, I think it started before that."

Maggie nodded. "I understand. He told me he'd sunk everything into the herd, hoping he can pay off the bills for Mama's treatment after the cattle are sold. But his health . . . He's only forty-seven. He's not exactly old. And if he's got the doctor coming every week—"

"That is only for the last month or so. And I have heard him say to Dr. Vargas that he should not drive out here so often, but the doctor wants to come. He gives him medicine, but your papa does not have me fix it for him. He does it himself. Powders, I think."

Maggie stood and shoved the handkerchief into her pocket. "Well, I'm going to find out exactly what's going on."

She marched out of the living room and crossed the big parlor. The door to her father's office was open. She glanced inside, but he wasn't there.

She went down the hallway and paused outside his bedroom. She felt horribly alone. Never before had she been on the opposite side of anything from Papa. In some ways, it felt worse than when she knew Mama was dying.

Lord, help me. Show me what to say.

She raised her hand and knocked.

"What?" he asked gruffly.

"It's Maggie. May I come in?"

After a moment she heard the bed creak. "Come ahead."

She opened the door. He was sitting on the edge of the bed, looking tousled.

"What is it?"

She stood before him, feeling guilty for no reason whatsoever. She hauled in a deep breath.

"Papa, I just found out that Dr. Vargas comes to see you often."

"So?"

"So I want to know what's going on. Dolores says you are ill, but she doesn't know what the trouble is. Please tell me."

"I don't see that it's any of your business."

Tears threatened to overwhelm her again. *Oh, please Lord!* Instead, she grasped at the anger that warred with the sadness inside her. "It is my business. This is my home, and you are all the family I have left. If you're going to be sick and I end up having to make decisions about the ranch, it will certainly be my business! You have no right to keep things from me. Now tell me!"

He started shaking his head when she was halfway through her tirade. By the time she'd finished, his face was dark red and he was struggling to rise.

"Don't get up, Papa. Just stay calm and tell me."

She placed a hand on his shoulder, and he sank back onto the bed. He was silent for a moment, avoiding her gaze. At last he looked up at her.

"I hoped we'd never have to have this conversation."

"Well, we do, Papa." The tears came, but she didn't care anymore. "Please talk to me! What is it?"

He let out a heavy sigh. "Cancer."

Maggie clenched her teeth.

"There's no cure," he said.

She sobbed. "Papa!"

He opened his arms, and she sat down beside him and buried her face against his shoulder. She cried for several minutes, unable to stop. At last she sat up and pulled out the crumpled handkerchief.

"I'm sorry, Papa."

Tears streaked his face, too. "Oh, Maggie, I hate this. I wanted to leave you a working ranch in good shape, not a pile of debts. And now the boys are threatening to walk out on us. I can't stand it. If it weren't for you . . ."

"What?" she asked, a new terror striking her.

He shrugged. "It wasn't supposed to be this way."

"No, it wasn't." She hugged him again. "Papa, I'm so sorry. Please don't worry about the ranch. It's *you* I need."

"But you won't have me for long, whether we like it or not. It's what made me tell you to come home, even though I knew you'd have a better time in San Francisco than you would here."

"No, Papa. I'm glad I came home. I wouldn't give up this time with you for anything. We'll work out something with the men."

He shook his head. "I don't see how. We can't give them what they want. And Alex! I never thought he'd do this to me."

"But if you told him why—"

"No! You mustn't."

She pulled away and studied his ashen face. "But why not, Papa? If the men knew you're sick—"

"I couldn't face them. Please, honey. Let me have this little bit of dignity."

She swallowed hard, her mind racing. "All right, Papa." She kissed his cheek, unable to say more.

CHAPTER SIX

When Alex rode into camp at last, only an hour was left before it was time to change the night riders. As tired as he was from the long ride to the ranch and back, he knew he couldn't sleep. One of the other men might as well get some rest. He exchanged Red for another horse from the remuda and trotted to the holding pens, where he met Nevada in the starlight.

"Turn in if you want. I'll take over."

"You're early," Nevada said.

"I was awake anyhow. Figured I might as well be out here."

"What did Porter say?"

"No change."

Nevada peered at him in the moonlight. "So you're really going to strike with us?"

"I'm thinking about it seriously."

"It's all I think about now," Nevada said.

Alex looked out over the quiet herd milling in the pens. "I never thought it was right to do something like that. To go against the man who's fed us and taken care of us for years."

"What he's doing isn't right. He betrayed us."

"I understand your feelings."

"Do you? We've been friends a long time, Alex. I always liked it here, and I like the people I work with. But I was earning a living. Now I'm not."

Alex blew out a long breath. "Go and get some shut-eye."

"Sure. But you know that if you don't walk with us, the boys are going to think you're as bad as Porter."

"If I don't side with you, it will be because I think God would have me stick with my employer."

"Oh, we're bringing God into this?"

Alex studied him in the moonlight. "How can you not?"

Nevada shrugged. "I figure God put us here on this earth to work. Porter's not letting us do that. He's wrong. Period."

"So God is on your side."

"That's the way I see it."

Nevada rode off toward the camp, and Alex watched him go. Would God really pick sides in this? More likely, He expected them to settle the matter peacefully. Neither side was going to budge, so far as Alex could see, and he was caught in the middle.

He rode slowly along the fence outside the holding pen. All was quiet tonight. He wished he'd brought his Bible out here, but he'd left it in his bedroll. Probably wasn't enough light to read by, anyway. He tried to remember the verses in Paul's letters about working for your master and doing what he said. Was he talking to slaves? Or to regular working men? Alex knew there were verses about working and not being lazy and providing for your family. But was it wrong to strike when the boss wouldn't pay you a decent wage? And was he, as foreman, wrong to sympathize with the men?

He figured he knew where Maggie stood in all this. As

Porter's daughter, she'd come down on his side, no matter what. She'd lost her mother, and Martin Porter was all the family she had left. Alex didn't know as he blamed her.

She was a very smart woman. At least, she'd been a smart girl. She'd said she could have convinced her father to listen to them. Did that mean she was advocating for the men? Maybe he should have listened. If he and Maggie had joined forces, they could have done something together.

Well, it was too late to go that route now.

He rode along, paying no mind to his horse or the cattle, slouching in the saddle. He met up with Tommy and exchanged laconic greetings. After a bit, Early rode out to take Tommy's place.

"Howdy," Alex said, and rode off toward the far end of the fence so he wouldn't have to talk to the older man.

When their relief came four hours later, Alex and Early rode back to the camp for breakfast. They were met by Nevada and the rest of the men. Alex could feel their unrest as he handed his mount over to Joe.

"We're done here, Alex," Nevada said.

Alex eyed him carefully and decided there was no changing his mind. He looked around at the others. "Does that go for all of you?"

"It sure does," Harry Jensen said.

Several of the others added their assent. A couple of them hung back and seemed to watch the others for cues. Bronc Tracey, the tall, dark-skinned cowboy was one, as was Stewie, their cook.

Alex shook his head. "I'd hate to see you do it. Boys, we agreed to do this job. You ought to at least finish the roundup. Don't leave it half done."

"We're going," Nevada said. "And as much as I like you, Alex, if you don't go with us, we won't let you stop us."

"Yeah," Tommy said. "We'll be sorry, but we've made up our minds. We're going, and that's that."

"In fact," Nevada said, "if you don't side with us, we're agreed—we need to tie you up while we do what we're going to do."

"What are you going to do?" Alex's pulse pounded, and dread flashed through him. Some of these men came from rough backgrounds.

"We figure we'll let the cattle loose," Harry said.

"You can't do that."

"Why can't we? If the boss won't listen to us, he'll pay."

"Yeah," Nevada said. "He'll be sorry he didn't give us what we asked for."

"Hold it." Alex held up his hands. Nevada was usually a reasonable man, but he sounded uncharacteristically childish now. "Isn't leaving him in the lurch bad enough? If you take off today, he'll be in a difficult situation. He'll have to get someone else to come in fast and finish the roundup. That won't be easy. Then he's got to hire a crew to get these critters to Fort Worth."

"Look, we know you want to be loyal to Porter," Nevada said. "But we have a better chance of making him listen if we leave him right when it hurts him the most."

"Yeah," Tommy said. "We'll hurt him in the pocketbook."

"And we need to ride to other ranches," Joe said. "We have to get to them before Porter does and get some support from the other cowhands."

"That's right," Early said. "If we don't get there first, Porter will hire cowboys away from his neighbors to do our jobs."

Nevada leveled his gaze at Alex. "So are you coming with us, or not?"

"Aren't you even going to eat breakfast first?"

"Half of us have eaten already." Nevada shouted to the

cook, "Stewie, get a plate for Alex." When he turned back to Alex, his face was grim. "I'm warning you, we'll be watching you. Don't get any ideas about running off to tell Porter. Either you're one of us now, or we'll leave you here tied up good."

"You'd really do that?" Alex stared at him. He'd always considered Nevada a friend he could count on. Suddenly he was an outcast, and men he had trusted planned to harm him.

The other men looked a little gray, but no one spoke up until Early said uneasily, "He could die if we do that."

Alex eyed Nevada askance, but even this man—the one he'd considered rock solid in supporting him when it came to bossing the men—didn't bat an eyelash.

Joe called out, "Rider coming!"

←———— ★ ————→

They all swung around toward the trail from the main ranch. A single horse cantered toward them. As the rider came closer, they all stood in silence. Before anyone spoke, Alex recognized the horse—and the expert horsewoman in the saddle.

Maggie.

She hadn't ought to be so far from the home ranch by herself. Did she think she could talk these men out of their plans? He had the feeling she wasn't here for the fun of it.

She pulled up a few yards from them in a puff of dust and bounced lightly to the ground. Like a born Texan, she dropped Duchess's reins and ambled toward them. Her expression was neutral, but her eyes jumped from Alex to the other men, weighing their demeanor.

"Morning, boys," she said.

Harry whipped off his hat. "Miss Maggie. Nice to have you home."

Several of the other men threw him rather disgusted glances.

Alex stepped forward. "Hello, Maggie. What brings you out here?"

"May I talk to you for a minute, Alex? Or are you busy?" She looked again at the knot of men, not one of whom looked remotely as if he'd done a lick of work that morning.

"Sure." Alex turned and caught Nevada's eye. "You fellas put things in order. We'll finish our discussion in a little bit."

Maggie said nothing about his unusual instruction. Alex wasn't sure he wanted to talk to her, but he surely didn't want her talking to the rest of the men. They were so riled up already, things could get ugly if she said the wrong thing. Even as pretty as she was, she represented the boss as far as they were concerned, and short of her father, Maggie was the worst person who could have entered the camp.

A dozen yards beyond the chuck wagon, Alex turned and faced her, making sure he could see what the men were doing. Several of them had headed toward the remuda, and a few filled their plates for a belated breakfast. But at least half a dozen just stood where he'd left them, gawking.

"What is it?"

Maggie frowned. She was standing so close, she had to tip her head back a little to look up at him. He could see the darker blue flecks in her eyes. Her creamy white skin reminded him of the differences between them, and how removed she'd been from ranch life for the last two years. She'd pulled back her hair, but a lock showed under the rim of her Stetson.

Alex cleared his throat and edged away just a bit. He hadn't been this close to a woman—not even Dolores—since he'd left his parents' place.

"You're going to strike today, aren't you?"

"We—uh—" He looked away. Should he consider her the enemy? Because she surely wasn't on the men's side. But if he took her father's part and decided to ride off with Maggie, what would they do? The disturbing image of him and Maggie tied up together all day in the blazing sun made his stomach sour. The boys wouldn't lay a hand on her, would they? He wasn't sure—they'd seemed mighty determined to keep him away from Mr. Porter while they carried out their plans.

In less than two seconds, her expression went from apprehensive to furious. "How could you do this to Papa?"

"I haven't done anything except try to talk these fellas down. But you might as well know it's not an easy job."

"They've decided, then?"

"Pretty much." Alex adjusted his hat so that it shaded his face more. Maybe the men couldn't read him the way he was trying to read Maggie.

"Well, you've got to call it off."

"Me? You think I have that power?"

"The men will listen to you."

"They're tired of listening to the boss and the boss's man. They're not giving me much of a choice in the matter."

"What do you mean?"

"If I go against them . . ." He sighed and lowered his chin. "Maggie, I think you should take Duchess and ride home. *Now*."

"What are you saying? Alex . . ." She reached out and grasped his forearm. He looked down at her hand, then at her face. Color flooded her cheeks. She let go and lowered her gaze. "Please, Alex. You need to help us. You're the only person the men will listen to. I know you're right, and they won't talk to Papa anymore. But it's not how they think it is."

"How is it, exactly?"

Her cheeks were scarlet now. She hesitated. "Do you need to know every detail?"

"If you expect me to try to turn the herd for you, yes."

He glanced toward the men by the campfire. Diego and

Harry were drinking coffee. Nevada, Tommy, and Joe were still watching them. What would they think, with Maggie holding on to him like she had and blushing? Tommy stared with disbelief, and Nevada's gaze held sheer contempt.

Alex backed up a step. "Maggie, these men are determined. I don't think they'll listen to me, unless I can go back to them and tell them your father has changed his mind. Has he done that?"

"Not . . . exactly." She looked up at him again, and now her eyes pleaded. "He made me promise not to tell you certain things. Alex, please. We need you. You *and* the men. Don't leave us now."

"I told you, I don't have a lot of choice. And if they walk, what good am I to your father?"

Tears glistened in her eyes. "I tried to get him to change his mind about Leo."

"What about Leo?" Alex glared at her. The injustice Porter had done the injured man went down hard with the men, him included.

"I was going to help Dolores take care of the little boys while Leo's at the doctor's office in town."

"You told me. Your pa wouldn't have it, and he sent them into town."

She nodded. "Dr. Vargas is keeping Leo there for at least two weeks. Sela needs to stay in town and help tend to him. The doctor's gone a lot, helping his other patients. After that, if things are going well, the doctor says they might be able to move Leo home."

"That sounds reasonable."

"He'll be laid up a long time. Sela will still need help, but they'll probably have to board in town. It would have been easier with them in their cabin, but . . ."

"He won't let them go back there?"

Maggie didn't look at him. "We'll have to see what happens when Leo's ready to go home. But in the meantime, I found a woman near the doctor's office who'll keep the boys for a week or so. If they behave, maybe she'll keep them until the doctor lets Leo go. And she'll let Sela sleep there if she wants to. But . . ."

"Did you see Leo?"

"No, but I talked to Sela." Maggie swiped a tear away. "Alex, this is really hard for her. The doctor says Leo may not ever be able to ride a horse again. She's worried about how he'll make a living after this."

Alex had considered Leo one of his best friends since he came to the Rocking P. He didn't like the idea that the cheerful man might not be able to earn money to support his family.

"I wish you'd told me last night."

"I . . . Papa . . ." She shook her head.

"I wish we could do something to help them," Alex said.

Maggie lowered her voice. "I gave her some money for food and incidentals. Papa wouldn't advance Leo's pay for her. I feel so bad. Alex, I've never seen him like this before. I have to believe he'll come around. What I gave Sela won't last long."

"Is your pa paying the doctor?"

"I don't think so. At least he hasn't agreed to yet. He was put out with me for helping them."

"That's cruel. It's . . . it's downright criminal."

Maggie cringed. "Please don't."

"What do you want me to say?"

Tears rolled down her cheeks. "I don't know. I—I paid the woman for a week's board for Sela and the boys. She can go over there and eat if she feels she can leave Leo long enough."

Alex swallowed hard. Maggie was doing a lot more than he'd realized, and he felt he'd been too hard on her. "That's— that's good of you."

She shook her head. "That and the little cash I gave Sela was all I had. It was my own pocket money, left over from my trip. I can't do any more for her, and I feel so terrible."

"I'll take up a collection among the men. And your pa had better give me Leo's wages on payday. I'll take them to him."

"But—"

"What?" It came out gruffer than he'd meant, but Alex couldn't contain the rage he felt toward her father and the tenderness for Maggie. Together, they made him feel as though he'd been caught on foot in the middle of a stampeding herd of longhorns.

"I was just thinking," she said. "You might not have a next payday if you strike."

"You think he'd withhold our pay? He owes us for half a month now."

"I hope he wouldn't. But he's very upset that you would do this to him. All of you men, but especially you, Alex."

Alex sighed and pulled his hat off. He wiped his forehead with his sleeve and put the hat back on. "I don't know what to say, Maggie."

"He told me . . ." She hesitated, as though she wondered whether she ought to tell him the truth. "There are things I can't talk about—personal things. But Papa told me that if you all strike, he'll ride over to the Herrera ranch and ask Juan and his men to help him finish the roundup and go in with him on the cattle drive."

Alex stomach sank. Mr. Porter was already planning what to do. He had no intention of meeting their demands. And he'd come to the conclusion that Alex would walk with the men.

"I'm sorry, Maggie. I didn't want it this way."

She nodded. "I'm afraid he'll fire you all if you strike, and not take you back, no matter what. Then we'll have twenty men without jobs. And Sela and the kids—what will happen to them? Leo isn't striking. It's not fair for him to be caught in this." Her lips quivered and she wiped her hand across her cheek again, smearing the tears. "Can't you stop this, Alex? Please!"

"I don't have that power, Maggie."

She sobbed, and his heart wrenched. It was bad enough feeling torn in half between the men and his employer. Something had to be wrong with the boss. Something awful. Otherwise he wouldn't act this way.

"Don't cry, Maggie."

She sniffed and tugged at the bandana around her neck. She took it off and mopped her face.

"That's better," Alex said. "Look, I'll ask the men one more time. You wait here."

She nodded.

Alex walked over to the campfire. More than anything he wanted to be able to give her some good news.

"Gather around, boys. I need to talk to you."

The men who hadn't scattered came over, eyeing him suspiciously.

"What's up?" Nevada asked.

"I'm going to ask you all one more time, and after this I'm done talking about it. Can we make a gesture of good faith and ask Mr. Porter one more time to work with us?"

"Not me," Early said.

"Me neither." Diego spat in the dust. "I've had it up to here, Alex." He made a chopping motion near his throat.

"I think it's gone too far," Bronc said, almost apologetically, looking past Alex toward Maggie.

Nevada gazed at Alex with hard, dark eyes. "Is Porter asking us to stay?"

"No."

"Then what more is there to talk about?"

"That's right," Tommy said. "We're striking, no matter what your *girlfriend* wants."

Alex lunged toward him, and Nevada grabbed his arm and held him back.

"Take it easy, Alex."

"I won't let anyone talk about Miss Maggie that way."

"It's not exactly an insult, is it—saying you're sweet on her?"

Alex gritted his teeth. "She might think it was."

"Oh, I doubt that," Nevada said. "Just climb down off that overgrown sense of chivalry."

Alex stood still, fuming. All of the men would make fun of him now, and he probably deserved it. But Maggie hadn't earned humiliation. He hoped she hadn't heard their remarks, but she'd certainly seen him jump on Tommy.

He pulled in a big breath. "You fellas be polite to Miss Maggie. She's not against us. She's only here to try to help her father, when he's too stubborn to help himself. That's kind of noble, don't you think? She could've stayed home."

Tommy's lip curled. "Yeah, well, maybe she should've."

Alex wanted to punch Tommy so badly he could barely keep from charging him again. But Nevada would stop him again. He took another deep breath. Nevada was a good friend. He knew when to act tough, and when that time came, nobody would be tougher. Nevada was a man you wanted at your back. He didn't want to make things worse between them when the men were like a powder keg waiting for someone to light the match.

"That's it," Nevada said softly. "Bide your time, pal."

Alex nodded. His friend was right. Vengeance was God's. When this was over—and he hoped, when they all went back to work again—he'd recommend that Tommy not be rehired.

In the meantime, if they insisted on striking, it was better to stick together.

Bronc said, "The way I see it, I ain't going to keep working for this outfit unless Porter promises to raise our pay. Rhonda and I aim to own our own place someday, and it won't happen at thirty bucks a month."

Harry nodded. "I hate to do it, Alex, but we can't get by on what he's giving us. You know that. Especially the family men."

"Yeah," Early said, stroking his long mustache. "We want to see Leo taken care of, if nothing else."

"I hear you, and I understand. Really I do." Alex clenched his jaw and looked at Maggie. She stood watching them, her face blotchy from her tears, but her eyes held resolution.

"Look, what if we say forty a month, but he gives Leo half pay?"

"Leo and any others hurt working for this outfit," Nevada said.

The other men murmured, and after a minute, Harry said, "I'd take it, Alex."

"Me too," Early said.

Alex looked over the cluster of men. Hardened, angry— all of them. He wouldn't dare ride off again and leave them to hash over their discontent without his tempering presence. The others who hadn't been in on the conversation might disagree when they heard of the offer they were making. That could make them furious, and they might do something destructive.

"Nevada," he said, "will you ride back with Maggie and present the revised demands to Mr. Porter?"

"What—forty a month, and what else do I tell him?"

"Either forty a month or thirty and we keep our herds, like before, and Leo can draw half pay until he's in the saddle again. The same for any man injured on the job."

"All right. But he'll say no."

Alex ignored Nevada's last comment. "If he accepts, we continue working as we were. If not, we're done tomorrow at sundown."

"Tomorrow?" Tommy asked. "Why not today?"

"Tomorrow's Friday, and we're supposed to take in the cattle we've rounded up. We do that, we get our pay, and then we leave."

"If he pays us," Nevada muttered.

Alex shot him a warming glance. "It will maybe make him more agreeable if he knows we'll do that."

"Suits me," Early said. He looked relieved.

Harry nodded. "I can live with that."

"Looks like I don't count," Tommy said. "We ought to walk right now."

"Settle down, Tommy." Nevada's stony face was enough to make the younger man close his mouth.

Alex decided he'd be foolish to wait for anyone else to speak.

"I'll tell Miss Maggie." He walked slowly toward her. She must have heard some of the men's remarks, or maybe she could read the outcome in his face. She broke their gaze and looked down at her boots.

"The men insist on some concessions, Maggie. I'm going to send Nevada Hatch back with you to see your pa with our last offer. If he turns us down this time, I can't hold the men. I'm trying to persuade them to at least bring in the cattle we've rounded up before we leave tomorrow, but I can't promise that will happen."

"But . . . you'll all keep working today?"

"I can't speak for all of them, but I sure will. And I'll try to keep the rest of them working, at least until we hear back from your pa."

Tears glistened in Maggie's eyes. "Please don't let them do this, Alex. It could ruin my father."

Just pulling in the next breath was painful, and he couldn't look her in the eye. "What do you think this will do to the men? Think of Leo, Maggie. Think of Sela and the kids. Is that how you want your family's employees to live?"

Nevada trotted his big bay horse over. "I'll be riding with you, Miss Maggie."

Maggie glared at Alex. Without another word, she turned and gathered her horse's reins. She lifted her left foot to the stirrup. Under other circumstances, Alex would have offered to give her a boost, but such an action might get him clobbered about now.

She swung up into the saddle and wheeled Duchess without so much as a glance in his direction. She clucked to the horse and took off at a canter. Nevada's horse shot off after hers. Alex stood watching until he could see only a puff of dust where they'd disappeared. He reminded himself to breathe. He had cattle to round up.

ommy and three of the other cowboys rode over to where Alex was checking his saddle girth.

"We're heading for the Bar D and the Lazy S to tell the men there what we're doing," Tommy said.

"Why don't you wait until Nevada comes back and we know for sure? Let's get this job done and leave with a clean slate."

Tommy shook his head. "If we wait, Porter will tell the other ranchers, and we won't be allowed to talk to their men."

That was likely true, but Alex hated to let them go and drum up support before he got this final confirmation. He realized he was clinging to a slim thread of hope that the strike would not go forward, but the odds were against him. He and Porter had parted last night with the understanding that they would strike, and he doubted that would change now. But if the Rocking P was the only ranch where the hands struck, plenty of other men would be ready to hire on with Porter.

"All right. But just you four. And come back by sundown and tell us how it goes."

Tommy nodded. He and the other three loped away, letting their high spirits escape in whoops. Maybe it was better to get them off Rocking P land for a spell.

As Alex mounted Red, Early rode over. "You and me for the creek bed, boss?"

Alex bit his lip. "If we strike, I'm not your boss."

Early nodded. "Remind me when we get the word."

"All right. Let's go."

For the next two hours, he tried not to think about the strike, or Porter's iron stance on the pay issue, or Maggie's tear-streaked face. He and Early popped cattle out of brush and drove them down ravines and over hills. When they brought in forty head to the corrals, Bronc was tending the gate with his left hand wrapped in a makeshift bandage.

"What happened?" Alex asked as soon as the cattle were confined.

"Oh, I was holding down a calf for Diego, and he singed me with the branding iron."

Alex winced. "How bad is it?"

"It won't keep me down, but I feel it."

Alex looked him over and decided to trust Bronc's assessment. "All right. Take it easy if you need to. I'll talk to Diego. He needs to be more careful."

"Oh, don't worry about him," Bronc said. "I gave him that message, loud and clear. Lucky you wasn't around when it happened."

Alex nodded grimly. Bronc's vocabulary got creative on occasion.

Alex turned Red out with the remuda and took a fresh horse, to give his personal mount a rest. He and Early rode out again to look for more strays. They had to go farther each time, and it was past noon the next time they reached camp. Alex handed his horse off to Joe. Half a dozen men were eating their dinner. Stewie had beans, side meat, flapjacks, and unlimited coffee ready.

"Nevada back yet?" Alex asked Joe at the corral gate.

"No sign of him."

Alex didn't like it, but he headed for the chuck wagon.

"Eat up, boys," Stewie called. "You may not know where your next meal is coming from."

Alex washed in the enameled washbasin and shook the droplets from his hair. After he'd scrubbed a layer of dust off his hands and wet his bandanna, he went to Stewie for his dinner.

"Are you walking with us if it comes to that, Stewie?"

The cook handed him his plate. "I reckon so. Hate to leave the Rocking P, but I also hate to think of what'll happen to me when I'm too old to cook. Shep's working around the main ranch, but I wonder how long Porter will keep him on. And he sure hasn't got room for two old geezers with rheumatism."

Alex sat down in the shade of the wagon to eat. Early got his plate and came to sit beside him. "Whatcha think now, boss?"

Alex took a gulp of coffee. "I think it's taking us longer to do this job without Tommy and the others. We're down six men now, counting Leo and Nevada. I sure hate to ride off and leave a job not done."

"That's kinda the point, ain't it? Show Porter how much he needs us?"

"I suppose."

"Listen, boss, I gotta tell ya, I didn't like the way they was talking this mornin'. If they start talking about roughin' you up again . . . well, I won't stand for it, ya hear?"

"Thanks, Early. I did wonder about you and Nevada. We go back a ways."

"Yup. Nevada, he wouldn't let 'em hurt you either. He just

didn't say nothin' so the boys wouldn't get any madder'n they were. He mighta let them tie you up, but I'm guessin' he'd've been the one to do the tyin'—not too tight, you know? And he'd knock down anyone who tried to seriously hurt you."

Alex wasn't sure the older man was right, but his words did bring a little comfort.

Tommy and the others came back with noncommittal news from the other cowboys they'd contacted. Most were happy to stay where they were, and no one wanted to come right out and declare in support of the strike. At least nobody else was eager to hire on at the Rocking P if the men left their jobs.

"We warned 'em about conditions here," Tommy said. "Porter will be lucky to find a single man to work for him after this."

When Alex went back for more beans, Stewie said, "How's it going?"

"You mean the roundup?"

"Well, yeah. Everything."

"Not bad. Not good, either."

"You boys aren't nearly done, are you?"

Alex shook his head. "It would take three or four more days to do it right, but I guess we're done once we take this cut in."

Stewie nodded. "I'm hoping Nevada brings us good news."

"Me too." Alex looked around at the men. No one seemed in a hurry to get back to work. Diego had gone off by himself, probably keeping out of Bronc's way. The rest sat within a few yards of the smoldering fire. "Got more coffee?" Alex asked.

Some folks thought it was foolish to drink hot coffee in the Texas heat, but they didn't have anything better, and when men dragged into camp tuckered out, something about the strong brew hit the spot.

"I'll get you some," Stewie said. "That fresh pot oughta be ready. Sit down and eat."

Alex ambled back to where Early still sat in the shade. Stewie grabbed a tin cup and walked over to the fire. They'd let it burn down to embers, just going enough to keep the food warm.

"Hey, boys, coffee's ready," he called.

Stewie lifted the coffeepot and turned toward the wagon. He didn't notice the empty spider he'd set off a few minutes earlier and he tripped over it. He had the presence of mind to fling the coffeepot away from him as he fell, but the contents sloshed out on the ground, sending a brown wave from his hands nearly to where Alex sat. A few drops splashed on Early's boots.

Stewie curled up and rubbed his shin, swearing mildly. Bronc chimed in with a stronger epithet.

"Oh, great." Tommy scowled at Stewie. "Nobody needs a clumsy cook."

Alex stood and walked over to extend a hand to Stewie. "You all right?"

"I think so." Stewie took his hand, and Alex pulled him up.

Early had followed Alex. He stooped and retrieved the coffeepot. "You got makin's for more?"

"Oh, sure." Stewie took the pot and headed for the back of the chuck wagon, muttering and limping.

"It's my turn to work the branding fire," Alex said to Early.

Early nodded and gazed toward the hills in the distance. "Reckon I'll see if Diego wants to ride up to Willow Canyon. They's probably a few cattle up there."

As the other men saddled their fresh mounts for the afternoon's work, no one mentioned Nevada. He should have been back by now. Alex grew more tense every time he thought about it, but he was glad no one brought up the subject.

As Harry mounted his horse, the cinch strap on his saddle broke, and the cowboy plummeted to the ground, saddle and all. He lay there for a moment with an injured air. Tommy, Bronc, Early, and Diego burst out laughing. After a moment, Harry joined them. For the first time that day, Alex cracked a smile.

"Well, now, boys," Harry said as he climbed to his feet and dusted off his pants, "I reckon I'll be a minute puttin' a new leather on there. See ya later."

"I've got one for you," Joe said. He kept some extra straps, rivets, a leather punch, and other supplies with his cache of horseshoes and nails in kegs mounted outside the chuck wagon.

Despite the small mishaps and the tense atmosphere, the men continued driving in cattle, culling them, and bringing the mavericks to the branding fire. Alex worked there with Joe and Tommy. The day had turned out hot and humid, and working around the fire had Alex thirsty, tired, and out of sorts in short order. He tried to keep the tone light and friendly, though when the men came in from the range they invariably asked if there was any word.

In the occasional lulls, Alex recorded the number of calves branded, cows released, steers added to the day's "cut," to be driven to the ranch and join the herd that would be sent to Fort Worth. Who would handle the cattle drive? He wondered if Mr. Porter was already lining up a new crew.

There must have been a better way to handle the men's complaints. Alex went over in his mind the men's rising discontent and his pleas to Mr. Porter. Step by step, they'd come to this impasse, and now he was in the awkward position of having to choose sides. And he'd chosen, irrevocably, to stand with the men. That meant, in all probability, being out of work within a day, without regular pay, and without a place to live. He supposed he could always go home to his father's ranch and take up freighting again, though he loathed it.

Even more distressing than the thought of being out of work, Alex knew he'd lost the respect of one of the men he admired most.

He didn't like the way Porter had behaved over the last few months. As much as a year ago, he'd seen signs that the boss was growing weary. Slowing down. Not working as hard as he used to. And last year's cattle sales had been disappointing.

Had financial losses brought him to this—where he wouldn't take care of the men who'd given him their labor and loyalty? He'd pushed the men too far, something Alex never would have thought Mr. Porter would do. When he looked back over the spread of years, he could see that the boss had changed drastically. It had happened so gradually, the newer men didn't even remember him as a generous, good-natured employer who would toil beside them from sunup to dark.

Alex had never had a claim on Maggie, and yet he felt he'd lost her too. He'd known she admired him when she was younger, but he'd followed the advice of his foreman then, and ignored her more blatant attempts to flirt. He'd treated her like a kid sister. Sure, she was cute then, and fun to be around. He'd always brightened when she came out to the corral to watch them breaking new horses or when he'd been assigned to keep an eye on her while she took a pleasure ride. But he didn't want a shred of distrust between him and the boss, so he'd been extra careful not to give any reason for offense. That had paid off and gotten him where he was today.

And now she was back. He might have earned the right to look at the boss's beautiful daughter as something more now— even the right to court her. But that couldn't happen when he was leading his boss's men in rebellion. Maggie was right— Porter would never forgive him now. He wasn't sure Maggie would either. That cut him to the quick.

An hour before sunset, Nevada came back alone. His horse jogged along slowly as though both he and the rider hated to return to camp. Harry spotted him first and called to Alex.

"Looks like Nevada's back. Took his time."

Alex laid down the Rocking P branding iron and walked out to meet Nevada before he reached the campfire.

"What's happening?"

Nevada frowned and shook his head. "Porter won't listen. Any man who won't keep working at thirty a month is fired immediately and can pick up his pay tomorrow. He says he'll have it ready. Today's the fifteenth, so we'll each get half a month's pay. That's it."

Alex stared at him. "It took you all day to get that out of him?"

Nevada shook his head and looked off toward the hills. "I rode into town after, to see Leo. The doctor's keeping him doped up because he's in so much pain."

"I'm sorry to hear that."

"Yeah, well Sela's sticking by him, but she looks real tired. She's got the baby with her all the time and nobody to help her. The doc's gone most of the day, seeing patients."

"Maggie got someone to watch the boys, though," Alex said.

Nevada nodded. "But they really need Leo's pay. I told her we'd see if we could get it for him tomorrow."

"And Porter won't change his mind?"

"Nope." Nevada pushed his hat back and met Alex's gaze. "We're in it, chum. No backing down now."

CHAPTER EIGHT

"Can't you just give a little, Papa? Nevada looked so angry when he left!"

"He's got no right to be angry. If anyone should be upset, it's me. I've given those men exactly what I promised them, nothing less. And what do I get? Tough talk and laziness."

Maggie decided not to debate that problem. The appropriation of the men's private herds was obviously a sore spot on both sides. Nevada Hatch had yelled so loudly that Maggie had heard him in her bedroom and come to see what the ruckus was about. If she were the ranch's owner, she wouldn't handle the matter the way her father had. But he was supposed to be wiser, with all his experience. She felt as though he was throwing away what he'd worked all his life to build.

The bleak thought that soon she *would* be the owner didn't cheer her. These men would be gone by then and she'd have a new crew. Without her father and the hands she'd known and trusted since girlhood, how could she run the Rocking P? She clutched the edge of his desk and tried to bring her thoughts back to the less terrifying problem at hand. She'd heard only the tail end of the latest argument, but the loudness and tone had made her fear the two men would come to blows.

"I never made maverick herds part of your wages," her father had said in icy tones. "Show me where it's written that I owe you a one of *my* cattle."

"But you've let the men keep them for at least ten years that I know about," Nevada had responded. "That's setting a pattern, and stopping it now without compensation is going back on your word." Maggie jumped at the sound of Nevada's fist hitting the desk.

"It's no such thing!" Papa's chair scraped the floor as he leapt to his feet.

Maggie knew she shouldn't interrupt as they argued on for a few more minutes; she wrung her hands and wondered if she ought to barge in. Her father's coughing bout tipped the scales. She'd marched into the office and invited Nevada Hatch to leave in none-too-cordial terms. Now her father drooped in his chair, still proud and unrelenting, though his enemy left the field.

"But, Papa, some of those men have families," she said. "What will they do?"

"They should have thought of that before they started this strike thing." Her father began to cough again. He pulled out a handkerchief and covered his face.

Maggie hurried to the side table and poured him a cup of water.

"Here. Drink this. And shouldn't you be taking the medicine Dr. Vargas left for you?"

He took the cup and gulped down some water, then resumed coughing. Nothing she could do for him seemed to help.

He sank back in his chair with his eyes closed, a grimace of pain distorting his features.

"I'll go for the medicine." She hurried out and down the hallway to his room for the packet. She'd made him tell her the instructions for mixing it yesterday, and for the last twenty-four hours, she'd browbeaten him into taking it on schedule. Other than that, she'd found few ways to comfort him. Sometimes even her presence seemed to pain him.

She carried the mixture back to the office and held the glass out to him. "Here you are. Maybe you should lie down, Papa."

"No, I've got work to do." He waved a hand, indicating the ledger and papers spread out over his desk. But he took the glass from her and downed his dose.

While he drank it, Maggie peered cautiously at the papers.

Lowering the glass, he winced. "That stuff is awful. Can't see how anything that bitter can help your insides."

"Next time the doctor comes, I'll ask him how it works. Can I help you with your work here? It might go faster."

"No, thanks. I figure all the hands will be in tomorrow morning for their pay, and I want to have it all ready, so there's no dillydallying. I want them paid off and out of here."

Maggie's heart sank. "But they're not done with the roundup, Papa. Let me ride out to their camp again and see if we can persuade them to at least finish the roundup."

"No. I'm done with them. I'll hire a new crew."

"Where?"

He frowned and picked up his pen. "I sent Shep over to Herrera and Bradley today. He'll rally my friends around me."

Maggie hoped he was right. "At least let me help you prepare the men's pay slips. Do you have the cash on hand?"

"Shep is bringing it. I told him to go to the bank first."

"Isn't that kind of dangerous, sending him alone to get so much money?"

"It's not our usual payday. Nobody will know we're getting it today."

Except Alex and his men, Maggie thought. She shoved aside the disloyal thought. The men may be unhappy and irresponsible enough to quit in the middle of roundup, but they wouldn't *steal* their own payroll.

The thought made her think about the men. How far would they go in opposing her father?

In her mind's eye, she saw a couple of the newer men. She'd never met them before—they hadn't been with the Rocking P when she'd left two years ago, but she'd seen them out at the roundup camp. One of them looked dangerously angry. And the older hands had looked worse than unhappy. Nevada's attitude today shouldn't have surprised her, after the things Alex had told her. But she'd always considered him one of their loyal employees and one of their best cowboys. How could he turn on the family so easily?

Or had it been easy? It came down to that, she reminded herself. This thing seemed sudden to her, but it wasn't. The men's grievances had simmered for months. She hoped that if they were really walking off the job, they would leave quietly and not do any mischief.

She pulled a chair over next to her papa. "Why don't you read me the names, and I'll write out the slips."

He frowned, but shoved a tablet toward her and reached for the ledger. "Harry Jensen."

Harry was one of their older cowboys, full of pithy wisdom and knowledge brought by experience. She wrote his name on the line at the top of the first sheet. "All right, what else?"

"Then the date."

She wrote it: May 15, 1884.

"And the amount." Her father hesitated. "Fifteen dollars."

She frowned at him. "Papa, they get thirty dollars a month."

"And they've worked fifteen days—if they worked today, which I'm not so sure about."

"Would it break us to give them a full month's pay?"

He sat still for a long moment. "Maggie, honey, we're already broke. I borrowed for last month's payroll. I'm hoping Nathan Wilson will advance me enough to pay them this time. If he won't . . . well, those boys are going to be a lot madder tomorrow than they are already."

"Oh, Papa." Tears sprang into Maggie's eyes. "Why, oh why did you send me to San Francisco? You knew this was coming!"

"I hoped I could find a way to stop it before you found out. I'm sorry." He hung his head.

Maggie rose and walked to the window. She stared out at the barnyard and watched as the golden filly trotted about the corral, tossing her regal head. She nipped playfully at Duchess, but the old mare ignored her.

The only possible way to keep from going under was to get the cattle to Fort Worth and sell them at a good price. The money might not pay off all her father's debts, but it would enable him to pay the men off and get by for a while. If she could buy some time, she could think about all the options. But they needed that extra time.

She whirled to face him. "Look, if we offered the men forty a month starting in June—without the small herds—and gave Leo and Sela an allowance while Leo's laid up, I think the men would stay. At least they might agree to finish the roundup and drive the cattle to Fort Worth. Once we sell the herd at the stockyards, we can pay off those who don't want to stay and cover the most pressing debts."

Her father shook his head. "Unless prices are phenomenally high this year, it won't be enough."

"But it will give us some time to work things out, Papa."

"I've been doing that for the last two years, don't you see?

I'm going to lose the ranch, Maggie. That's what it comes down to."

She did some quick figuring for the payroll they were now preparing in her head. Eighteen men, at least—maybe more—at fifteen dollars each.

"Dolores and Shep will stay, won't they? I mean, we don't have to pay them tomorrow."

Her father grunted. "As far as I know, they're loyal. But Shep's always been close to the other men. I guess we'll see about him."

"And how much is Alex getting now?"

"Forty a month."

She nodded, thinking that the foreman's pay should be raised to at least fifty dollars a month.

"Well, do you think if we ask them to hold off and do the drive, and we'll pay them for the full month but at their old rate—"

"What are you saying, old rate? I can't raise it. I told you that."

"But if they agreed to stay, even just through the cattle drive, that would put us into the next month. We could promise they'd get forty starting in June. And Alex—"

Her father shoved himself up out of his chair. "*Enough*. I'm not giving in to them. Not one penny. We pay them off tomorrow and I start fresh."

He walked unsteadily out of the office. Maggie walked slowly to his desk and sat down in his chair. She looked down at the ledger with the names listed. Alex Bright, foreman, was at the top. She reached out and touched his name on the cool paper.

Her father felt betrayed by all these men, she realized. Harry Jenson, Joe Moore, Nevada Hatch, Early Shaw, all of them. But especially by Alex, the kid he'd chosen to replace

Jack Hubble, the foreman who had been with him since the beginning. Alex, the promising young man her father had mentored and invested time in.

Alex, the man to whom his daughter had lost her heart. Of course, he didn't know that. Did he?

She knew Papa wouldn't give an inch. That would be a sign of weakness, and weakness was the one thing he wanted so desperately not to show. It was overtaking him, stripping him of his strength, his manhood, his wealth, his authority. No, Martin Porter would not give an inch of Rocking P ground. And if she let on to anyone else that he was ill, probably dying, she'd be on the list of traitors too.

She decided to saddle Duchess and ride to the Herrera ranch, four miles away. Carlotta would listen to her and offer a different perspective.

In her room, she changed quickly into her riding costume and braided her hair. She went out through the kitchen, stopping long enough to apprise Dolores of her plans.

"Oh, good," Dolores said. "Señorita Carlotta is just what you need. You cannot be sad around that one."

Maggie rode Duchess as fast as she dared push the old mare. She'd have to ask Shep if there was a younger horse she could ride when she needed to push her mount. Probably the rest of their horses were all out at the roundup camp. She wondered about the golden filly. She looked to be about three years old, perfect age for the roundup.

She made it to Carlotta's home in half an hour, but Duchess was wheezing and drenched in sweat. She'd have to go slower on the way home, and the hours were fleeing. She wondered if Shep had returned yet with the men's pay.

Carlotta invited her to her room, which consisted of a large, airy suite with a door that opened on the courtyard. They settled in the feminine sitting area, a room unlike

Maggie's plainly furnished bedroom. Carlotta favored ruffles and lace—on cushions, curtains, and the skirt of her bed and dressing table. The four-poster bed was shrouded in filmy waves of embroidered tulle. Every time she visited, Maggie was put in mind of a bridal chamber. Carlotta kept her femininity, especially in social gatherings. Yet she could rein, ride, and rope with her father's *vaqueros*.

The Herrera family had several housemaids to help with the children, the cooking, housework, and laundry. Some of them were relatives that Carlotta's parents had hired with an eye to finding husbands for the girls in Texas. One of them brought a tray bearing a pot of chocolate and a plate of lacy sugar cookies. She opened the doors to the courtyard so the air could flow through the room and then left Maggie and her hostess alone.

"Have you finished your dress?" Maggie asked as Carlotta poured out the hot chocolate.

Carlotta laughed. "Not yet. It was only yesterday that you saw it. And I took this morning off to ride with Enrique Marquez."

Maggie should have guessed, since Carlotta was wearing an eye-catching black and silver riding costume. She frowned, trying to place the name. "Who is he? I don't know him."

"He is Señor Bradley's wrangler."

"Oh, I see." Obviously the Bradley ranch had had a change of personnel since Maggie had been away. "Is he handsome?"

"Somewhat."

"But why isn't he out on their roundup?"

Carlotta waved a hand in dismissal. "Finished. They leave tomorrow on their cattle drive, and he wanted to see me before he went."

"How romantic," Maggie said. "Have your father's men finished their roundup?"

"Oh, yes. They have gone already."

Maggie gulped. "Our cattle aren't ready, I'm afraid. We're . . . running behind."

"Ah. Too bad." Carlotta smiled. "You did not come back so soon to talk of men and dresses. What brings you here?"

"It's Papa. He's ill."

Carlotta sobered. "Is part of the problem his sadness perhaps?"

"He is grieving deeply," Maggie said, "but the illness is real. Carlotta, it's bad. Very bad. I lost Mama last year, and I'm afraid I'm going to lose Papa, too."

"Oh, my dear." Carlotta put her arms around Maggie and patted her back. "I am so sorry to hear this."

"So am I. And he doesn't want anyone to know, so I shouldn't have told you."

"I will keep it our secret," Carlotta said, her dark eyes solemn.

"Thank you." Maggie sniffed and blinked hard to hold back tears. "I had to talk to *someone* about it. Things are not going well at the ranch—not well at all. One of the men was injured—you know Leo Eagleton."

"Yes. His wife, Sela, is a friend of mine. Mama brought her from Mexico ten years ago, and she married the gallant cowboy."

Maggie smiled. "Did you hear what happened?"

"No. Tell me."

Maggie detailed what she knew of Leo's injuries and ended up telling Carlotta the whole story—how her father wouldn't let the men go for the doctor but made Sela drive her husband to town in the wagon, and how he had refused to pay the doctor's bill or allow Sela to leave the children at the ranch while she tended her husband in town.

"Oh, my, that does sound quite coldhearted," Carlotta said.

"Martin Porter was always tightfisted, but this is beyond anything I would have imagined."

Quite shocked, Maggie blinked at her. "Do you really think that? I always thought Papa was a good boss and that he cared about the men." She took out her handkerchief and wiped her eyes. "Two years ago I'd have said Papa could never behave this way."

To her astonishment, Carlotta laughed. "Dearest, I know you have always loved your father, but from what my father says, he may be a good cattleman, but he's a bit stubborn. You have to realize, a man like that is too bullheaded to back down now."

"The men say they'll walk off the job tomorrow, and the roundup isn't finished."

Carlotta's face puckered. "That's not so good, but there's nothing you can do about that. Just let your papa handle it. This is his doing, and he must get himself out of it."

Maggie's lips trembled and she clamped them firmly together.

"What?" Carlotta said.

"I'm sorry—you must think me an infant, with all this crying. But what if Papa can't get out of this muddle? I think he's tried for at least a year, but it's no good. The bills for Mama's care, and . . ."

"My dear, I'm so sorry." Carlotta at last took her seriously. "I did not realize how bad it was. Tell me all, and perhaps we can think of something."

"You mustn't say a word," Maggie cautioned. "Papa is so proud—"

"Oh, yes," Carlotta said. "He is that. I like your father, but his pride—that has made trouble for him, perhaps? He has been too proud to come to his friends for help? My father would have helped him if he'd known."

"I fear you're right. He said he would ask your father if the men went on strike, but I'm sure he hasn't said a word about his debts or his illness." Maggie hesitated. "He mentioned when I came home that he would ask Juan for help if he needed men . . ."

Carlotta grimaced. "Ours are mostly gone on the drive. I don't know if your father asked mine to have our men take any of his cattle along."

"They wouldn't have been ready," Maggie said. "And he wouldn't have asked his friend to delay for his sake."

"That is a pity. They won't be back for a couple of weeks, so there's not really anyone to spare right now. I can ask my father—"

"No, don't do that. I don't want Papa to think I'm going behind his back. Carlotta, I've been out to roundup camps before. Papa used to take me every spring. I've seen what the men do."

"Yes?"

"You know, I'm a pretty good rider."

"I'd call you an expert."

"Well, thank you," Maggie said. "I can rope, too. I learned as a child."

"As did all of us ranchers' children. What are you thinking?"

"Well, it occurred to me that a lot of ranch women do have the skills needed to round up and brand cattle, as you said."

"You mean . . ."

"Yes," Maggie said. "Women could do this job."

CHAPTER NINE

*C*arlotta's lovely dark eyes widened. "Margaret Porter! Are you saying we should go round up your father's cattle?"

"Why not? We could do it. Papa is too ill to do the job, but we could get some of our friends and finish the roundup. The men are probably close to being done with it. They've been out there all week, and I know they've brought in a couple of cuts and put them in the north pasture already."

"But really—ladies out there in their skirts and sidesaddles, herding steers and—and branding calves? I can't imagine it."

Maggie looked around at her friend's lavish furnishings. Though Carlotta lived in feminine luxury, she could ride as well as she could dance. Maggie laid her hand on her sleeve. "Think about it. If we could just bring in the last few cattle, then the herd would be ready for the drive to Fort Worth. I doubt there are many calves left unbranded. But I can find out how many they've brought in and about how many should still be out there. Meanwhile, Papa could be hiring some men to do that cattle drive for him."

"Or maybe your men would see their folly and come back." Carlotta's eyes flickered. "If the word spread that women were doing their jobs as well as they did them . . ." Her eyes gleamed. "What about your so-handsome foreman, Alex Bright? Is he striking along with the cowboys?"

Maggie couldn't meet her gaze. "I tried to talk him out of it, but he feels a loyalty to the men—especially after what happened to Leo."

"Too bad," Carlotta said. "I trust you used all your powers of persuasion."

Maggie gulped. "That depends on what you mean. The truth is, I begged him."

"And he would not listen? For shame! Alex is not the man I thought he was. Did you cry?"

"Perhaps a little."

"And did he kiss you?"

Maggie pulled back and stared at her. "Well, *no*."

"Pity." Carlotta looked ready to expound on feminine wiles, but a gentle knock came at the door.

"Carlotta? I have something for you." Her mother's voice sounded carefree and indulgent.

"Come in, Mamacita," Carlotta called.

Señora Herrera entered carrying a small basket.

"Here we are," she said, offering the basket to Maggie. "Blanca and I have been trying a new recipe I got from her mother. Sugared pecans. You girls must try them and tell us what you think."

"Thank you." Maggie chose a couple of pecan halves from the basket. She took it that Blanca was another of Señora Herrera's stream of pampered servants.

"Mama, you have to hear Maggie's plan," Carlotta said.

"Oh, what is this?" Señora Herrera sat down and set the basket on the table. She flicked her fan open and waved it gracefully. "Tell me, Maggie."

"Well, I thought perhaps Carlotta and I could get some of our friends to help me bring Papa's cattle in—that is, if the men really do walk off the job tonight."

"*What?* Your men refuse to work?"

"Yes. They're threatening a strike."

The señora frowned. "My husband mentioned this to me, that some of the *vaqueros* were talking of it, and I thought it was nonsense."

"I'm afraid not," Maggie said. "One of our men rode in from the roundup camp this morning to speak to Papa about it, and it seems they are serious. If Papa won't raise their wages—and he can't afford to—they will leave tomorrow and not return. And they have not brought in all the cattle. Some are still in the holding pens at the roundup camp."

"You see, Mama?" Carlotta said gaily. "Someone needs to go let the cattle out of the pens tomorrow and bring them back to Señor Porter's ranch."

"And who will drive them to the stockyards?" her mother asked.

"Papa hopes to hire someone else to take them to Fort Worth," Maggie said.

Señora Herrera shook her head. "And you think girls can do that? Bring them to the ranch?"

"I think we could," Maggie said. "Of course, it might involve a little more—there are probably some still out on the range, and there may be a few to be branded, but—"

"Branded? Surely you girls cannot handle the branding irons. It is too dangerous."

"I've watched them many times." Maggie looked toward Carlotta for support. "I believe we could do it. And even if we didn't do any branding, at least we could make sure all of Papa's cattle are in and ready for the drive."

"I think it would be fun," Carlotta said, leaning over the basket and scanning the contents. "I would help you." She picked up a pecan half and popped it into her mouth.

Her mother fanned herself, her forehead wrinkled. "But what would my husband say?"

"Now, Mama, you know I've been restless lately. Our men are gone on the cattle drive, and it's very boring to be here at home with no cowboys around to flirt with." Carlotta laughed, but her mother did not seem to be amused.

"I promise I would make her behave, Señora," Maggie said.

"Of course I would behave. We could get a dozen women together easily and go finish the Porters' roundup. It would be good to get out and do something—and something useful!"

"If your brother was old enough to go with you—"

"Oh, Mama, please!" Carlotta waved her hand. "Helio is only seven, and we will not be tending babies while we work. We will be too busy. Isn't that so, Maggie?"

"Well . . . "

"It will be a lark! I will ride over to the Lazy S this afternoon and enlist Lucy Shuman and her sister."

Carlotta now seemed more enthused with the idea than she was, but Maggie couldn't think of a better plan.

"I could stop in Brady on my way home and spread the word."

"Yes," Carlotta said eagerly. "Tell Nancy Jeffers and Consuela Rigas. They are both good riders, and they can get the news out to their friends. Oh, and Poppy Wilson."

"The banker's daughter?" Maggie asked.

"Yes, I saw her last week and she told me she was bored to death. She'd love an excuse to get out of town for a few days, I'm sure."

After an hour's visit, Maggie did as suggested and spent some time in the little town of Brady. She stopped at the hotel, the mercantile, and the bank to tell the owners' wives and daughters of the plan. Last of all, she went into the house where Dr. Vargas practiced medicine.

Rhonda Tracey, Bronc's wife, sat at a small desk in the patients' sitting room. The doctor employed her to schedule appointments, assist him when needed, clean the office, and tend minor ailments when the doctor was out on house calls. She greeted Maggie warily when she entered the front room.

"Hello, Miss Porter. Are you here to see the Eagletons?"

"Yes, thank you." Maggie wondered whether she ought to say anything to Rhonda about the strike. Did Rhonda even know? Perhaps she did and now looked upon Maggie as an adversary.

"I'll tell Miss Sela."

While Rhonda disappeared through the doorway to the hall, Maggie smiled at two patients waiting to see the doctor. She didn't know either of them, another sign that she'd been away far too long. A minute later, Rhonda came back.

"Miss Sela's feeding her baby, and she says for you to come on back there. Mr. Leo's decent, and you know the way."

"I sure do." Maggie made her way to the back bedroom where Dr. Vargas housed patients who needed prolonged care.

"Señorita Maggie!" Sela didn't rise from her chair, where she was nursing the baby, but she smiled her welcome. Her lovely face was lined with fatigue, and her hair was pulled back in a careless knot. "Come in. See how well my Leo is doing?"

Leo smiled sheepishly from the bed, where he was propped up with pillows behind him. "*Buenos dias*, Señorita." His words were slurred and his eyelids heavy.

"Hello, Leo," Maggie said. "I'm glad to see you're making progress."

He shrugged. "The leg hurts, but what can I say?"

"He had his medication not long ago," Sela said. "That's why he is so jolly now. Soon he'll be sleeping."

"That's it," Leo said. "Either I hurt, or I sleep."

"Yes," Sela said. "For a few minutes after he takes the medicine, it doesn't hurt so bad, and he is still awake. That is the only time we can talk."

"Hmm. Maybe Dr. Vargas can adjust the dose," Maggie said. "You ought to have more time awake without so much pain." She crossed to the window and sat down on the broad sill.

Sela shrugged. "He says that after a few more days, it will not hurt so much, and then Leo will stay awake longer without needing it so soon."

"I'm sure he knows best." Maggie smiled at her. "I can't stay long. I need to get home before supper, but I wanted to tell you what is happening with the men."

"They are striking?" Leo's speech slurred, and his eyelids drooped. "Nevada came by this morning, and he told us."

"Oh. I see." Maggie looked from him to Sela.

"It is true," Sela said. "He told us he rode in to see your father, and Mr. Porter wouldn't listen to him. The men wanted to leave today, but your father cannot have the money to pay them until tomorrow, so they will go then. If they don't work today, he won't pay them at all."

"That ain't right." Leo yawned.

"No, but Nevada said he thinks they will work the day. But they're not going to finish the roundup."

Maggie sighed. "That's what Alex told me this morning. I'm very sad to see this happening. But Carlotta and I have decided that we'll get some of our friends together tomorrow to help us finish the roundup."

"You will need more than one day." Leo yawned again.

"Do you think so? I'd hoped it was nearly done. Well, Sela,

if any other women come by, could you please tell them that we need anyone who can ride and rope to be at my house at ten o'clock?"

"Wait a minute," Sela said. "You mean you're getting women to do this? I thought you meant you and Carlotta would ask your men friends for help."

Maggie chuckled. "I don't have that many men friends since I've been away two years. And most of the ones I do have will be tending to their own cattle. No, Carlotta and I are riding out to the camp ourselves. I need to help Papa with the payroll first thing in the morning, but that will give the women time to gather at the ranch, and Shep will pack some supplies for us. We'll talk over our plans and set out as soon as we can. We hope some other girls will help us."

Sela put the baby up to her shoulder and patted the infant's back. "I wish I could go and help you."

"No you don't," Leo said. He gazed at Maggie, his eyes not completely focusing. "I am striking with the other men. I may be laid up, but I'm striking. You hear me, Sela?" He glared at his wife.

Sela raised one hand. "I hear you, Leo. I guess you're right. I can't go out and help your boss if you are siding against him."

Maggie sympathized with the couple, and wondered if everyone would hate her because of her father's actions. And would the people in Brady take sides and line up for or against them?

"I guess I'd better get going," she said. "Leo, I hope you feel better soon. Sela, how are the boys doing?"

"All right. They are a little bored, I think. I hope they will behave for Mrs. Cutler."

Maggie went over and patted her shoulder. "I don't have time to stop in and see them today, but I will the next time I'm in town. Is there anything you need?"

"We're getting by. Thank you for everything you've done, Maggie. I know this is hard for you."

Maggie smiled as tears pricked her eyes. "Thank you. Difficult as it is, I'm sure you and Leo have the harder part right now. I'm praying for you."

"And I am praying that your father will make peace with the men."

"Bless you." Maggie glanced toward the bed. Leo's eyes were closed, and he appeared to have drifted into sleep.

She went out to get Duchess and rode home, planning a hundred details to make the roundup happen.

When she arrived at the ranch, Alex's red gelding was tied to the hitching rail out front. She took Duchess to the corral, unsaddled her, and turned her out. Promising herself she'd return to rub the mare down and feed her soon, she hurried into the house.

The door to her father's office was open, and Alex's broad back took up most of the doorway. She strode across the parlor and peered around his arm. Her father stood behind the desk, glaring at Alex, and Alex's posture was just as rigid.

"I'm sorry it came to this," Alex said. "I can't let the men down, Mr. Porter."

Her father's eyes narrowed. Maggie wasn't sure whether he'd noticed her or not.

"I'm sorry, too, Alex," he said. "But if that's the way you feel, it's been nice knowing you." He opened the top desk drawer and dropped a twenty-dollar bill and a five on the desk. "That should cover what I owe you as of today."

Alex stood still for a long moment.

"What's the matter?"

"I hoped it wasn't too late. That we could still talk. Maybe work something out so that the men can keep working."

"Forget it," Papa said. "I'm not raising wages. Any man who

leaves the job and doesn't come in for his pay tomorrow morning won't ever get a cent out of me."

Maggie couldn't see Alex's face, but she did see the tension in his body. At last he stepped forward and took the money from the desktop.

Part of her wanted to weep. The other part wanted to pound Alex to a pulp. Of course he'd be foolish to leave without the money that was rightfully his—especially if it was the last pay he'd get in the foreseeable future. But couldn't he throw back his shoulders and tell her father he'd stand with him and see this thing through? Papa would have no one now—no one but her, and maybe Dolores and Shep. He needed a strong young man like Alex—someone who could not only do a hard day's work, but someone who could lead the hired men, either the ones they had now or new ones they'd hire for the drive.

Alex turned and headed for the door. Maggie jumped aside, but instead of following him, she grabbed his forearm when he passed her and ran to keep up with his long strides.

"Alex, please—"

He glanced down at her and kept walking. "We had our say this morning, Maggie. I thought you understood."

"But when we hire new men, we'll need someone to lead them—"

They'd reached the front door, and he threw it open. "It won't be me. You'll have to hire a new foreman too."

She let go of his arm and watched him go down the steps. "Don't the men realize they're better off sticking with us?"

"No, they don't realize that. No more than your father realizes what's good for him and his ranch."

"Nevada said some pretty choice words to Papa this morning."

"I wish he hadn't done that, but it doesn't surprise me."

Alex walked to the hitching rail and reached for his horse's reins.

"I saw Leo today. He says he's striking with you boys."

Alex paused then and looked at her. "I'd expect that of him. He's a good man."

"Yes, he is. What will happen to him and Sela?"

Alex hesitated. "You'd best discuss that with your pa. But I did mean to ask him for Leo's pay so we could take it to him."

"But if Leo says he's striking, Papa won't do anything to help him."

"He's not doing anything now. So why is that worse?" Alex put his foot in the stirrup.

Maggie stepped forward and clutched one of the porch posts, feeling a little lightheaded. "I'll see that Leo is paid. But Alex, Sela's exhausted. What if Papa won't let them move back into their cabin?"

He swung into the saddle and gazed down at her. "The men will all give part of their last pay to help out Leo and Sela. After that, I can't guarantee anything. But so far as we're able, we'll take care of our own. That's more than I can say for the Porters right now."

He turned Red and urged him into a lope. Maggie stood on the steps with tears streaming down her cheeks, watching the puff of dust he raised move farther and farther away.

CHAPTER TEN

*M*aggie blotted the tears from her face and hurried back to her father's office. He sat hunched over in his chair, holding his stomach.

"Papa, are you all right?"

He grunted as though that question didn't deserve an answer.

Maggie knelt beside him. "Are you in pain?"

"My medicine."

"I'll get it. Sit still." She flew to his room, quickly mixed the dose, and carried the glass back to him. Was he following a schedule for the medicine, or just taking it whenever his pain reached a level that kept him from functioning? "Here. Take this, and I'll help you get to bed."

"I'm not going to bed *now*."

"You should rest." Her hands shook as she held out the glass.

"It's nearly supper time," he said. "Dolores will fuss if I don't go to the table."

Maggie wasn't sure whether to tell Dolores to leave him alone or to bless her for keeping her father going on his regular routine.

"I'll go see if she's nearly ready. But as soon as you eat, you're going to lie down."

In the kitchen, Maggie found Dolores getting ready to put the meal on the table.

"Oh, that looks so good." Maggie eyed the beef stew, biscuits, and pureed squash.

"Thank you, *querida*. I just hope your father will eat a little tonight. I try so hard to make his favorite foods, but so many times lately he hasn't felt like eating."

"It's part of his illness, I think."

"I think so, too." Dolores put the basket of biscuits in her hands. "He says nothing tastes good anymore."

"I tried to get him to lie down, but he insists on eating at the table. I'll tell him supper is ready. Maybe tonight he will not be able to resist your cooking."

Maggie placed the biscuits on the dining table and went back to the office for her father. This time he didn't protest, but leaned on her shoulder as they went through the parlor to the dining table. Though he didn't eat a normal portion, he did get down half a biscuit and several spoonfuls of stew. Maggie noted that he ate almost all of the squash Dolores had put on his plate.

"Carlotta and I talked about the strike this afternoon," she said as Dolores brought them dishes of custard. She tried to keep a cheerful tone.

"Oh?" her father asked. "Shep tells me Señor Herrera can't spare any men for my roundup. He's sent his herd to Fort Worth already. I . . . hoped we'd be ready to send our cattle with his, but we were late getting started this spring. And I expect Juan's herd was already as big as he'd want it to be. You get a herd too big, and it's hard to find feed and water for them all."

"Oh, Papa, you mustn't worry about it. Carlotta is going to help me find a new crew to finish the roundup. Maybe by the time it's done, some of the men from other ranches will be free to help. You can have Shep looking in the meantime for some to join our outfit for the drive."

Her father's eyebrows drew together in a frown. "Where will you dig up men for the roundup? Shep went to three ranches today, and no one could spare any cowpunchers. Frankly, I think their men are in sympathy with our bunch and refused to come and help us, but their bosses didn't want to admit it."

"That may be," Maggie said.

"Yes, and if the cowboys on the other ranches strike too, this whole county will be in a mess." Papa stared at his dish of custard without seeming to see it. He didn't even bother to pick up his spoon. "If I weren't desperate for cash, I'd say we should wait until fall."

Maggie wasn't sure she could make him feel better, but perhaps she could at least make him smile. "I don't know about the other ranches, but I know who will do ours. I'm going to hire a crew of women."

"What?" His jaw dropped, and he stared at her with stricken eyes.

She knew she had only moments to persuade him that it was a good idea. If he made up his mind that it wouldn't work, or that he couldn't bear people's ridicule, he would crush her plan.

"Carlotta's coming here tomorrow, and so are some of our friends. I spread the word in town today. I hope to get enough ladies who can ride and rope to at least bring our herd in from the holding pens. Once the roundup is done, we'll worry about workers for the drive."

Her father barked a short laugh. "If you can do that, girl, I'll pay your ladies a dollar a day. Don't know where I'll get it from, but the story alone should be worth a small loan from the banker."

Maggie smiled. "I'm sure my . . . my cowgirl crew will be happy to hear it."

———— ★ ————

The sun slid toward the western horizon as the men gathered around the campfire to eat their last meal together in the Rocking P's roundup camp.

"I don't even feel like going in for my pay in the morning," Tommy said. He forked beans into his mouth and scowled as he chewed.

"Me neither. I don't want to see Porter again," Bronc said.

Alex held his cup steady while Stewie filled it with coffee, then turned to face the men. "If anybody wants my advice, which you probably don't—"

"Sure we do, Alex." Nevada stood and carried his empty plate to Stewie's washtub. Alex gave him a nod of thanks. Nevada had stood by him in this, for the most part. He wouldn't stick with Porter, but he wouldn't let the men take their discontent too far, either, and Alex was grateful for that.

"All right, here's what I think. You should all swallow your pride for an hour. You'll need that last pay to live on while we strike. And if all of us chip in a dollar or two, we can help Leo out. I'm sure Doc Vargas would appreciate it if we gave him a little something toward Leo's bill."

"That's a good idea." Nevada came back with a full cup of coffee. "And it'll rub Porter's nose in it if he sees us helping out someone he refused to take care of."

Alex wondered if that would make a difference. With the mood Mr. Porter was in now, it was more likely he'd see it as a sign that they didn't need higher pay. Anyone who could give away his money must have too much of it. But he didn't voice that thought.

"Alex is right," Early said. "I don't know about you fellas, but I'm going to get my pay. I want to eat."

"We should all take some food from the chuck wagon," Tommy said.

"That ain't ours if we ain't working for Porter anymore," Harry said.

"He won't miss a few beans and a little coffee." Tommy threw the dregs of his coffee out on the grass.

"I say we let the cattle we've rounded up out of the pens," Diego said.

Tommy grinned. "Yeah, and stampede 'em, too."

Nevada stepped toward Tommy. "Lookahere, boy, I intend to go in there tomorrow morning and get my pay like a man. And to do that, I want to be able to look Porter in the eye and know that every day I *did* work for him, I gave him his money's worth."

Harry looked around at the younger men. "Which is it? Keep your pay for this month, or destroy the hard work we've done here the past few days?"

Alex held his breath, not daring to speak.

"I'm drawing my pay," Early said.

"Me too." Stewie walked over to the back of the chuck wagon. "Anyone who wants a doughnut better come get it now. I only made three dozen, and I reckon they'll go fast."

The men swarmed the wagon for their treats, and Alex drew a deep breath. Nevada hadn't moved. Alex looked over at him.

"Thanks."

"It's only right."

"That was close, though."

Nevada nodded. "It was. Much as I begrudge Porter for the way he's treated us, I don't think it's fair to make him do this work all over again. Not if we're taking pay for it."

"Right." Alex looked toward the pens. "If we leave the cattle penned, though, they'll be without water until someone comes and lets them out."

"That's up to Porter to get them up near the house. He's got the ones we already took in, in that north pasture with the stream."

"Yeah, that's where we were planning to leave them until we got them all collected for the drive." Alex heaved out a big sigh. "I wasn't going back tomorrow, since the boss paid me today, but maybe I should. We need to tell him we're leaving the cattle penned."

←——— ★ ———→

The next morning, Alex rode around all of the pens. They'd released the cows and young stock that would roam the range for another year. Only those headed for the stockyards remained in the enclosures.

"We ought to just drive them in," he said to Nevada. "It wouldn't take more than an extra hour."

"More like two, and the men are all worked up to leave. They've made up their minds they're done working for Porter—they don't want to get stuck doing a drive this morning. Besides—Porter won't include today in our pay."

That clinched it for Alex. He gave in and rode back to the campfire with Nevada. Every man had his own horse saddled and ready to go. Stewie had put away all his gear and closed up the chuck wagon. He would ride one of the remuda horses back to the ranch. They'd leave the camp just as it was, for whoever came to finish the job.

When he was sure all was in order, Alex gave the order for

the men to mount up and ride to the ranch house to get their pay. Then they could go to the bunkhouse and pack up the rest of their personal belongings.

"What about the extra horses in the remuda?" Joe asked.

Alex looked at Nevada. "What do you say?"

"I thought we were leaving them out here for whoever comes to finish the job."

"Or we could drive them in to the ranch," Alex said.

Nevada shook his head. "That would look too much like sympathy for Porter."

"Well, I got sympathy for the horses," Joe said.

"I'll help you water them all before we go," Alex told him.

It took them half an hour. The men were long gone. Nevada stayed, too, while Alex double-checked the gates and totaled up the numbers he'd kept on the roundup. Nine hundred fifty-six steers brought in, and two hundred twenty cows he thought should be culled from the breeding herd. They had branded more than four hundred calves and unmarked strays, most of which were this year's crop, and castrated the bull calves. They'd let the young stock go to grow for another year or two. Yearling and older unbranded cattle, they'd put the Rocking P brand on and brought in. Of course there were still another five or six hundred marketable steers roaming around on the Rocking P range. Even so, the final count on cattle they had herded to the pasture or the holding pens was 1,176. Not a bad herd to start out with on the drive.

With Joe and Nevada, Alex rode to the ranch. A black-topped buggy he was sure belonged to Dr. Vargas sat in front of the house, as did two wagons. Several saddle horses he didn't recognize browsed hay in the corral. Were some of the other ranchers here, plotting with Porter on how to deal with the strike?

Most of the other men were gone, but Early and Harry were still in the bunkhouse, packing their extra clothes and sundries.

"Did everyone get paid?" Alex asked.

"Yeah," Harry said, "but me and Early had to wait a while. When we finally got in, it was Miss Porter who gave us our money. We didn't see her pa. Then the doc came. I'm wondering if the old man's all right."

Alex wondered too. Mr. Porter must be ill, if he'd prevailed on Maggie to pay the men off. That would explain the doctor's buggy. But what about the other wagons?

"Do you know who else is in there?" he asked, as Harry and Early headed out the door.

Early looked back and smiled. "Looked like a hen party to me."

Alex stared after him, but it was too late to catch him and press him for more information. Maybe some of the town ladies had come to comfort Maggie.

He filled a basin from the rain barrel outside and washed his face and hands. He put on his last clean shirt, combed his hair, and headed for the house.

Joe and Nevada met him in the yard.

"You all set?" Alex asked.

"Yeah," Nevada said. "Want us to wait for you? We thought we'd go into Brady."

"Go ahead," Alex said. He probably wouldn't be here long, but he wasn't in the mood to watch most of the other men drink up the short pay they'd just received.

The two cowboys moved on toward the corral. Bracing himself for the coming encounter, Alex walked toward the house and stopped at the steps leading up to the broad veranda.

The door opened, and Maggie came out. She was wearing the same skirt she'd worn when she rode Duchess to the roundup camp, with a red-checked blouse. She looked very young and fresh—almost like she had three or four years ago—before she went away.

"Howdy," he said, and felt foolish for saying it.

"Good morning. I saw you from the window. Since you got your pay yesterday, I thought I'd come out here. Papa asked me to make sure you brought him your final count from the roundup."

"Got it right here." Alex fished the folded paper out of his pocket. "Is your pa sick?"

She pressed her lips together and nodded. "The doctor is with him now."

"I'm sorry."

He wanted to know whose rigs were tied up before the house, but it really wasn't any of his business. Still, the idea remained that some of the neighboring ranchers were inside pledging to help Porter and planning ways to counter the strike.

"Thank you. Would you like to sit down for a minute?" Maggie took a seat in one of the rustic rockers on the veranda and unfolded the paper. Alex sat down in the one next to it. His stomach churned—she made him more nervous than her father did.

"Is it serious?" he asked.

She looked up from the paper. "What? Oh, yes. I'm afraid it is."

He nodded. He'd figured it must be. "Maggie, I—" He stopped. There was nothing to say, really. He couldn't offer his support, not with the stand he'd taken on the men's behalf. And Porter wouldn't want his help now anyway.

The sound of female laughter issued from the parlor window, and he swiveled his head toward it. Not everyone at the Rocking P was somber today, it seemed.

<hr/>

Maggie jumped up as the sound of her friends' laughter poured out the window. "Excuse me just a minute."

She hurried inside without opening the door far enough for Alex to see much of anything. A moment later she closed the parlor window gently. She didn't want the foreman to think she and her friends were in here celebrating the men's betrayal.

"Is everything all right, Maggie?" Poppy Wilson asked.

"Yes, I just have to meet one last time with the foreman."

"Well, find out how they left things in the camp," Poppy said.

"Oh, I will."

Carlotta rose and came over to whisper, "That Alex Bright, he is too absolutely handsome. Can't you persuade him to stay?"

Maggie felt a blush coming on. She lifted the latch. "No, I'm sure he's made up his mind."

"But with a little flirtation, perhaps—a promise of more later . . ."

"That's scandalous," Maggie hissed. "If your mother could hear you!"

Carlotta laughed. "All right, let him go then. It's your loss."

Maggie went out onto the porch and closed the door firmly. Alex unfolded his long legs and stood.

"Oh, don't get up," she said, too late.

He almost smiled, and she wished he hadn't. Her heart fluttered like a goose trying to take off from the pond.

"Sounds like a party in there."

"Oh, some of my friends came to welcome me home. I'm afraid it turned out to be a bad time, with Papa sick and you men needing your last pay and all."

"I'm sorry. I'll get out of here as quickly as I can."

That reminded her of the paper she still held in her hand. Flustered, she sat in the rocker and smoothed it out on her knee. "This looks good. More than eleven hundred head of cattle in the pasture. How many did Papa expect for the drive?"

"Maybe eighteen hundred. That figure includes the bunch we left penned out at the roundup camp, but there are still several hundred to be rounded up."

"Oh." She pressed her lips together, hoping her dismay didn't show. She'd hoped the men were almost done with the roundup.

"Have you got someone to take over?" Alex asked.

"Are you offering to stay?"

"No."

Again her spirits plummeted. She struggled to produce a smile. "Actually we have found *someone*. I don't have as many . . . as many cowpunchers as are leaving, but I think a dozen can finish the roundup within a few days, and we should be able to get more help for the drive."

"That's good. I'm . . . glad you could get someone." Alex's eyebrows were slightly cocked, and she wondered if he believed her. He shifted in his chair. "Oh, by the way, we left the camp in good order. The chuck wagon's all tidy and closed up, so that no cows can come along and stick their heads in. And the remuda horses are penned up out there, too, in a pen near the one where the cattle are."

"Oh." She hadn't really thought about scores of cattle out there waiting to be released. She'd assumed all the ones they'd rounded up were in the pasture now.

"Uh . . . how long do you think they'll be all right in the pens?"

"Well, we watered the horses this morning."

She bit her lip. "I'm not sure our new crew can get out there before tomorrow morning. I'd hoped for this afternoon, but we'll need to . . . to organize things and . . . and get their supplies ready." He must think she was a rather cavalier ranch manager to be hosting a party when she had a new crew of cowpunchers to break in.

"Is your father planning to go to the roundup camp?" Alex asked.

She looked down at the paper, unable to meet his gaze. "I honestly don't think he's up to it."

"That's too bad. I wish . . ." He stopped and grimaced then went on. "I really mean this, Maggie. I wish I could help you out. But I can't. The men would . . . well, I just can't."

She nodded. She'd seen the men's faces yesterday when she'd gone to the camp to plead with him. Some of them had vented their anger today when they'd come in to pick up their wages. She was mildly surprised that they hadn't turned the livestock loose on the range and wrecked all the equipment. How much influence had Alex had to exert to keep them from stealing the Porters blind? If they'd taken the extra horses, she wouldn't have been able to stop them.

"Alex, I appreciate very much the work you've done here and your loyalty to the family, even though you feel you must go with the men."

"Do you?" He gazed into her eyes with such longing that she knew how bitter was his struggle. "Maggie, if there was any other way—"

"I know." She reached out and clasped his hand for a moment then withdrew her own. One glance out the window by Carlotta or Poppy and she'd be teased for the rest of her life—or until she married someone, whichever came first. At the moment, her prospects of becoming a spinster rancher looked pretty good. "Well, perhaps we can get someone to go out there tonight and water the stock, even if we can't bring them in until tomorrow."

Alex eyed her in silence so long that she had to look away.

"You're going out there yourself?"

"Well, yes. I thought I would. Since the new hands won't be familiar with the roundup camp or anything."

"Look, Shep and a couple of other men could do that. It would take them a while. But are you sure you've got a crew lined up? I mean, if your father's that sick . . ."

Tears spilled over and rolled down her cheeks. She ducked her head and wiped them away with her sleeve.

"He *is* that sick, isn't he?" Alex said softly. He touched her shoulder. "Maggie, I'm so sorry this is happening. It's going against everything I am to walk away from here and not help you."

"I know." Somehow his words made her feel better, but more tears splashed on her skirt. She fumbled in her pocket for a handkerchief. "We'll be all right."

Alex nodded. "Listen, there's enough grub stashed in the chuck wagon for three or four days. I asked Stewie before we left camp. He says there's beans, coffee, and quite a bit of other stuff. You might want to send some fresh meat along. That doesn't keep well in this heat."

"Thank you." She sniffed.

Alex detailed a few places where he thought she ought to check for small bands of cattle. "We didn't get up into the hills much, and there's probably three or four hundred Rocking P cattle up there." He paused for a moment. "Maggie, I . . . I'll be praying for you and your father."

Startled, she gazed up into his troubled brown eyes. "That means a lot."

He nodded. "Those cattle in the pens . . . They'll be fine until morning without water. If part of your crew could go right out there and bring them to the pasture first thing tomorrow, they'd probably do all right."

"And the horses?"

He gritted his teeth. "Just water them first thing. I don't like to see horses go that long without water, but if you have to . . ."

"I'm sure the new people we've found can handle it."

"All right." Alex rose, and she jumped up to stand beside him. "You did well to find new cowboys so quick."

He didn't look happy. She realized that this news didn't bode well for the striking men. Of course, if Alex and the others knew that the new roundup crew consisted of women, they'd laugh their heads off. She supposed they'd find out soon enough, since one of the men's wives and a couple of their sweethearts had signed on for the roundup and were now sitting in the parlor with Carlotta and the others. But she'd let him find that out in his own time.

"What will you do now, Alex?"

He sighed and shifted the angle of his hat. "Thought I'd stick around Brady a while and see how things go with the strike. The other men want to get as much support as they can. They all hope they can come back to work here after a bit, with better wages."

"I hope so too, but I can't promise anything."

"I understand." He paused and gave her that crooked smile of his. "Good-bye, Maggie."

"Good-bye."

She longed to fling her arms around him. But that was out of the question. She wanted to at least tell him that she hoped she'd see him again, but somehow that didn't seem the best thing for the acting manager of the ranch to say to the foreman leading the strike against her.

He walked down the steps and ambled across the yard to the corral near the bunkhouse, where the red roan stood. He gathered the reins and swung into the saddle.

Behind her, the door creaked open.

"Hey," Carlotta said, "are you coming back? Dolores wants to know what she should prepare for us to take for food tomorrow. And the girls all want you to tell them how to convince their mamas and their husbands that splitting their skirts is not immodest."

Alex turned Red and paused for a moment. Maggie wondered if he'd heard what Carlotta said. He lifted his hat, and Maggie raised her hand and she turned to Carlotta with a smile, hoping her friend wouldn't notice the traces of her recent tears.

"Right. I think we're in good shape on the food, actually." She needed to catch Dr. Vargas for an update on her father's condition before he left, but for now she had to focus on the roundup. She bustled back inside with Carlotta, ready to work.

CHAPTER ELEVEN

*M*aggie rose before daylight and dressed in her riding outfit. She picked up the saddlebags and bedroll she'd prepared the night before and her small lantern and lugged them into the hallway. She paused before her father's door and set down her bundles. Quietly, she entered his bedroom and tiptoed to the bedside.

His face was gray in the lantern light, but he breathed evenly. The doctor had increased his medication for pain and insisted she give him a hefty dose of laudanum in the evening so that he could sleep through the night.

Maggie bent and grazed his cheek with her fingertips. She hated to leave him now. Only Shep would be here to tend him and give him his medicine. Dolores had decided at ten o'clock the night before, as she and Maggie washed up the dishes they'd made cooking for the roundup crew, that she would accompany the cowgirls and cook for them at the camp. Now Maggie wondered if they'd made the right decision. If Papa took a turn for the worse, who would go for Dr. Vargas, and how would they get word to Maggie at the camp, an hour's ride away?

Dear Lord, please watch over him until I come back. She tucked the quilt about his shoulders.

"I'll see you in a few days, Papa."

She slipped out of the room and down to the kitchen. Dolores was already there, despite their late night and the extra work she'd put in.

"Good morning, *querida*. I have eggs and biscuits for you, and the coffee will be ready any minute."

Maggie kissed her cheek. "Thank you so much. I know it's going to be a comfort, having you along with us, but do you think we're wise to leave Shep here alone with Papa?"

"The doctor says your papa needs to rest. We will let him do that. No one will bother him about payrolls and strikes and who will drive the herd to the stockyards. *Si*?"

Maggie smiled. "*Si.*"

"And when we come back, he will feel better, and we will work out what to do next."

"I guess you're right." Maggie got a plate and filled it with food. As she sat down at the kitchen table, the back door opened and Shep came in.

"Mornin', Miss Maggie." He turned to Dolores. "I got all your goodies packed in sacks and tied onto the pack saddles. I wish you'd just let me take you out there in the buckboard."

"No," Dolores said. "Mr. Porter needs you here. We'll be fine with those two extra horses."

"Yes, Shep, don't worry about it. We'll get out to the camp just fine, with all of Dolores's cookies and biscuits and gingerbread intact."

"And I left plenty for you and the boss in that cupboard." Dolores pointed to the big wooden cupboard that held many of her baking supplies. "If Mr. Porter feels like eating, you give him anything that he thinks would taste good. Don't worry about giving him too many sweets."

"Would I worry about something like that?" Shep scowled at her.

"Maybe I should stay here." Dolores looked anxiously at Maggie.

"You do what you want. I'm sure we ladies can cook out there, but if you came it would free up one more person to help with the roundup—and I know our meals would go much more smoothly than if you weren't along."

Dolores pulled in a deep breath. "I will go."

Maggie ate her breakfast, but Dolores scurried about, adding more things to a sack.

"Where you going to put that?" Shep asked as he filled his own plate. "I've got the loads all packed and balanced."

"I'll carry it behind my saddle," Dolores said.

Shep was still sputtering when they heard horses approaching. Maggie rushed to the window. "It's Carlotta and her friend Consuela, and someone else. Oh, I think it's Sarah Bradley."

"That girl," Dolores said. "She's in love with your cowboy, Tommy Drescher."

"Really?" Maggie had known the rancher's daughter for many years, but Tommy was one of the Rocking P's newer hands, and she'd barely met him. But unless she was mistaken, he was the one who had angered Alex the morning she rode to the roundup camp. "Is it serious?"

"He rides over to their ranch every time he gets a day off," Shep said. "Her father don't like him, though."

"I wonder why she'd work for us when Tommy's striking?" Maggie turned away from the window.

"Maybe trying to earn a little something, since he won't be." Dolores shook her head and shoved a ladle into her sack.

"More likely to make her father mad," Shep said.

Poppy Wilson rode up just behind the other three, and Maggie hurried to the door. She knew that a few of the girls who had attended yesterday's meeting viewed the roundup as a lark or a way to shock their families. Thyra Reid, for instance. Her husband owned the feed store, and he was quite possessive of Thyra. Maggie suspected she'd joined the roundup crew as a show of independence.

Sarah had dismounted and met her at the bottom of the steps.

"Hey, Maggie! I see you have plenty of supplies packed. I brought some tinned fruit and a triple batch of biscuits."

"Thank you, Sarah." Maggie gave her a quick hug. "Hey, you're packing iron." She warily eyed the gun belt the girl wore.

"My pa says if we're going to be out on the range with no menfolk, we'd best be ready to shoot a snake or two."

Maggie turned to Dolores, who stood on the porch putting on a pair of worn chaps Maggie suspected Shep had donated.

"Dolores, should I take a gun along?" She hadn't fired one in ages, but Papa had taught her to handle a revolver and a rifle in her teen years.

Dolores shrugged. "If you want."

Shep came around the back end of one of the packhorses. "I put your father's shotgun on the packsaddle, Miss Maggie. Right here." He touched the stock that jutted from a saddle scabbard. "You want a handgun too? Might not be a bad idea."

"Put it in my pack," Maggie said. "I don't want to wear it."

"Awright. I'll get one out of your pa's office." Shep went inside.

While they exchanged greetings and last-minute instructions, three more women rode up. Shep brought out a holstered revolver and two boxes of cartridges.

"Reckon all your pa's belts are too big for you, Miss Maggie, but you can run your belt through this holster when you want it." Shep nodded toward Maggie's middle, where she had a comfortable old leather belt at the waist of her split skirt.

"I wish I'd thought to bring a gun," Carlotta said.

Poppy Wilson looked over her trim ensemble, which included silver conchos on her hatband and short silver spurs. "You won't need one. If a rattler sees you, he'll be so dazzled he'll forget to strike."

"At least you look like a cowpuncher," Bitty Hale, the postmaster's wife said, adjusting the shapeless felt hat she wore. "Some of us have to use sidesaddles."

"Who cares?" Sarah said. "We are going to have so much fun!"

Maggie hoped they wouldn't be disillusioned when they realized how much work the roundup would entail.

"Miss Maggie," Shep said in a low voice, "there's one other thing we haven't talked about."

"What is it?"

He glanced toward the knot of horsewomen and tugged her a few steps away.

"Have you gals thought about who's going to castrate them mavericks?"

Maggie stared at him for a moment. She hadn't given it a thought. Blood rushed to her cheeks. "Well, no, not really."

Shep nodded. "That's one thing maybe I shoulda brought up sooner. I don't want to embarrass ya. Now, if Dolores wanted to stay here, I could go with ya and do the dirty work, so to speak."

Maggie looked toward Dolores, who was laughing with the other women as Carlotta helped her adjust her stirrups.

"I don't think you could talk her into staying home now, Shep. She's set on going."

He let out a mournful sigh. "Well, now, that Sarah Bradley might jump right in and do it. Her and John Key's sister. But if you want to drive 'em home as is, so to speak, I can take care of 'em here later on, I suppose. But usually the cowpokes do it at the camp and let 'em loose again."

Maggie considered that. It would be a burden on Shep to have to do the messy work alone here at the ranch and then drive the calves back out to the range.

"How about this," Shep said. "When you think you've got all you're goin' to have, send word and I'll come out and help you. Whoever fetches me can sit with your pa if he's not up and about by then."

They left it at that. Within a half hour, nearly a dozen women had gathered. Several of them rode sidesaddle. Most of the younger women and the others who came from ranches wore divided skirts and rode astride on stock saddles. All had their bedrolls and a few extra clothes and provisions.

"One thing's for sure," Poppy Wilson said, after they'd compared what they'd brought, from Sarah's double batch of johnnycake to her stash of pickles and jelly, "we're going to eat well on this campout."

"Do you think any more are coming?" Maggie asked Carlotta.

"I wouldn't be surprised. A couple of girls who can't come are going to keep spreading the word in town and to the ranches. But I don't think we should wait any longer."

"All right." Maggie turned to the others. "Ladies, let's get to work."

Throughout the hour-long ride to the camp, Maggie's companions kept up a cheerful chatter. In her mind, she went over the tasks they needed to accomplish and tried to decide which women were best suited to each. She hoped they would not be sorely disillusioned when they saw the working conditions.

Lost in thought she wondered if she was leading them into a foolhardy errand. They stopped twice to wait while women adjusted their bundles or tightened their cinches, but they arrived at the camp without a mishap.

"Well now," Dolores said as they trotted into the area between the chuck wagon and the holding pens. "This doesn't look too bad. The boys left everything tidy."

The cattle milled about in their pens, and the extra horses trotted back and forth fitfully in the corral, whinnying and tossing their heads.

"Those horses, they are glad to see us, no?" Carlotta said.

"Yes, and we need to water them right away." Maggie turned and surveyed her crew. Most of the women had dismounted and were stretching. "Ladies, our first order of business is to unload our gear. Everyone will please pile her things behind the chuck wagon, out of the way. There will be some time at nooning when you can decide where you want to sleep, but we need to do some work right away."

The women gathered around Maggie, who remained astride her horse.

"Just tell us what you want us to do, Maggie," Sarah said stretching her arms over her head.

They'd discussed a division of work the day before, but only half the women had been at the meeting. Maggie pulled a piece of paper and the stub of a pencil from her skirt pocket and consulted the notes she'd written then.

"We need three crews. I need half of you—the ones who can ride well and rope if needed—to herd this cut of cattle back to the ranch. I'm making Carlotta the head of that group, because she can outride any cowpuncher in Texas."

The women all laughed.

"I don't know about that," Carlotta said, "but I think we can do this."

"Pick five more women to go with you," Maggie said.

"Can I pick you?"

"I think you can."

Carlotta nodded and faced the other women. "All right, I choose Maggie, Sarah, Hannah, Nancy, and Consuela."

"Very good," Maggie said. "We'll meet with you over near the gate to the big holding pen in ten minutes. Now, for those left in camp, Dolores will be in charge here while we're gone."

Dolores flushed but said nothing. The others nodded solemnly.

"Poppy," Maggie said, "I believe you're pretty good with horses. You and three others will be responsible for getting the remuda watered. Those horses are vital to our job, but it's going to take some work. The water's about a half mile away, and you can either harness a team and haul the water in barrels with the chuck wagon, or you can string the horses together and take them to the source."

With about thirty extra horses to take care of, that would be a major job, especially since the horses were parched and would no doubt be hard to handle on the way to the stream.

"I'll leave the details up to you, Poppy. You're a smart girl. But remember—safety is more important than efficiency."

Poppy nodded.

"And Dolores, I'll let you pick one lady to help you set up the kitchen area, get a fire going, and prepare for lunch. Use this fire pit for cooking, and please keep a pot of coffee and one of hot water for tea going all the time. That fire pit over there" —she pointed to one about fifty yards away—"is the one the men used for their branding fire. We'll do the same. Now, if anyone finishes their task before Carlotta's group returns, feel free to ride out and look for bunches of cattle. Keep in mind that the closest ones you find are probably culls from the ones the men already brought in and worked over."

"I'll choose Celine to help me, if nobody objects," Dolores said.

"I'd like that." Celine, the young wife of the Herreras' *vaquero* Franco Martinez, joined Dolores with a smile on her face. "I'll do whatever you want me to, but those longhorns, they make me nervous."

Dolores patted her shoulder. "You and me, we'll cook up a good dinner, *si?*"

A few minutes later, Maggie and Carlotta and their rest of their team were on their way to the holding pens. The cattle lowed piteously and shuffled about.

"It's going to be wild when we let them out," Maggie said. "Is everybody comfortable with their horse?"

The women nodded.

Carlotta said, "All right then, I will open the gate on this pen. Let's get a couple of you on each side, so that when they come out you can start steering them home. We want to go directly back to the Porters' ranch and put them in the pasture as quickly as possible."

Maggie took the side away from where the gate would swing, with Nancy Jeffers, whom she considered to be one of the least skilled riders in the group, and Sarah Bradley, a rancher's daughter who knew what was what. On the other side, with Carlotta, were Hannah Ervine, who'd grown up on a ranch, and Consuela Rigas, Carlotta's friend.

As soon as the gap between the gate and the post was wide enough, the cattle poured through. Maggie, on Duchess, did her best to head off those that wanted to head for the open range. Sarah and Carlotta managed to get the leaders going in the right direction, but Duchess was too slow to do the job well. Maggie loped after a group of six meandering steers and knew she'd never catch them. To her surprise, the inexperienced Nancy galloped past her, rode right in front of the charging steers and cut them off. The two of them were able to direct the six back into the herd still escaping from the pen.

Once the main part of the livestock was headed toward the ranch, the others willingly followed. While Carlotta and the others went on with them, Maggie and Sarah opened the second pen and let out the smaller group of cattle penned in it.

"How many cattle have we got in this cut?" Sarah yelled.

"About three hundred," Maggie said, going by what Alex had told her the evening before.

The two bunches blended into one herd. They hadn't gone far before Poppy and her team rode up behind them, each leading several horses from the remuda strung together with lariats. Maggie saw the chance to rest Duchess and make use of a fresh cow pony.

She rode up to Sarah and said, "I'm going to see if I can swap horses."

Sarah nodded, and Maggie rode off to join Poppy and the others with the remuda. "After you water them, I want a new mount," she yelled to Poppy.

Poppy nodded. "Go on with the cattle and I'll bring you one after they drink."

"Go quick," Maggie said. "The cattle have to cross the stream, and they'll make a mess of it. Go upstream a little from the crossing."

It only took her a minute to catch up with the herd. She rode at the back, eating dust and urging the stragglers to catch up.

The cattle all but stampeded into the shallow water and shoved each other as they vied to quench their thirst. They spread out down the length of the stream for a couple of hundred yards. Maggie stayed on the near side of the stream to head off any who finished drinking and tried to go back the way they'd come. She'd been at this task for about ten minutes when Poppy trotted toward her from farther upstream, leading a feisty-looking pinto.

"He looks rarin' to go," Maggie said.

"He's spirited," Poppy agreed, pulling the gelding up alongside her mount. "I hope he's not too much of a handful for you. He was so pretty, I admit I picked him for his looks."

Maggie laughed and hopped to the ground. "You have to be careful of that—with horses and with men. I can't wait to try him out. Not that I don't love Duchess, but she's past her prime, and I don't think she's quite up to this game." She flipped her stirrup up and hooked it over the saddle horn as she spoke and set about untying the leather strap. As soon it the cinch was free, she pulled the saddle and blanket off Duchess and carried them over to the pinto.

"Hold him close," she told Poppy. In a couple of minutes, she had Duchess's saddle and bridle on the pinto and had transferred the lead rope to Duchess. "Thanks a lot. I'll see you in a few hours."

She swung into the saddle and set off after the herd that was now moving slowly away from the stream. She helped Hannah and Consuela drive the last of the cattle up the far bank of the stream. The pinto responded to her hand and leg signals so well, she almost lost her balance when he pivoted to head off an errant steer.

"You're something!" She patted the horse's withers. Since she didn't know his name, she decided to call him Speck.

It took three hours to get the herd to the north pasture. Maggie was exhausted, and some of the women, especially the older ones like Nancy and Hannah, looked ready to fall out of their saddles.

"Well, the men might have done it faster," Carlotta said, "but we didn't lose one critter."

Maggie smiled. The women had put all their stamina into chasing and heading off the rebellious animals that wanted to leave the herd and go back to the open range.

"Tomorrow will be easier," she said. "We'll get more efficient as we go."

She was tempted to ride a little farther to the ranch house and check on her father, but she restrained the impulse. They'd been gone only about five hours, and she needed to make the most she could of this day.

They returned to camp shortly after noon. Dolores and Celine had dinner ready and had served the women who had watered the horses and begun rounding up more cattle. They had only put twenty new animals in the pens, but it was a start.

Carlotta gave an amusing account of their morning drive while the women in her group filled their plates.

As they settled down to eat, Poppy called out, "Somebody's coming."

Along the road toward the ranch and Brady, several riders trotted toward them. Within seconds Maggie could tell most of the six wore skirts. The women in the camp set aside their dishes and gathered to greet the newcomers.

"Hey," Mariah Key, the leader, yelled as she pulled up on her compact pinto. "I heard you needed women to do a man's job today."

Maggie grinned. "Glad to have you." Mariah's brother, John Key, had a ranch a few miles east of Brady. "I see your family's well represented."

"Yes, Lottie and I are here for the day, and I can stay on if you need me. Lottie will have to go back tonight."

Lottie Key, Mariah's sister-in-law, rode up beside Mariah and dismounted. "Hello, Maggie. Glad you're home. John said I can't stay away all night. He's afraid the children will fuss."

Maggie and the others greeted the six newcomers. Dolores asked if they'd eaten. Most of them had, but they didn't turn down cookies and coffee.

When Maggie went to refill her cup and get dessert, Carlotta met her at the chuck wagon.

"This is great," Carlotta said. "We've got nearly as many hands as the men had."

Maggie grinned. "So we ought to get the work done in twice the time they would have."

"You mean half the time don't you?"

"I wish." Maggie walked out to the fire. The women all turned toward her expectantly and stopped talking. Maggie addressed her cowhands. "Our morning tasks are done, and we have some reinforcements. Three ladies are only here from now until sundown, and I want to put everyone to the greatest use we can. Do I have two volunteers to stay here and prepare the branding fire? If you're not adept at riding and you can't rope at all, this might be a good place for you, though I must say everyone did their jobs admirably this morning."

Thyra and Rhonda raised their hands.

"Thanks. The fire pit the men used for branding is over there." She pointed to the ring of stones fifty feet away. "We'll need a wood fire that will burn down to hot coals, about like you'd want for baking bread. Poppy tells me that in the bunch they rounded up this morning, there's only one calf in need of branding. Maybe we should take care of that before the rest of us go out looking for more cattle."

"That's a good idea," Bitty said. "Some of us haven't got much of a notion what to do."

"I don't want to watch," Lottie said.

Mariah laughed. "Don't mind Lottie. She's softhearted."

"It's all right, Lottie," Maggie said. "We won't make you do the branding, or even watch if you don't want to. But the more of us who can handle each job the better, and the faster we'll get finished."

"You can put your branding iron in my cook fire if you want, for this one," Dolores said, "but after that, I want you out of my hair while I get supper ready."

Maggie walked to the other fire ring and selected the Rocking P branding iron that lay on the grass. She took it back and shoved the business end into the coals.

"All right, I need someone who can cut cattle to help me get that little rascal out of there."

Carlotta volunteered and ran to fetch her horse. She and Maggie rode into the holding pen with the other women watching and cheering them on from outside the fence. Carlotta cut the calf out, away from its mother and the other full-grown cattle, and Maggie dropped a loop of her lariat neatly over its head. Instead of throwing it inside the pen, she coiled in half the length of her rope and led the balky calf to the gate. Poppy opened it, and while Carlotta held the other cattle back, Maggie led the calf toward the branding fire.

"Those of you waiting here can catch the calves when they come in if you want," she said. "Throw and brand them, and then let them go."

"What if they won't leave their mothers?" Hannah asked.

"If the mama is in good shape to keep producing, let them both go. We'll see them again next year."

"Hey, Maggie, I think the branding iron's ready," Rhonda called from the cook fire, where Dolores was fanning the coals.

"She's pretty near orange," Dolores said.

Maggie led the calf closer. "Who knows how to throw a calf?"

"Reckon I do," Sarah said.

"I'll help you." Mariah stepped up beside Sarah.

"All right, everyone watch how they do it," Maggie called,

dismounting. "We want to make this process go as quickly and painlessly as possible, for the calves and for you."

The women watched in fascination as Sarah walked up to the bleating calf and leaned over its neck. She grabbed it and threw her weight against it, knocking the calf off its feet. As soon as it hit the ground, she placed one knee on its neck to prevent it from rising. Mariah leaned on the calf's hindquarters and held its legs down. The calf writhed but couldn't get up.

"Good job," Carlotta yelled.

Maggie, meanwhile, had run to the fire. She took the branding iron and carried it quickly to where the calf lay panting in the grass. He looked bigger down here than he had from the back of her horse.

"Hold him steady," she told Sarah and Mariah.

Maggie circled the calf and eyed its flank, wondering if she could do this right. If she didn't hurry, the iron would be too cool. She hauled in a deep breath and pressed the hot Rocking P symbol to the calf's hip.

The spotted calf lowed desperately, and Maggie wanted to drop the iron. But she knew you had to keep it there long enough to singe off the hair and permanently mark the skin, though not so long that you burned through to the tissue beneath. She swallowed hard, counted mentally one-two-three as the calf struggled, and pulled the iron away. The brand was a touch blurry, but definitely recognizable. Mariah and Sarah jumped up. The calf leaped to his feet and crow-hopped away, blatting.

The other women erupted in cheering. Maggie straightened, feeling a little queasy.

"Here you go," Celine said, holding out a tin cup full of liquid.

Maggie took it and gulped down the lukewarm water. "Thanks." She wiped the sweat from her brow. Then she took stock of the talent she had before her and split up the women who were going to ride out searching for more cattle. Four groups of three or four women rode out together with instructions from Maggie on where to search. All pledged to return to camp before dark.

Poppy, Nancy, and Bitty rode with Maggie, and even though the "town" women were less adept than Maggie, they were able to locate and drive in two dozen cattle. Among them were three calves and a yearling not yet branded, as well as a steer with the Lazy S brand.

Maggie was pleased to find that two other teams had come in, and nearly forty more cattle shifted about in the largest holding pen.

"I'm afraid we brought in a few that have already been worked," Sarah told her after Maggie's cut was secure in the pen, "but we got two mavericks and one calf from this year's crop branded."

"Good work," Maggie said. "How many of them look good for the drive?"

"Maybe twenty."

Sarah, Thyra, and Rhonda set about preparing to brand the calves. With each calf the women improved their technique. When they turned the last one loose, Dolores banged on a kettle with her ladle.

"Come and get it!"

"Carlotta's not in yet." Maggie looked anxiously toward the line of hills to the east.

The sun was nearly set, but she thought she could make out a dust cloud hanging near the base of the hills.

Mariah came and stood beside her. "That's got to be them."

"I think I'll ride out and meet them," Maggie said. "They must be exhausted."

"Well, Lottie, me, and Thyra need to head home as soon as

we eat. If we can come back tomorrow, we will."

"Thanks so much for your work today," Maggie said.

Mariah grinned. "We enjoyed it."

She went to get her dinner plate. Maggie searched the distant range again. She was sure now—someone was coming, and from the amount of dust they raised, there had to be quite a few animals on the move.

She walked past the chuck wagon on her way to the remuda of horses. "Dolores, I think Carlotta and the others are heading in with their cut. I'm going to go see if they need help."

"We'll have plenty of chow when you're done," Dolores said.

Maggie threw her saddle on a horse that didn't have sweat stains and rode out at a lope. The others were scarcely a mile out from camp, and she was soon close enough to recognize the riders. Carlotta waved at her, then bolted off on her pinto to head off a rebellious steer.

Maggie moved in to help control the herd. As they approach the camp, Bitty ran to hold the gate for them. As soon as the cattle were all inside the pen, the women who'd brought them in went to unsaddle and get their supper.

"You've got almost fifty head," Maggie said to Carlotta. "That's wonderful! Where did you find them?"

Carlotta smiled. "We had about a dozen that we found in a canyon between the hills. We'd started back when we met up with some of my father's *vaqueros*. They said they'd seen quite a few Rocking P cattle on the Bar-H range, and they would get them for us. We were only a mile away, so we went along slowly while they rode back and brought out your cattle. But then it took us a long time to get back here with so many."

"That was nice of them," Maggie said. "We've got a few of theirs, but not many. We have more of the Bradleys'."

"Oh, and that mustang Consuela is riding threw a shoe."

"Great." Maggie grimaced. "I don't think we have anyone along with blacksmithing skills." She had cleaned her horses' feet ever since she'd learned to ride and had even trimmed a few, but she'd never learned the art of shoeing. They always had plenty of men around who could do it, and it was very hard work. As a girl, she hadn't cared to delve into it.

Carlotta shrugged. "We'll have to rest that horse until we can get him shod."

"Yes. Tomorrow or the next day, maybe we'll take the herd in, and we can take the horse back to the ranch then. If Shep can't shoe him, he can take him to the blacksmith in town. I'm not even sure who's been doing the farrier work for Papa lately." Before Maggie had left with her mother, they'd employed a cowboy who took care of those duties, but she hadn't seen him when she helped with the payroll yesterday. He must have moved on while she was away.

"How are you doing?" she asked Dolores as the cook loaded her plate.

"Oh, my bones are tired, but I expect yours are feeling worse."

Maggie smiled. "You're right, I'm played out."

Thanks to her daily rides since she'd come home, her legs weren't as sore as they might have been. Her arms were another story. Twirling a lariat, throwing calves bigger than she was, and holding them down had her feeling bruised and weary.

"Hey, Maggie," Hannah called. "Come sit down, lady. You look beat."

Maggie went to her and settled on the grass between her and Bitty.

"I may be tuckered out, but this is the most fun I've had in ages," Bitty said.

"I'm so proud of everybody." Maggie opened her biscuit and

slathered it with apple butter. "I did a quick estimate, and I think we brought in around two hundred cattle today. That's not counting the ones we let loose again. I mean two hundred to sell."

"Yay!" Sarah applauded, and the other women joined in.

"Hooray for the cowgirls!" Hannah yelled.

Carlotta came and sat down facing them. "I really think we can do this, Maggie. I admit I had my doubts at first."

"Well, we might not have brought in as many as the men would have," Bitty said, "but I think we did pretty good."

"We did." Maggie took a bite of her biscuit. She would have to cull the cattle carefully in the morning, when the light was good, to make sure they took only the ones her father would want to send to the stockyards, but for the first time she was sure they could do a creditable job. She smiled at Carlotta. "What did your father say about you coming out here?"

Carlotta shrugged. "He was a little skeptical."

Celine said, "I think my Franco was more upset than Señor Juan."

"Well, my papa didn't come right out and say that we couldn't handle it," Carlotta told them, "but I could tell he was thinking that."

"Was he upset that you're taking a man's job?" Hannah asked.

"No. In fact, he felt bad that he told Maggie's papa he couldn't send any men over. But most of them are off on the drive now anyway."

Maggie bit her lower lip. They'd be latecomers at the stockyards, and they might get lower prices. She hoped the money wasn't drying up by the time the Rocking P cattle got there.

How they would get to Fort Worth was still unsettled. She hadn't given up all hope that the cowboys would be back to work by then. But if not . . .

She looked around at her band of lady cowpunchers and wondered how many of these women would be willing to leave their families for a month or more of dangerous work on the trail.

CHAPTER TWELVE

lex and Nevada laid out their bedrolls on a bluff overlooking a creek. They didn't camp too close to the water, or they'd have been trampled by loose livestock going to drink at dawn.

Nevada built a small campfire, and Alex took from his pack two tins of beans he'd bought and peeled off the labels so they wouldn't catch fire. He opened the lids and set the cans down inside the edge of the fire ring. Neither of them had a proper coffeepot, so Nevada put water in his little tin pan and stirred in a spoonful of ground coffee.

They let the beans and coffee simmer while they tended their horses and stashed their saddles under some juniper branches in case it rained. After a half hour of rotating the cans now and then, Alex pulled them out, using his riding gloves for pot holders and squinting against the smoke.

"Not half bad," he proclaimed after the first spoonful.

"Not as good as Stewie's," Nevada said.

The coffee wasn't really potable, but Alex didn't want to

insult his friend their first night out, so he drank his share and spit out the grounds.

"What you planning to do tomorrow?" Nevada asked.

"I dunno." Alex set his can of beans aside and leaned back on his elbows. "I can't see much point in staying around here. Porter's not going to take us back. He's hired a new crew already."

"How'd he get enough punchers that fast?"

"Beats me."

Nevada shook his head. "I never thought we were doing ourselves out of work. You reckon we'll all have to move on to some other ranch?"

"I do. And maybe a ways off. The other ranchmen around here likely won't want to hire us." Alex watched the fire for a minute then said, "I s'pose I could go home and haul freight with my pa."

"Freightin'? That's no good."

Alex didn't like the prospect. He'd left home because his father and his partner had left off running the stagecoach stop after the railroad went through and put their full energy into the business they'd started out with in the early 1850s—hauling freight with mule teams. Their ranch wasn't big enough to run many cattle on, and the Bright-Garza operation was now strictly a freighting station.

He wished he could go back to work for Martin Porter. The Rocking P used to be a good outfit. It could be again. He didn't like the fact that he couldn't see Maggie again, either. He smiled at the memory of how she'd ridden alone all the way out to the camp to see him. Feisty little thing. He already missed her.

"I wonder if their new men got out there and watered the remuda."

Nevada leaned forward and tossed a dry stick into the fire.

"You wanna ride to the camp in the mornin' and see? Be awful if they let those horses go thirsty."

"All right. But let's drop in and see Leo first. Maggie Porter gave me his pay yesterday. I want to give it to him myself."

"Sure thing." Nevada stretched. "Reckon we'll be safe riding into camp? Maybe we should pick up a couple of the other boys."

———— ★ ————

"Maggie!" Carlotta yelled. "Hannah fell off her horse."

Maggie ran toward the corral. They hadn't even gotten out of camp this morning, and things were going wrong. Hannah was leaning on Rhonda's shoulder while she hobbled toward the gate. Rhonda, the woman who kept house for Dr. Vargas and assisted with his patients, had an arm about her. Mariah and Sarah were trying to catch a chestnut gelding that darted about with a saddle hanging down on its ribs. It squealed and kicked at every horse that came near it.

"Be careful," Maggie called and then almost bit her tongue. Those two were ranch women and knew better than to get in the way of an angry horse's heels. She turned to open the gate for Hannah and Rhonda, but Carlotta had beaten her to it. "Are you all right?"

"Well, my ankle hurts, but I think it'll be all right," Hannah said.

"Got the wind knocked out of her," Carlotta told Maggie.

"Let's get your boot off before it swells too much," Rhonda said.

"But then I might not be able to get it back on."

Rhonda led her toward the chuck wagon. "Trust me, you don't want to have me cut it off later."

Hannah sat down near the wagon and grimaced as Rhonda eased her boot off.

"There we go." Rhonda tossed the boot aside and peeled back Hannah's stocking.

"That doesn't look too bad," Carlotta said, leaning in close.

"The bruises will take awhile to show." Rhonda gently felt Hannah's ankle.

"Ouch." Hannah gritted her teeth.

"I'm going to get a wet cloth from Dolores," Rhonda said.

"I'll get it." Maggie hurried to the back of the wagon, where Dolores was washing dishes. She explained the problem, and Dolores soaked a linen dish towel in water for her.

"That's as cool as we've got."

"Thanks," Maggie said. She wrung the towel out and took it to Rhonda. Hannah's ankle was beginning to puff up, and it looked redder than it had a minute earlier.

Rhonda took the cloth and wrapped it around Hannah's foot and ankle. "Leave that on there ten minutes, then we'll soak it again."

"Hannah, you'd better stay in camp this morning," Maggie said.

"I don't think it's broken," Rhonda told her, "but it'll probably swell up more and be sore for a while."

"I think Dolores has some willow bark," Maggie said.

"I'll ask her to make you some tea," Carlotta offered and spun away to make the request.

Maggie touched Rhonda's shoulder. "Thank you. It's a relief to have someone here who knows about nursing."

When they'd made Hannah as comfortable as possible, Carlotta walked toward the horse corral with Maggie. "You want us to go ahead out?"

"Yes, take half the women and check that ravine between Knob Hill and the Bradleys' boundary. In fact, there are about a dozen Bradley cattle in the second pen. Might as well take them home. It'll take you an hour or two to get them over there, but the ravine was one of the places Alex told me they hadn't worked yet, so you'll be close to Bradleys' anyway."

Carlotta nodded. "Maybe we'd better take some food."

"Not a bad idea—and make sure all the girls have full canteens. I'll take the rest and go south."

When Maggie rode in about noon with her team of four other women, Carlotta's band hadn't returned, but that didn't surprise her. Her own team had found about forty cattle and brought them in.

This was slow work, and she wasn't sure it was worth keeping all these women out here away from their families and their chores. Inexperience and other factors—green horses in the remuda, unskilled workers, and the vastness of the range—kept them from being efficient.

As they headed their cut into the holding pen, she wondered what Alex and the other men were up to today. *What would happen to them? Would they be able to find other jobs?* She was quite certain her father would hold their defection against them and not hire them back. And Alex would probably never forgive her. By hiring the women, she'd made him expendable and undermined the effect of the men's strike.

She couldn't help hoping he would understand that she did this for her father. Maybe someday she could tell him the whole story.

She was surprised to see Hannah tending the gate for them. Her ankle was wrapped in strips of cloth, and she wore a moccasin on that foot. She smiled cheerfully at Maggie.

"Good job!"

"How's your ankle?" Maggie asked as she rode out of the pen.

"Well, it hurts, but not so much that I can't help out. Dolores loaned me a moccasin because my boot wouldn't go on over the bandage."

"Shouldn't you stay off that foot?"

Hannah shrugged. "Rhonda thinks it's not too bad. Really, it doesn't hurt that much now. But if it's all the same to you, I'll be helping Dolores for a while. Celine said she could ride out with you this afternoon."

Maggie was washing up for her midday meal when Carlotta's team returned with about two dozen steers.

"The pickings are slim out there now," she told Maggie. "Most of the cattle we saw were cows or young stock."

"Maggie!"

She turned toward Dolores's voice. The cook pointed toward the trail that led toward the creek. Four riders approached.

Maggie and Carlotta walked out into the open space between the branding fire pit and the chuck wagon. Maggie adjusted her hat so the brim shaded her eyes, but she didn't recognize the men.

"Do you know them?" she murmured to Carlotta.

"Not sure. I think—yes, they're Bar D men. I know that palomino."

Maggie had to smile. She'd have expected Carlotta to know the men better than she did the horses, but she'd underestimated her friend this time.

"It's their foreman," Carlotta added in a whisper as the men drew near. "He's called Grit."

"Gents," Maggie called out. "Can we help you?"

Grit shoved his hat back a half inch, and the other men touched their hat brims.

"Ma'am. We heared your men had some Bar D cattle over here."

Maggie frowned. "Not so far as I know. If the Rocking P men brought in any of your beeves, I'm sure they must have thrown them over to your range. But since I've been out here, we haven't seen any."

"Whatchoo mean, since you bin out here?"

Grit's eyes narrowed and he looked her up and down in a way that made Maggie cringe. For the first time, she wished she'd worn her sidearm and not left it with her bedroll during the day.

"Where's your men at, anyhow?" Grit asked. "I hain't seen Alex for an age."

"Didn't ya hear?" one of the other cowpunchers drawled. "The Rockin' P men are strikin'."

Grit smiled. "That's right, I did hear somethin' about that. You tellin' me you got women workin' the roundup now? Or are you gals just out here to tidy up after the men?"

Maggie clenched her teeth.

Carlotta strode forward and stood before Grit's horse with her hands on her hips. "You watch yourself, mister. Do you know who you're addressing? That's Miss Porter, and she's the owner of this ranch, so you just hold your tongue."

"Hey, boss, that's Herrera's daughter," one of Grit's men said. "You don't want to mess with her, or her padre will run you out of Texas."

"Ha!" Grit grinned. "I thought you looked familiar." His eyes lingered on Carlotta. "Whatchoo doin' out here, señorita?"

"We're doing more work than you *vaqueros* are." Carlotta's taunting prompted Maggie to step up beside her.

"I assure you gentlemen that if we find any drifted cattle with the Bar D brand, we'll send them home."

"You sure you hain't branding any of our calves?" Grit looked toward the fence. "Maybe my boys oughta take a look in your holding pens, just to make sure."

"No, I don't think that's a good idea," Maggie said. This wasn't like the old days of the open range, when the men from various ranches got together to do their roundup and sort out the cattle. Now many of the boundaries were fenced. Her father held grazing rights to the range they were working on, and sometimes a few head from other ranches wandered over here, but the herds didn't mix like they used to.

She held the foreman's stare. Grit may have honorable intentions, but she had a bad feeling about the entire encounter. If these men sympathized with the strikers, perhaps they'd ridden over from the ranch ten miles distant to give the new workers a hard time. They could end up making far more trouble than Alex and his departing men had made.

"Oh, I think we need to see what you've got." Grit nodded to the man on his right. He and another of the cowboys turned their horses and trotted over to the pen.

Maggie glared at Grit, clenching her fists involuntarily. "This is outrageous. Take your men and get off the Rocking P."

Grit smiled. "Last I heard, your old man owned this range, not you." He looked toward the corral. "Whatcha got, Shorty?"

One of the cowboys near the gate called, "Looks like they've got a couple dozen mavericks that might belong to us. You want us to cut 'em out?"

CHAPTER THIRTEEN

*N*ot one of those cattle is yours." Maggie lifted her chin and planted her feet firmly as she watched the leader, but inside she quivered. What had she gotten these women into?

Carlotta spat a stream of Spanish at the cow-punchers near the gate, and Maggie laid a hand on her arm.

"Take it easy, Carlotta." She had no time to pray, but she sent up a wordless cry for help and fixed Grit with a glare. "It's true that the Rocking P property and range rights are in my father's name, but I have full authority from him. I suggest you and your men leave. Now. You're not taking any cattle out of our herd. If we find any—"

"Riders coming," Bitty yelled.

Maggie's heart sank. A few more men from the Bar D— or any other outfit in sympathy with the strikers—would tip the balance of power. More than ever she wished she'd worn her father's revolver or could lay hands on the shotgun still in the scabbard on her saddle.

She looked toward the stream, but no one came along that trail. She shifted her gaze toward the ranch and town. Half a dozen horses were coming up fast. She held her breath. Things could get uglier in a hurry.

"It's Alex," Dolores cried, and Carlotta sucked in a deep breath.

Maggie's heart pounded. Did Alex mean support—or more trouble? She straightened her shoulders. "As I was about to say, you can tell Mr. Danfield we'll send any of his strays home at the end of our roundup."

The six newcomers rode up and halted their horses. Alex looked from Grit to Maggie and back.

"Afternoon, ladies," Alex said. "What's the story here?"

"Nothing we can't handle." Maggie looked him over, trying to read some motive for this visit, but she couldn't find any clues. Only his brown eyes seemed different as he met Grit's gaze—tough and challenging, though he sat relaxed in the saddle. Nevada Hatch, beside him, was another story. Maggie got the impression of a cat, sleek and disinterested, but ready to spring in an instant.

"We heard over to the Bar D that Porter had fired you punchers and hired a new crew, so we thought we'd ride over and make sure they weren't branding none of our strays." Grit nodded at Alex. "Never thought I'd find a bunch of females trying to take your place—and your pay."

Nevada Hatch crossed his wrists and leaned on his saddle horn. "Thought we'd better come see if the ladies needed a hand, seein' as they're trying to do a man's job out here."

Maggie shifted her gaze to Alex. "I suppose you told the other ranches about us and sent these buckaroos over to make trouble."

Alex's jaw dropped. "No such thing. We just heard about it in town. We had no idea you were out here 'til an hour ago, did we, fellas?" He glanced around at his companions.

"We sure didn't," Harry Jensen said. "I heard it when I dropped in to see Leo. We just assumed your pa hired some men, Miss Maggie."

"Well, we'd like to get on with our work and get the job done," she said.

"That right?" Grit smiled. "Boys, get them mavericks, and we'll mosey along."

"No, you don't." Sarah Bradley stepped out from the shadow of the chuck wagon with her revolver leveled at Grit. "Those are all Rocking P cattle. If you take one of them, we'll shoot you for rustlers."

Dolores stepped up beside Sarah holding Maggie's shotgun. She trained it on the men near the holding pen gate. Maggie's stomach knotted, and she made herself breathe slowly.

Mariah Key and Poppy Wilson ambled forward holding revolvers pointed at the men.

"That's right," Poppy said. "We may be wearing skirts, but we know how to defend Mr. Porter's herd."

"Whoa, now!" Grit sat a little straighter and eyed Alex uncertainly.

"Don't look at me for help," Alex said. "I was bossing this camp until yesterday morning, and there weren't any Bar D cattle in the pens when I left. We'd sent about a dozen head over to your ranch the day before, though."

"Hmpf." Grit hauled in a deep breath. "All right. Shorty, I guess we were mistaken. Come on, boys." He narrowed his gaze at Maggie. "Ain't often a man pulls iron on another puncher. I won't forget this."

"Just stay on your own range, and you won't have any trouble," Sarah said, holding her gun steady.

Grit pivoted his horse and took off at a lope, with his three men right behind him.

Maggie let out a deep sigh.

"Well, boss, what do you want us to do now?" Sarah asked. Dolores had lowered the shotgun, but Sarah still held her revolver.

"Thank you all," Maggie said. "I don't think the Rocking P men will harm us." She looked expectantly at Alex and his companions.

"Oh, no, ma'am," Alex said.

"We sure wouldn't," Early echoed.

Maggie nodded and turned to the women. "Let's get those calves branded before anyone else comes along and tries to claim them."

The women put their guns away. Dolores went back to the chuck wagon. Most of the others headed for the remuda or the branding fire.

Maggie turned back to the lingering Rocking P men. Alex was looking over the camp.

"Well, as you can see, we're doing all right," she said.

He nodded.

"Are you surprised?" Carlotta asked.

"A little. Is there anything you need help with?"

Maggie frowned at him. Alex seemed serious, but Nevada Hatch sat there watching her and Carlotta with a smile that bordered on a smirk.

"Are you men asking for your jobs back?"

Alex raised a hand in dismissal. "No, ma'am. We're still striking."

The glimmer of hope Maggie had felt winked out. "Then go away."

"That's right. You're not welcome here," Carlotta said.

Instead of turning Red around and riding out, Alex swung down from the saddle. "Could I speak to you for a minute?"

Maggie hesitated. "We have a lot of work to do."

"I understand." He didn't move.

Maggie tried to stuff down her irritation. She didn't want Alex to play with her feelings. Had he known the Bar D men would be here? And had he come to look like the cavalry and gain her favor, or to make trouble?

"All right. What do you want?"

"I just want to assure you that we did not send those hombres out here. I truly didn't know you ladies were doing the job until Leo told us. I have to admire you for taking this on."

Maggie pressed her lips together. She didn't want to spill to him that her father couldn't get any other men to do the work, thanks largely to the strikers' pleas for sympathy at the other ranches. But she couldn't claim she was doing it just for fun.

"How long had those fellows from the Bar D been here?"

"Not long." She couldn't avoid his searing gaze. "We'd have handled it, but I have to admit your arrival made it a little easier."

He nodded. "Did you get that bunch out of the ravine over near Knob Hill?"

"We did. Thank you." There were so many things he could tell her that would make this job easier. But Maggie couldn't bring herself to ask him for that information. After all, she was out here to make sure his striking wouldn't hurt the ranch. She wished he and Nevada and the others hadn't come. Several of her cowgirls were dawdling around the chuck wagon and looking over the men who'd ridden in with Alex, and her own insides roiled. She cared deeply for this man, but they stood on opposite sides now—and Alex was making it hard to see exactly where the line was. One thing for certain, she wouldn't be able to concentrate on her work today.

"Look, we stopped at the ranch house on the way here," he said.

"What for?"

"Shep must have heard us riding by. He came outside and flagged us down."

Maggie gulped. "Is everything all right?"

"He asked me to tell you that your pa is holding his own."

Maggie closed her eyes for a moment. "Thank you. I've been wondering."

"He—uh—he also asked me to see if you were ready for him to come out and—and do the job he said he'd do for you." Alex cleared his throat and didn't quite meet her gaze. "Look, Maggie, how many bull calves you got? These fellas and I could take care of it for you—"

"But you men said you wouldn't work here."

He huffed out a breath. "I guess we'd better get moving then."

"Right. You should."

Alex held her gaze for a moment, and Maggie forced herself to turn away. She walked toward the corral, where Poppy had a horse saddled for her.

"Thanks, Poppy. I'm going to leave a couple of extra women in camp with you and Dolores and Hannah this afternoon. If any more punchers from other outfits come nosing around, you send them packing, all right?"

"We sure will," Poppy said.

At the sound of galloping hooves, she turned in time to see Alex and his friends riding away toward Brady. Maggie let out a deep breath. Had she just severed the flimsy thread that had tethered her to Alex?

"Yippee!" Sarah, mounted and ready to ride, yelled and rode her horse in a circle around the camp. A few of the others joined in, yelling and laughing. Celine danced about the cook fire.

"What's going on?" Maggie called.

"They're just letting off steam," Dolores said. "Celebrating, since you all chased the cowboys out of here."

Maggie shook her head. She didn't feel like celebrating. She checked her supplies and donned the worn leather chaps she'd borrowed from Shep. The canyons and arroyos she planned to scour were full of brush and prickly pear. The horse Poppy had picked for her was a scrubby dark bay. He looked tough. Maggie mounted and rode to the center of camp.

"Ladies," she called, "you haven't so much won a victory as you have passed a test. There may be more of those, so keep your wits about you. Now, gather 'round while I give new assignments."

She led five other women out with her to check several isolated areas. By late afternoon they had collected a large bunch of strays.

"Let's move them along," she told the others. "We want to be back in camp before sunset."

They hustled the herd, with the pointers trotting at the sides of the moving column, riding up on any cattle that tried to stop and graze. A yearling darted out from the herd and ran for freedom. Nancy whirled her horse and galloped after him. At breakneck speed, the horse pivoted again, and Nancy flew off her sidesaddle.

Maggie charged toward her, ignoring the escaping steer. As she pulled her horse up, Nancy sat up and blinked at her.

"Are you all right?" Maggie jumped down and knelt beside her.

Nancy pulled in several deep breaths.

"Nancy?" Maggie looked toward the small herd. The other women kept the cattle moving, but one horsewoman had spotted them and was riding back to check on them.

"Yes, I'll be fine." Nancy smiled, still gasping. "It's been a long time since I did *that*."

"Are you sure you're all right?"

Nancy put out her hand, and Maggie grasped it and pulled her to her feet.

Bitty rode up. "What happened?"

Nancy gave a halfhearted wave.

"She took a spill," Maggie said. "Can you get her horse?"

The dun gelding Nancy had been riding stood switching its tail about twenty yards away. Bitty trotted off to catch it.

"Does anything hurt?" Maggie asked.

Nancy shook her head. "My pride. But no. I only needed to catch my breath."

"Maybe you should rest," Maggie said.

"No, there is plenty of time for that after we get the cut in. But I tell you this: I am going to ride astride. My husband wouldn't let me leave home unless I rode the sidesaddle, but he does not understand."

"Maybe you can use Hannah's saddle. I doubt she'll be riding tomorrow."

Bitty brought Nancy's horse over.

Maggie eyed her keenly. "Are you sure—"

"Hush now." Nancy seized the reins. "Give me a boost, will you?"

Soon the three caught up to the herd and continued on to the roundup camp. The women kept them moving much better than they had yesterday. Maggie wondered if she would have to take the cattle to Fort Worth herself. It seemed less likely every day that she would be able to hire a male crew to do it. How many of her generous cowgirls could she conscript?

At least the railroad would pick up the cattle in Fort Worth now. The ranchers no longer had to drive them all the way to Kansas or Colorado or some other distant place to sell them. But with her inexperienced drovers, she figured the journey of two hundred fifty miles could take up to a month. Would these women be willing to leave home for that long? And how safe would they be on the trail, away from the comparatively secure Rocking P range?

Lottie held the gate while they herded the cattle into the pen. The steers protested and tried to dodge the enclosure. It took the women a good twenty minutes to turn back all the rebellious animals and force them inside.

"My husband and some of his men came from the Key ranch with thirty of your cattle," Lottie said. "There were half a dozen calves in there, so we branded them and let the cows and their babies loose."

"Great." Maggie looked toward the animals inside the fence. "Did they collect their strays from the other pen?"

"They sure did."

"Good—we won't have to drift them back to your ranch. Thank John for me when you see him, won't you?"

Maggie's back ached. She wished she could have a bath and sink into bed—her bed at home, with the warm quilts, fresh-smelling sheets, and plump featherbed. She rode to the remuda corral, handed her horse off to Sarah, and staggered to the chuck wagon, where she downed a dipperful of cool water.

"How's Hannah?" she asked Dolores.

"That girl's not doing too well." Dolores wiped her hands on her apron and picked up a pot holder. "Just my opinion, but I think she should see Doc Vargas."

"Oh?" Maggie looked around and spotted Hannah, lying on her bedroll in the shade beneath the wagon. She knelt and peered under. "Hi."

"Hello." Hannah sounded groggy.

"Does it hurt a lot now?" Maggie asked.

"Pretty bad."

"I'm sorry. I'm going to see about getting you back to town."

"I don't think I can ride that far," Hannah said.

"You'd have to go in the wagon."

Hannah clenched her teeth but didn't protest.

Maggie went back to Dolores. "Has Rhonda looked at her ankle again?"

"I don't think she's come in yet."

Maggie went to the branding fire, where Carlotta and Bitty were putting the Rocking P mark on the two mavericks they'd brought in their cut from the canyon. Nancy sat nearby, watching and rubbing her left wrist.

"You *are* hurt," Maggie said.

Nancy shrugged. "It's not bad. I didn't notice it at first, I was so angry that I'd fallen off."

"Do we need to wrap it?"

"I don't think so."

"All right." Maggie turned to Carlotta. "Can you go over the tally with me when you're done here? I think we need to get Hannah to the doctor, and I'm considering all of us going and taking in what cattle we have."

"You mean, end the roundup?"

"Yes. We're still short a couple hundred head of what we hoped for, but any cattle that are left are way up in the hills. We could wander around all week and only come up with a few more."

"That's true."

Maggie took out her notepad and they walked over to the large holding pen. "All right, the cuts we brought in yesterday and today, minus any strays, breeding cows, and young stock, will give us the marketable animals." Starting with the count Alex had given in his final report, she totaled up the numbers for the herd now in the north pasture and their day herd.

She and Carlotta went over the figures and decided their figures were as precise as they could manage.

"Well, Papa hoped for a few more," Maggie said, "but sixteen hundred head isn't bad."

"That will be a good drive," Carlotta assured her. "You need to get them to the stockyards while prices are still high."

Maggie knew theirs would be one of the last herds to arrive this spring. More ranchers would make their drives in the fall, but the Rocking P couldn't wait that long. They needed an infusion of cash as quickly as possible.

"I say we drive these beeves in tonight."

"You're in a big hurry. Why not wait until morning?"

Maggie looked at the sky. "I'm afraid we're in for a storm later. The wind's picked up. It could be miserable out here tonight. And we don't want the cattle to panic."

"At least they would be in the pen." Carlotta squinted toward the lowering sun. "It would be dark by the time we got there, and if the lightning started, we might lose control of the herd."

"That's why I think we should start now."

Carlotta shook her head. "The ladies have worked all day. They'll want to eat supper at least."

Maggie sighed. "I guess you're right."

"As usual." Carlotta's dazzling smile flashed.

"I'll remind you of that tonight, when it's pouring rain and we're trying to keep the cattle calm."

Maggie took the dark-to-midnight watch with Sarah, Bitty, and Consuela. Thunder rumbled in the distance, and toward the end of their watch, the sky clouded over. Lightning split and stabbed on the horizon.

Maggie and the three others rode slowly around the perimeter of the large pens, speaking in steady, low tones to the cattle. As long as the storm stayed several miles away, the longhorns kept fairly quiet, though they shifted about a lot.

Across the herd, Consuela's lovely soprano voice wafted to

Maggie in a haunting Spanish ballad. After that, Bitty sang one of her favorite hymns. From off to her right, Sarah's alto joined in, and Maggie couldn't resist adding harmony of her own.

When Poppy and three more women came to relieve them, Maggie gave instructions to wake her if things got rowdy.

"Don't worry," Poppy told her. "If they start stampeding, you'll wake up in a hurry."

Maggie rolled into her blankets near the chuck wagon. What would they all do if they had a downpour? A few of them could squeeze into the chuck wagon, she supposed, but the truth was, they'd be needed to control the cattle. She was grateful for the holding pens. In the old days, when the roundup was done on the open range without benefit of fences, keeping the herd together in a storm was nigh impossible. And they might face that exact challenge on the cattle drive.

She realized that she'd accepted the idea of making the cattle drive with her female supporters—as many as would undertake the adventure with her. Maybe she'd broach that to them in the morning at breakfast, before they left for the ranch. They should be thinking about it. She'd need to leave on the drive soon, to avoid the heat of midsummer. She wanted the cattle to arrive at the stockyards in good condition.

She awoke when raindrops splattered in her face. She wouldn't sleep anymore, so she might as well get up. Quickly she stowed her bedroll and pulled on a coat. Rhonda joined her as she hurried to tack up a horse. Before long, most of the other women came to help with the herd.

For the rest of the night, they circulated around the pens. An exceptionally loud thunderclap set the herd to running across the large pen. At one point a huge steer challenged the fence. The sound of wood splintering reached Maggie over the drumming of the rain and the lowing of the unhappy cattle. She and six other women converged on the spot. The angry steer bellowed and prepared to charge the weakened fence again.

"We've got to hold them," Maggie yelled to the others.

They spread out along the fence line and kept their horses moving back and forth, so that the cattle would be well aware of their presence. While the rain drummed down, the women sang hymns and lullabies and protected the fractured section of the fence.

At last the rain let up and the thunder drifted away to become only an infrequent growl in the distance. All the cattle remained in the pens, but the cowgirls were drenched.

CHAPTER FOURTEEN

The following morning they started out cold, wet, and hungry. When at last the cattle were in the north pasture only half a mile from the ranch house, Maggie turned her cowgirl crew toward home with a smaller herd of maverick calves and their mothers. These they drove into a pen nearer the home ranch as rain began to fall once more. The bedraggled women reached the ranch house near noon and ran the remuda into the corral beside the barn.

Maggie turned to address the other women. "Well done, ladies! We'll all go in the house and get warmed up and have something to eat."

"We're a mess," Sarah said. "We ought to just go to your bunkhouse to dry out and change our clothes."

"Nonsense!" Maggie turned to Dolores. "You can rassle up something for lunch, can't you?"

"You bet I can," Dolores said.

When they rode up to the front of the house, Maggie was

so tired she wasn't sure she could walk inside. The door opened, and Shep hurried out and across the porch.

"Ladies! Welcome back. I wondered how you were making it, out there in the storm last night."

Maggie grabbed his arm for support. "We did all right, Shep, but we're worn out. We want to come in and get changed and have a bite to eat."

"Well, you're in luck. I've got a big kettle of hot soup on the stove. I had it in mind to ride out to the camp in the buck-board this afternoon if I could get someone to stay with your pa."

"How is he?"

Shep shook his head. "It ain't good, Miss Maggie. I'm sorry to say it, but that's one reason I thought to go out to camp. I wanted to tell you to come see him if you could."

The other women had gathered around, and Shep seemed to suddenly take notice of them. He put on a smile and called, "You all come right in. We've got a couple of rooms you can change in, and I'll get you some hot water. And then we'll sit you down for some food."

"Yippee!" Bitty's screech made them all laugh.

"Let's put our horses in the barn, girls," Maggie said. "There should be plenty of feed in there for them."

They all took the horses they'd been riding across the barn-yard and led them inside.

"They can go out again after we feed and water them," Sarah said.

"No, there are plenty of empty stalls." Maggie took a quick survey. The only horse in the barn was the palomino filly. Its stall was clean, and the golden filly whickered and came over to the half-door to nuzzle Maggie's hand.

"She's gorgeous," Carlotta said, coming up behind Maggie.

"Yes. I never found out who she belongs to. I'll have to ask

Shep. He must have been taking care of her since the hands left."

"You go in and see your papa. I'll take care of your horse."

Maggie shook her head. "I'll do it."

"No, go on." Carlotta pushed her toward the door. "You need to see him. I heard what Shep said."

"Thanks." Maggie flitted between the horses and the women carrying saddles and brushes. She jogged across the yard in the drizzle and went in the kitchen door. As Shep had said, a huge pot of soup simmered on the wood stove, and the pleasant fragrance made her stomach clench. Chicken, unless she was mistaken. Good old Shep! Several kettles of water were also heating.

She met him in the hallway on her way to her room.

"I put a pitcher of warm water on your washstand," Shep said. "You get cleaned up and go to your pa."

"Thank you. Is he so much worse, Shep?"

He grimaced. "The doctor came out last night and told me to increase his medication, but that makes him groggy all the time."

"He *is* worse, then," Maggie said.

"I think it's as much the news as it is his health."

"What news?"

"He got a letter yesterday. It gave him a setback, I'm afraid."

Maggie's chest tightened. "Who was it from?"

"That hospital place your mother went to." Shep clenched his teeth. "I don't usually go snoopin', Maggie, but after your pa read that letter he slumped down in his chair and dropped it on the floor. I got him to bed, and afterward . . . well, it was lying there, and I went to pick it up, and I saw what it said."

"It's all right, Shep." She patted his arm. "You're looking out for us, and I don't blame you for seeing that."

He nodded. "Thanks."

"So tell me—was it another bill?"

"Kind of. It was a letter that sounded all legal like. I put it in on his desk. You want me to fetch it for you?"

"I'll go in there and read it after I see Papa. Just tell me the gist of it."

"Well . . ." Shep inhaled deeply. "It sounded to me like they're sayin' if your pa don't pay what's owed, they'll start proceedings to take his property."

She caught her breath. "This ranch means everything to Papa."

"No, *you* mean everything to him. More than anything, he can't stand the thought of dying and leaving you penniless, with no home. He's counting on the cattle drive, Maggie. If you can't get those cattle sold and make the people he owes back off, I think that would do him in. He needs to know you'll be all right when he's gone."

As she washed up and changed out of her trail clothes, Maggie thought about her situation. She was grateful that she had faithful employees like Shep and Dolores to see her through this difficult time. If the men had stayed loyal to the Rocking P, she wouldn't have half the worries she now faced. Alex and the cowpunchers would take care of the herd for her, and she could stay with her father.

Seeing Alex again yesterday had only confirmed what she'd known since she came home from San Francisco—she loved him. Now it seemed to be futile. Those men, especially Alex, could never come back to the ranch. Her father wouldn't let Alex through the front door if he returned. Papa certainly wouldn't trust him with his financial future.

She opened her armoire and gazed at her choice of dresses. Side by side were the black mourning dresses she'd worn after Mama died and the gay ball gowns Iris had coaxed her into wearing in San Francisco. She hated the sight of the expensive attire she'd bought to wear in the city.

She touched the sleeve of one of the black dresses. Would she be in mourning again soon?

Today was not the day to grieve. She shoved the mourning gowns to one side and took out a less somber dress. She loved the blue polished cotton, though the full skirt was a bit impractical for the ranch. Papa liked to see her in blue, and today she would do anything she could to please him.

She pulled it on and struggled to fasten the buttons in the back. In San Francisco, Iris or her maid had buttoned Maggie's dresses. She'd forgotten about that. On the ranch, she always wore ones that buttoned or hooked in the front, so she could dress herself. At last it felt right, and she used her hand mirror and the large looking glass over her dresser to make sure. She picked up a fan and her tally notebook and went out into the hall.

From the parlor, she heard the sound of the women's voices.

"Miss Hannah and Miss Celine, you come with me and I'll show you where you can change," Dolores was saying. Maggie thought ruefully that someone should be taking care of Dolores.

She went to her father's door, confident that Dolores and Shep would make the other women comfortable.

Papa drowsed in his bed, and she took the chair beside it. He looked thin and pale. Perhaps she imagined it, but his breathing seemed shallow, too.

A few minutes later a tap sounded on the door, and Dolores opened it a few inches.

"Can I get you anything?"

"No, I'm fine." Maggie stood and went to the door. "He's sleeping, and I don't want to wake him."

"Maybe you should come eat with us," Dolores said. "Rhonda and I have put Hannah to bed in the guest room."

"Good. I don't want to make her ride all the way to town in this rain."

"Yes, we'll hope it's cleared off by morning, and then we can get her to Dr. Vargas. Shall we put the rest of the ladies in the bunkhouse? I hate to, but we don't have enough beds anywhere else."

Dolores smiled. "It's a little rough out there, but I'm sure they'll find it a lot nicer than sleeping on the ground."

"Maggie?" At her father's question, she turned back to the bed.

"Yes, Papa, it's me. We've brought the cattle in. They're all in the pasture now."

"I thought you'd be out there a few more days."

"Well, if you want us to go back out, we can, but we've got most of them. I thought it might be more important to get the cattle to the stockyards quickly than to round up the last hundred or so."

He frowned, but after a few seconds he said, "I s'pose so."

She took the seat next to his bed and reached to touch his hand. "So, you haven't been feeling well since I left."

His mouth twitched. After a long moment, he said, "You make me proud, girl."

Tears welled in Maggie's eyes. There was so much she wanted to say, but she kept quiet, stroking his hand gently until she was sure he'd lapsed back into sleep. She rose and tiptoed out.

The women were gathering at the long wooden dining table. Bitty and Carlotta were putting the finishing touches on the table settings used to feed the cowhands over the years. Shep, Celine, and Dolores brought dishes from the kitchen.

"Sit right here, Miss Maggie," Dolores said, touching the back of the chair at the head of the table—her father's chair.

It seemed wrong to Maggie, but there wouldn't be enough

chairs if no one sat there, and she supposed it would soon be her rightful place. She sat down, and the others found seats around the long table. She knew she would croak and choke up if she tried to pray aloud.

"Sarah. Would you?"

Sarah nodded and bowed her head. "Lord, we thank thee for thy mercy in bringing us and the cattle in safely. We ask that thou lay thy hand of compassion and healing on Mr. Porter. And we thank thee for this meal and for the one who prepared it. Amen."

Soft amens echoed around the table, and they began to pass the serving dishes.

"There's plenty of soup and johnnycake," Shep said, "and I've got a cake in the oven, so eat up."

Maggie eyed the table with satisfaction. Somehow, he'd found time to get out pickles, honey, jam, and sauerkraut, too.

"So, are we going back to the roundup in the morning?" Sarah asked.

"I'll have to go home, I'm afraid," Lottie said.

Maggie shook her head. "I don't think we'll go back. I saw Papa for a minute. He's quite ill, and his medicine makes him sleepy, but he seemed to agree with me that the most impor-tant thing now is to get those cattle to the stockyards. If we go out on the range again, we might pick up another hundred or two hundred head, but I don't think it's worth it."

"We're late starting the drive anyway," Sarah said. "My father's cattle went two weeks ago."

"And mine last Saturday," Carlotta said.

"Yes." Maggie looked down the table at all the expectant faces. They'd given her so much already. How could she ask more of them?

"Will you try to hire some men in town?" Bitty asked.

Maggie smiled, but her lips trembled. "I doubt I can get very many, at least on short notice."

"But if you don't hit the trail soon," Sarah said, "yours will be the last ones to the railhead, and you won't get top dollar for the stock."

"We'll probably be last as it is." Maggie reached for her glass and took a sip of water. "I'll be taking the herd myself. I don't know whether any of you can help me. If not, I suppose I'll need to spend a few days trying to hire some men. But I'd prefer to head out day after tomorrow." She looked to Shep, who was setting a platter of sliced ham on the table. "Do you think we have the supplies on hand and can restock the chuck wagon tomorrow, Shep?"

"We sure can. I made sure to get extra grub when I was in town. I didn't know what you was planning, but I figured somebody was going to need a stake for the drive."

She nodded. "Well then, anyone interested in trailing to Fort Worth with me?"

The women glanced at each other. Celine and Bitty looked as though the idea had never occurred to them, but Sarah was smiling and looking to see who else was game.

Shep cleared his throat, and Maggie looked to him.

"Miss Maggie, if you don't mind, I'd like to go with them on the drive. I know I'm old, and I move a little slow, but I'd be proud to be part of the Rocking P drive again. You could stay here with your father."

Maggie stood and walked over to him. She put her arms around him and gave him a big hug. "Thank you, dear friend. It would cheer my heart to have you along. You're trail savvy, and I'll feel a whole lot safer knowing you're close by. But I need to go myself. I'll be there in Papa's place. I think we need a Porter on the drive."

"I'll stay here and tend to your father, if you can get another cook," Dolores said. "I loved being out with you ladies the last few days, but my bones are weary."

Maggie went over and hugged her too. "Thank you. I don't think I could go unless one of you was with him."

"Do I get a hug too?" Sarah pushed back her chair and stood, extending her arms to Maggie.

"Count me in, *chica*." Carlotta stood as well.

"Would we get a chance to shop in Fort Worth when we get there?" Mariah asked.

Maggie laughed. "My dear, I'd be happy to spend a day or two helping you spend your wages when this is over."

Hannah and a couple of others had to decline, but when the count was complete, Maggie had herself, Shep, and eight other women on board. She had hopes of bringing in a couple more, but they'd get by with that if they had to.

Most of the women went home the next morning to see their families, do laundry, and prepare for the drive. Nancy insisted that her wrist would be fine without benefit of the doctor's ministrations and rode for home.

Shep prepared a pallet in the bed of the buckboard for Hannah, so that they could drive her to Brady when they went for supplies.

Maggie decided to ride in the back of the wagon with her, and they tied Hannah's saddle horse to the back.

"How is your father this morning?" Hannah asked as they set out.

"He's feeling better," Maggie said. "Dolores took him his breakfast on a tray, but he said he wanted to get up and have dinner with me later. He looked much stronger when I saw him."

"That's good." Hannah lay back on her pillow. "Ma's going to have a fit when she sees that I'm hurt. But Pa will just laugh and say I'm a pampered princess, riding home like this."

"You did a good job, and I'm very sorry you were injured."

"Don't worry, Maggie. I'll be fine."

"Well, we're going to stop at the doctor's, so he can take a look before we take you home."

← ★ →

When they reached the office, Sela Eagleton brought out a pair of crutches. She and Shep helped Hannah up the steps and into the doctor's examining room. When Sela came back to the waiting area, she smiled at Maggie and Shep.

"How are things going at the ranch?"

"Not bad," Maggie said.

"You finished the roundup for your father, yes?"

"That's right. We've got all the cattle in now."

"Them gals did a fine job," Shep said.

Sela smiled. "That is good. Are you sending them to buyers? Leo said you would have trouble finding men to drive them to Fort Worth for you, since most of the ranchers have already sent their herds."

"Oh, we'll manage," Maggie said.

Shep winked at her. "How's old Leo doing?"

"Well, he is still in bad shape—condition, the doctor says. Not good. But he is better. The doctor has not given up hope that he will walk again."

"I certainly hope he'll be able to," Maggie said. The prospect of Sela working to support the family for years to come alarmed her.

"We hope to get him up in the wheelchair this afternoon. The doctor says he can sit outside for a while. He is feeling a little stronger now."

"That's good," Shep said.

"And how are *you* doing, Sela?" Maggie eyed her drawn face closely.

"I am doing well. Rhonda came about an hour ago and said she will come back to work tomorrow. I was happy to earn a few dollars while she was gone."

"I'm glad it worked out for you. How are the children?"

"Pretty good," Sela said. "My mother came up to help with them."

"Oh, that's wonderful. It must be good to have her here."

"It is. I was quite—I am not sure how to say it. There was too much, you know?"

"Overwhelmed?" Maggie suggested.

"Yes. That is a good word, I think. But with the money Alex and Nevada brought from the men, I was able to rent a small house for a month. Mama is staying there with them. She brings little Angelina in for me to nurse."

"That's . . . nice." Maggie couldn't help feeling that she and her father contrasted badly with the men and their show of compassion for the family.

Sela pushed back her dark hair and looked at Shep. "If you would like to see Leo, I think he would be pleased."

"Sure, I'll be happy to see the old sidewinder."

Shep followed Sela down the hallway. A moment later, the front door opened. Maggie looked toward it and stopped breathing. Alex Bright stood in the doorway, scowling at her.

CHAPTER FIFTEEN

lex paused in the doorway and let his eyes adjust to the dim interior of the doctor's house. He wrinkled his nose. A sharp smell hung in the air, like some kind of medicine. Only one person sat in the waiting area—Maggie Porter.

He stepped inside and closed the door.

"Maggie."

"Alex." Her forehead puckered in a frown.

"Is—" He glanced toward the empty chair where Rhonda or Sela usually sat, then toward the hallway. "I hope your father's not worse."

"I'm here with a friend."

"Oh." Alex took off his hat and sat in a chair as far from Maggie's as he could get. He wouldn't want her to think he was making overtures. That might give her another excuse to tell him off. He balanced his hat on his knee and tried to avoid looking at her, but he couldn't, and he glanced her way again.

Maggie was staring toward the desk. She'd got a little sunburn, but she looked healthy. Maybe a little less elegant than when she'd first come home, but it suited her.

"So . . . how's the roundup going?" he asked after a minute of silence.

"Fine."

He nodded. They kept quiet, sitting across the room from each other, looking at the wallpaper, wooden floor, and benches. A couple of minutes later, Dr. Vargas came out, and Alex rose.

"Hello, Miss Porter," the doctor said. He nodded at Alex. "Mr. Bright."

"I'm just here to see Leo," Alex said quickly.

"Ah. You may go on through."

Alex walked past him. As he turned into the hallway, he heard the doctor say to Maggie, "While Mrs. Eagleton helps Mrs. Ervine, I wondered if I could have a private word with you."

He wondered what that was about. Hannah Ervine must be in the treatment room. . . . None of his business, but it didn't sound as if everything was as "fine" as Maggie let on.

He knocked softly on the door to Leo's room.

"Come in," called a familiar voice.

Alex opened the door and grinned. "Hey, Shep!" He stepped in and grasped the old cowpuncher's hand. "Great to see you."

He felt a slight nudge of disloyalty. Could he stay friends with Shep and still support the strikers? This whole thing was tearing him up. Whenever he saw Shep or Maggie, he wished he was on their side. He liked life a lot better when there weren't any sides.

←——— ★ ———→

In a tiny room that held only a desk, two chairs, and ceiling-high shelves full of books and boxes of papers, Dr. Vargas faced Maggie with a troubled face.

"Miss Porter, how is your father today?"

"I think he's a little better—better than he was last night, that is. I've been away for a few days, and Shep said he was quite ill while I was gone. I hope he's on the mend now."

Dr. Vargas nodded gravely. "I saw him yesterday morning, and I recommended to Shep that he increase Mr. Porter's pain medication."

"It's very bad, isn't it, Doctor?"

"I have wondered how much your father has told you."

"He told me that he has cancer, and there is no cure. Please tell me—what does this mean? Is he dying? He certainly made it sound that way."

The doctor sighed. "To be honest, I don't expect him to live more than a few months. It could be very sudden. Sometimes patients surprise us and have a protracted illness, but I believe your father's condition is quite advanced. You mustn't hope that he'll recover, Miss Porter. It just doesn't happen with this disease."

Maggie nodded, fighting tears. "I understand. Now, what can I do to help him?"

"I've given him a tonic that some physicians claim has helped their patients. By that I mean it might possibly help slow the ravages of the disease. Its value has not been proven, but I felt it was worth trying. The pain medication—it's a laudanum-based syrup—is about all we can do to lessen his suffering. But as you probably know, it makes him drowsy and less alert. And your father hates that."

"Yes."

"Other than that," Dr. Vargas said, "make him comfortable. Shep and Dolores have been very good about helping him and caring for him during his worst times."

"They certainly have," Maggie said. "I'm grateful to have friends so true."

"I'm glad you see them that way, not merely as employees. They'll stand by you too, Miss Porter, when your father is gone."

Maggie reached out and gave his hand a brief squeeze. "Thank you." Her eyes filled. Again she wondered whether leaving home now was the right choice. Torn, she did not want to miss Papa's final days, but she knew that if she didn't make the cattle drive, they had no one who would.

The doctor tapped his fingers on the desktop. "I know he's worried about finances, but I've tried to tell him to let that go. He can't do much about it now, and it would be too bad if he spent his last days in turmoil over bills and such."

"I'm trying to help ease his mind on that score." Maggie smiled as brightly as she could, considering she felt on the verge of violent weeping. "I'm making arrangements today to get the cattle to the buyers in Fort Worth so that we can pay off at least a part of his debts for my mother's treatment."

"That should comfort him a bit." He eyed her keenly. "Rhonda Tracey dropped by here a short time ago. She seemed to think you were headed for Fort Worth yourself."

Maggie gulped. "Yes, sir. I can't see any other way."

He spread his hands. "I'm sorry, Maggie, to see it come to this. If there's anything I can do, let me know. And don't fret over paying my bill right away. I'm a patient man."

She offered almost a smile to the doctor and rose. "Thank you."

The doctor walked with her to the door. "I'll continue to see him as often as I can. I plan to drive out that way tomorrow."

Maggie went out into the hallway. Sela was just helping Hannah out to the waiting area.

"The doctor says Miss Hannah can go home, but she needs to stay off her feet for a couple of weeks," Sela said.

Hannah smiled. "He says I can take the crutches home and bring them back when I can bear weight on my ankle without it hurting."

"I guess we're ready to go then," Maggie said.

"Would you like me to tell Shep you're ready?" Sela asked.

"Thank you, and give my best to Leo. I won't bother him this morning, but I wish him well." Maggie opened the door and held it for Hannah. She was relieved when Shep appeared a moment later, without Alex. She wasn't sure she could face him again right now.

They bundled Hannah into the wagon and left her and her horse and gear at her parents' house. Maggie and Shep went on to the general store for the supplies needed at the ranch and on the cattle drive. Maggie also went to the bank for enough cash to pay off the women who had helped with the roundup.

The bank's owner, who was Poppy Wilson's father, stood behind the window.

"Well, Miss Porter!" He gave her a wide smile. "I saw Poppy for a moment this morning before I left home. She seems to have had a grand time on the roundup."

"Yes, and I hope she'll go with me to Fort Worth. Did she speak to you about that?"

Mr. Wilson frowned. "Sounds a mite risky, you ladies going off like that, away from home."

"Shep Rooney's going with us," Maggie said. "I think we'll be perfectly safe."

He arched his eyebrows and looked down at the check she had written. "Well, I never had much success in trying to curb Poppy's activities. . . . You know, your father is scraping the bottom of his accounts."

Maggie gritted her teeth. "Well, yes, I did know. I hoped there was enough there for me to pay off the ladies who helped me this week. We're taking a good-sized herd to Fort Worth, so I should be able to cover all of the ranch's local bills when we return. But I do want to pay my cowgirls."

Mr. Wilson set a ledger up on the counter and flipped through it. "I can't give you more than twenty dollars. I'm sorry."

"All right. I'll only pay those who worked the last few days but can't go on the drive. I think that will cover it."

"What about food and such for the trail?"

She felt her cheeks flush and glanced around. Only one other customer remained in the bank, and he was heading for the door.

"I'm counting on Mr. Riddle at the store to extend credit just a bit longer."

"Ah." He nodded his head.

The way he said it made Maggie's heart sink. Just how much did her father owe the local merchants, anyway? She'd make it her business to find out and clear those debts if it killed her.

Mr. Wilson handed over the money in one-dollar bills, and she thanked him and hurried out to the wagon. At the mercantile, Mr. Riddle didn't seem averse to filling her order, so Maggie and Shep gave him their lengthy list.

While Shep and Riddle's son—Carlotta's erstwhile suitor—loaded the wagon, Maggie ventured to approach the storekeeper again.

"Oh, Mr. Riddle, I don't know if you heard, but I'm sending my father's spring herd to market, and I'll want to settle the Rocking P's account with you when that's done. Could you give me an idea of how much is owed, please?"

"Certainly. It's four hundred seventy-eight dollars and ten cents, counting what you're taking this morning."

She blinked. "So much." It was a very large amount, but

she'd honestly thought it could be worse. What startled her most was the fact that he had rattled off the amount so blithely, without even peeking at the ledger. He must have anticipated her asking, or at least been thinking about it while he totted up her bill.

"Thank you. It shouldn't be more than three or four weeks before I can take care of that." She went out into the sun and climbed aboard the wagon to wait for Shep. Their errands took all morning, and it was half past one when they returned to the ranch with a wagon full of supplies and a bundle of mail.

"I'm sorry we're late," she called to Dolores as they drove up.

Dolores waved from the kitchen doorway. "It's all right. Your father's up and ready to eat dinner with you."

"You go on," Shep said. "I'll get this stuff unloaded later, when you're ready to supervise. Most of it's going right into the chuck wagon."

Maggie washed up and went straight to the dining table. Her father was seated in his usual place, at the head of the table. Maggie's spirits lifted, just seeing him there.

"You look well." She leaned down and kissed his cheek.

"I may not be well, but I feel better." He gave her a tired smile. "Dolores says she's made chicken and dumplings, and I'm hankering for it."

Maggie smiled. Papa hadn't sounded so eager for food since she'd come home from San Francisco. He asked the blessing, then tucked his linen napkin into his shirt collar.

"So, you're heading out again tomorrow?"

"That's the plan."

Dolores brought a tureen of hot chicken in gravy and set it on the table. The snowy dumplings bobbed in the dish, and the fragrance made Maggie's mouth water.

"Dolores, I don't know how you managed everything you did this morning, but I'm glad you did."

The cook smiled. "It wasn't hard, once all you ladies got out from underfoot. I have to admit it's nice being back in my kitchen—even though I enjoyed the roundup."

"Well, don't get any ideas about traipsing off on the cattle drive," her father said.

"How's Hannah?" Dolores asked.

"She'll be fine. She has to use crutches for a couple of weeks."

Dolores retreated to the kitchen. As Maggie and her father began to eat, she noted that he consumed only a small portion of food. She didn't comment but talked pleasantly about the people she'd seen in town and her anticipation of the drive.

"I'm glad you'll have Shep along," her father said, "though we'll miss him here."

"Papa, maybe you should see if one of the men would come back to work around the barn. You've got a few horses that will need to be tended." She didn't say that Dolores might need someone who could ride for the doctor, or in an emergency, help her lift him into bed.

"No."

That was all he said, and she didn't press him. But she knew that she and Dolores would both feel better if a reliable man was on call. Someone strong and honest. *Alex*.

———— ★ ————

Alex and Nevada sat on their horses, watching from the knoll west of the ranch house. They kept beneath the overhanging branches of a big cottonwood. Anyone would have to look sharp to spot them up there, with dawn just breaking.

"She's a spunky gal," Nevada said. "Didn't think she had it in her."

"Maggie Porter's got a lot of steel in her spine." Alex shook his head. No use wallowing in regrets. Maggie was lost to him, and so was his job.

"This will kill the strike, you know."

Alex glanced over at his friend. "That's what I'm thinking. I heard some of the men have drifted off to look for other jobs already. Harry told me yesterday he was heading for Wyoming."

"Too bad. If the girls get those cattle to Fort Worth without any mishaps, Porter will no doubt start hiring other punchers."

"We can't do anything about it," Alex said.

"Can't we?"

They sat in silence for a couple more minutes, watching the activity below. At least ten women had ridden up to the Porters' house. Two wagons were hitched—the chuck wagon and the buckboard that would haul the bedrolls and miscellaneous gear for the drive. The remuda in the corral near the barn looked a bit slim to Alex—if they had a dozen punchers, they'd have only three horses each. He hoped Maggie wasn't trying to make the drive with fewer hands than that. He liked to have half a dozen horses per man on a cattle drive, but on a short trip like this they could probably make it with three each.

"Whatdaya reckon it would take to get our jobs back?" Nevada asked.

Alex shook his head. "Mr. Porter doesn't want us back. He's past that."

Nevada eyed him sharply. "You really liked him, didn't you?"

"Didn't you? In the old days, I mean."

After a moment, Nevada said, "He wasn't a bad boss. Not until this last year or two. After the missus took sick and went away, seems like he went with her."

"Yeah."

"Makes me want to do whatever we can to make sure his cattle drive falls apart."

Alex looked over at him. "What are you saying?"

"We could keep Miss High-and-Mighty Maggie from ever gettin' those beeves to Fort Worth."

"You sound like Tommy now."

"We've seen the back of him."

"Good thing," Alex said. Tommy's ideas for destroying the work of the roundup still bothered him. "I wouldn't do anything to hurt Maggie and her friends."

"Oh, I'm not talking about hurtin' the ladies. Just making their job harder."

"No. That's just spiteful."

"All right, not stop them, maybe . . . but just slow them down. Make them work a little harder. That's our pay they're earning, Alex."

"But it's our own fault." Alex looked over at Nevada's grim face. "We walked away from the job. We made that choice. It's not Maggie's fault she has to do this."

Nevada just stared at the ranch in the valley. Another woman came up the road that led to the nearest ranch—Bradleys'. She led a horse behind her bay. An extra personal mount, probably.

"That must be Sarah," Alex said.

Nevada grunted. "Can't believe all these women can just pack up and leave their families for a month or more."

"Me either."

Alex knew that some of the cowgirls were single, like ranchers' daughters Carlotta Herrera and Sarah Bradley. A few were married. Others had families in town. He'd spotted John Key's wife and sister among them at the roundup, as well as the postmaster's wife, Bitty Hale, and Nathan Wilson's daughter. Then there was Rhonda, the doctor's helper who'd given over her place to Sela while she worked the roundup. Was she going on the drive, too?

"One thing I gotta say, Maggie's friends have stuck by her. This has got to be a hardship for some of them."

"I heard Shep Rooney's going with 'em," Nevada said.

Alex nodded. "That's what I hear."

"So they found out they need at least one man, I guess, even if he's old and gimpy."

Alex said nothing, but he did wonder who would tend to things around the home place while Shep was gone. Had anyone worked the palomino filly he'd been training since he left for the roundup? That beautiful horse would forget everything she'd learned if no one rode her. He'd hoped to have the filly ready for Maggie when she came home, but he hadn't had time to put the finishing touches on its training.

"Come on," Nevada said. "I can't stand to watch 'em." He turned his horse away.

Alex lingered another moment under the cottonwood. He got a final glimpse of Maggie—mounting a black-and-white pinto. She'd picked a good, stout horse. He lifted his hat and settled it back on his head.

"Godspeed, Maggie."

CHAPTER SIXTEEN

The sun was nearly overhead by the time they got all of the cattle bunched up and driven out of the pasture. Shep had stuck around to help them, and Maggie was grateful—without him they might never have gotten under way.

As soon as the last of the sixteen hundred cattle was through the gate of the north pasture, he climbed aboard the chuck wagon and struck out with the team trotting. He would get ahead of the herd and scout a good place for them to camp tonight. Maggie hated to lose him as a point man with the cattle, but she was sure his leg bothered him. Asking him to spend more time in the saddle would be cruel.

Celine Martinez, who was married to one of the Herreras' men, drove the buckboard, and the two of them were out of sight within thirty minutes, while Maggie and her lady cow-punchers concentrated on getting the cattle moving in the right direction.

For the first day, they would edge along the Rocking P

land and then the Bradley ranch. The idea was to get the cattle far enough away from their home territory that they wouldn't try to drift back there during the night.

If they made good time, they'd head across open range for twenty miles or so beyond that. The ranchers with grazing rights allowed drives to pass through. Later on, Maggie would have to deal with those not so accommodating. In this era of fencing and increased farming, the open range was shrinking faster than Maggie had realized.

The evening before, Shep and Papa had gone over maps with her, planning the route. Instead of a straight line, they would have to drive the herd where the landowners would allow it. There might be places where they'd have to pay a toll.

"At least nowadays we won't have to worry much about the Injuns," Shep said.

Maggie was glad—she'd heard some of the stories the older men told of the drives ten or twenty years ago. If they got to market with half the original herd, they counted themselves lucky. Of course, those were the days of thousand-mile or longer drives. But the women could still meet with plenty of hazards along the way.

Maggie asked the women to gather around. "Lord," she prayed, "we ask for thy blessing on our travels. Guide us with thy hand, keep us safe, and if it be thy will, grant us success." A chorus of amens followed her simple prayer.

She let Sarah and Mariah ride near the front of the herd, a coveted spot. The women would rotate positions during the course of the journey, but these two knew the local terrain well, and she especially wanted Sarah up front if they met with any cowboys from her family's ranch.

Carlotta volunteered to ride drag with her for the first few miles. Cowboys detested the task because they had to eat dust as they followed the herd and constantly harry the rebellious cattle that wanted to veer off and the slower ones that wanted to stop and eat. While grazing was allowed along the way—otherwise the animals would arrive gaunt at the stockyards—it had to be discouraged the first day in order to get them farther up the trail.

"If you want to ride back and see your papa one more time, you should go now," Carlotta called to her when they came to the boundary of the Rocking P.

Maggie shook her head. "We said our good-byes this morning."

Carlotta nodded. "I know you don't want to leave him so long, especially while he is ill."

"I don't like it, but I have to do this for him . . . and Dolores will take good care of him."

"*Si*. We all will pray that he gets better while we are gone."

"Thank you." Maggie remembered the doctor's words and knew she shouldn't hope too strongly for that. Just the thought dragged her spirits down, and she drove herself to focus on the work before her.

Since it was nearly noon when they had all of the cattle in motion, Maggie decided not to stop for dinner. She passed the word for Poppy Wilson to ride up to the chuck wagon around two o'clock and bring back rations the women could eat in the saddle. Shep sent dried fruit, biscuits, strips of jerky, and cookies. Each of them carried a canteen of water, so they did all right, but Maggie looked forward to the hot meal Shep would prepare for supper.

As they crossed over the Bradleys' range, Sarah's father and two of his men rode out to meet them. Maggie was now riding swing position, along one side of the moving herd. Sarah waved to her, and she loped her horse up to join them.

"I expected you a couple of hours ago," Mr. Bradley said as the two women rode up.

"It took longer to get going than we thought," Sarah said. "The Porters' pasture is huge, and about a quarter of the herd had gone to the far corner of it. It took us a while to drive them all out."

"Well, I'm glad it wasn't anything more serious than that." He cast a critical eye over the beef cattle plodding past him. "The herd looks to be in good flesh. I hope the prices have held for you."

"Thank you," Maggie said.

Mr. Bradley gave her a rueful smile. "If my own hands were back from our drive, I'd lend you a few. I'm sorry I can't spare the ones I've got left here. Your pa was so late getting ready, I thought he'd decided to wait until fall. Otherwise, we could have taken some of your cattle with ours."

"It's all right. We'll make it. We've got Shep Rooney."

"Oh, Shep's a good man to have around. He's got a head full of wisdom."

Maggie smiled. "He's an asset, for sure."

Mr. Bradley and the two cowboys rode along with them for an hour, and Maggie began to relax. When a dozen steers bolted and tried to turn back to their home range, the men quickly turned them back into the herd. Maggie appreciated their effort, but she wondered if the women could have executed the maneuver so swiftly. She couldn't help but wonder if she was overly optimistic.

Mr. Bradley rode back to her position when he was ready to return home.

"You take good care of my girl, won't you, Miss Maggie?"

"I sure will."

He nodded. "She told me about your run-in with the Bar D men. Be careful, and don't take any guff from anyone."

"Thanks—I'll remember that."

The rancher frowned. "Well, I hate to let you go, but I

s'pose you'll be all right. Sarah's a good shot, and I expect you and Carlotta Herrera are too."

"Not half bad, Mr. Bradley. Mariah Key is another one who knows which end of a gun is which."

"All right. I'll get moving. See you in a few weeks."

He and his cowpunchers waved and loped away from the herd.

Maggie let her horse walk along at a leisurely pace, watching the cattle to make sure they all kept heading in the right direction. She'd hoped to make at least ten miles today, but now that goal seemed out of reach. Mr. Bradley had suggested they stop for the night just inside his far boundary. That was eight miles from where they started. She'd have to be content with that, since it looked like they wouldn't be able to make the planned stop before dark.

She hailed Bitty, and she rode over to walk her horse alongside Maggie's.

"Can you ride ahead and see where Shep and Celine are settled? I don't think we'll make it farther than the creek on the Key ranch line."

Bitty cantered off ahead of the cattle, and Maggie wished she'd undertaken the pleasant task herself. To be free from the dust and the lowing, shifting herd for half an hour would make a nice break.

She laughed aloud. They'd been out half a day, and she was already tired of running cattle. That was a bad sign.

They neared a watering hole that held a substantial amount of water, and the leaders of the herd veered toward it. Maggie had instructed her cowgirls to let the cattle drink at such spots, but not to let them linger. A few weeks from now, ponds like this one would be dry, so it was a blessing, but it also was a bother for the women. It kept the cattle from continuing on toward their goal. The camping place was on the edge of a creek, so the cattle would be able to drink again there.

It proved harder than she'd anticipated to get the herd away from the pond. As surely as the women drove a bunch away, they circled back toward the water. At last the drovers managed to push them onward, but the pond had cost them at least an hour.

When they rode into camp, the sun was down and twilight had fallen. Maggie slid from the saddle, weary to the bone.

She quickly made night herd assignments. She'd ended up with twelve people, counting herself, Shep, and Celine. Rhonda had unexpectedly received her husband's blessing, along with her employer's, to take part in the cattle drive. Maggie was delighted to have her along, since the skills she'd learned in Dr. Vargas's office amounted almost to those of a nurse. Mariah Key had also brought along her cousin, Helen Branch, who was visiting from Mason County. Though they would miss Lottie Key, Mariah's sister-in-law, Helen's deft touch with horses was a welcome addition.

They could make three night-herd shifts, but this close to home Maggie chose to divide the workers into two shifts of six people. If the herd broke for home now, they could lose two days rounding them up and bringing them this far again.

She assigned herself to the first shift, but Carlotta came to her as the gathering broke up to eat supper and then take up night watch or retire to their bedrolls.

"You need to sleep first, Maggie."

"I won't ask the others to keep watch while I rest. The trail boss shouldn't do that."

"You're fooling yourself. The boss gives the worst assignments to the newest hands."

"Maybe when there are plenty of punchers to choose from, though I'm sure they always put one or two experienced men on a crew. But we don't have any spare workers,

Carlotta. I want all my ladies to be fresh and rested."

"And we need you to be feeling good, too. Come on, you've had a long day."

"No longer than anyone else," Maggie said. "You all got up at least as early as I did this morning, and you rode to my house before we started."

Carlotta scowled at her. "You want to fight? Are you forgetting I have four sisters? You can't win a spat with *me*. And I say I take the first watch and *you sleep*."

"I can't—"

"Stop that. You can. And I insist. I know you, Margaret Porter. You lay awake half of last night going over the list of supplies and the route we'll take, didn't you?"

Maggie couldn't deny it—all of that and her father's illness, the ranch's debts, and the way Alex had avoided looking at her in the doctor's office.

"And that's not saying how much time you spent praying for your papa," Carlotta added, as though she could read Maggie's mind—or part of it, anyway. "Those cattle are tired, too, and it won't be hard for us to watch them without you. Now, go get your plate and eat up. And then you are going to rest."

Maggie glared at her for all of five seconds. Tears spurted into her eyes, and she blinked at them, startled and disconcerted. "All right." Her voice quavered, and she blinked harder.

Carlotta put her arms around her and patted her back. "There now. It's going to be all right. We're going to do fine— and you are not the only one praying, you know."

———— ★ ————

Maggie slept a good, solid four hours, lying on her two blankets and with one of Carlotta's covering her. She'd brought a small pillow, having learned her lesson on the roundup. Most of the other women had, too. Since they had the buckboard along for a "hoodlum wagon," to carry their gear, they had plenty of room for such things. Most of the ladies had even brought a change of respectable clothing to wear when they reached Fort Worth. Mariah Key had never been to the city and was determined to cut a fashionable figure when she got there.

Celine was puttering about the cook fire when Carlotta made the rounds, waking the six who had slept through the first shift of night herding. Almost as soon as Maggie had abandoned her bedroll, Celine put a cup of hot coffee in her hands.

"Thank you," Maggie said.

Celine smiled. "I'm on watch with you now. Thought we could all use a cup of coffee to wake us up." She turned to offer some to the other women.

"Things are quiet with the herd," Carlotta reported. "A lot of them are lying down, but some are grazing. We mostly rode among them and tried to discourage them from spreading out too much."

"Good." Some of the women had no experience with containing a herd outside fences. "I appreciate your letting me sleep."

Carlotta smiled, her teeth gleaming in the moonlight. "Feel better?"

"Much."

Shep strolled over with a tin cup in his hand. "I'm on your shift, Miss Maggie, but I don't know as I can stay in the saddle that long."

"I don't want you to," she said. "Just have a horse saddled and ready in case we need you quick, all right? Otherwise, I think we'll be fine with five of us out there."

"I could come out there, but I don't know how much good I'd do sitting around."

Maggie shook her head. "You take it easy, Shep. We're counting on you having a big breakfast ready when we come in."

He grinned at her. "Now, that I can do."

Maggie turned to speak to Carlotta again, but her friend was already taking her boots off.

"I'll see you later." Maggie gulped down the rest of her coffee and took her cup to the back of the chuck wagon. When she reached the corral, Mariah and her cousin, Helen, were saddling horses.

"I've got this nice big gray ready for you, Miss Porter," Helen said.

"Oh, please, call me Maggie. And thank you very much." Maggie looked the horse over. He was huge—maybe seventeen hands—and he was wearing her saddle. She hoped he could cut and turn as tightly as the smaller mustangs could.

She rode out with Mariah, Helen, Bitty, and Celine, and walked the gray leisurely among the grazing cattle. After about a half hour, she heard Celine singing a Spanish ballad. Her clear, sweet tones hung over the herd like a blessing. A little later, Mariah started a hymn, and Maggie joined in. The stars shone so bright overhead, they looked solid, like jewels against a velvet gown. *This can work*, she thought. With God's help, she'd do this job and then straighten things out with her father. In the starlight she almost believed she might someday be able to make amends with Alex too.

A yell came suddenly from off to her left. It was Bitty, she thought. Maggie urged her horse to trot toward the commotion. They did *not* want a stampede tonight.

The cattle on Bitty's side of the herd were restless. Maggie spoke in low, firm tones as she rode through them. When she was close enough, she saw Bitty and another horsewoman out away from the herd, chasing a handful of steers.

"Get back there, you!" Bitty's voice carried, and Maggie gritted her teeth.

The two women had turned the bunch by the time she reached them. Maggie called softly to Bitty, "Got trouble?"

"That one old cow has a mind of her own, and she got six or eight others to follow her."

"Let's keep an eye on her." Maggie turned her horse and fell in beside Bitty. "Maybe we should keep her near the back of the herd tomorrow. And Bitty—don't yell at them, all right? One screech could set the whole herd off on a quiet night like this."

Bitty's head drooped. "Sorry, Maggie."

"It's all right. The rest didn't seem too agitated this time. But it doesn't take much to set them off, and out here in the open, we could be days rounding them up."

After that, Maggie tried to circulate more around the edges of the herd. Halfway through their shift, her stamina flagged and she slumped in the saddle. Tomorrow night they could form three shifts of four people, she hoped—although she didn't want to increase the risk of trouble.

"How you doin', Miss Maggie?"

Shep was approaching on one of the cow ponies, and she trotted the gray gelding toward him.

"Hello, Shep. It's going pretty well, but I'm starting to wonder if I'm crazy."

"Why so?"

"Some of these ladies have never worked cattle until this week, and . . . well, I guess it's a little too late to worry about that, isn't it?"

He chuckled. "I think you're doing a good job. Tomorrow you'll do even better. It always takes a crew a few days to settle into doing things right on the drive."

"Thanks. I hope you've gotten some sleep."

"Oh, yeah, I'm about ready to build up the cook fire. I'm doing eggs this mornin'—probably the only time you'll get 'em until Fort Worth. And Dolores made enough sourdough buns for a go-round."

"Sounds good."

He headed his pony back toward the camp, and Maggie resumed her rounds. Soft singing reached her, and she lifted her eyes once more to the sky. As she rode, she hummed and prayed. She had so many things on her mind, she doubted she could list them all off between now and breakfast. Mostly she prayed for Papa and for safety on the drive.

"Lord, if You want us to get by, please let me get a good price for these cattle," she whispered. In a few months, she'd be boss of the Rocking P. Would she be able to hire some dependable men as permanent employees, or had the Porter outfit lost all respect among the cowboys in McCulloch County? She hoped the strikers' complaints wouldn't keep other men from hiring on with her. She reached for her canteen and took a long swallow of water. She could advertise for cowpunchers and put in the ad the fact that she'd pay higher wages. Maybe that would draw in some decent men. Shep could help her decide which ones she could trust.

It came to her that she would hold the authority to hire back the striking men if she wanted to. And if they'd sign on with her. *Would they be willing to work under a woman rancher? And would they trust her to treat them right, after all her father's missteps?*

She remembered Alex's promise to pray for her. That brought a sliver of comfort and a huge pile of loneliness. *Was he out looking for a new job? Had he gone back to Fort Chadbourne to work with his father? Or would he hire on at one of her neighbors' ranches? Whoever got Alex Bright in the shuffle would be blessed.*

The thought that he might leave the area, disillusioned and bitter, weighed on her mind. She might never see him again.

←——— ★ ———→

"The women didn't set any records today," Nevada said. Alex said nothing but looked out toward where Maggie's herd lay. He could hear the distant lowing of cattle when the wind was right. They'd stopped just inside Jim Bradley's north boundary line. Probably a smart choice, since he was pretty sure Bradley's daughter was riding along. Maggie had some skilled women on her crew. He hoped she had enough with trail sense— and enough hands period—to take the drive through. Manpower, or in this case, womanpower, was important on the trail.

"Eight miles isn't so bad the first day," Early Shaw drawled. "Lotta times it takes a few days to hit your stride."

"Yeah, they got farther than Joe predicted," Alex said. Joe Moore had joined them on Nevada's invitation. With Early, they were four strong—not enough to man a cattle drive, but enough to tip the scales if Maggie had any more incidents like the one with the Bar D men.

"I'm going to hit the sack," Nevada said.

They walked back to their campfire. Joe had coffee steaming and had gotten out his tin cup and a bag of hard rolls he'd bought in Brady that morning.

"If you're serious about following them all the way to Fort Worth, we'd best stock up on comestibles," he said to Alex.

"Sure. We can stop at the next town. Might need a packhorse, though."

"Can't afford it," Nevada said.

"Yeah, let's just pack enough food for two or three days," Early told him. "We can ride into towns along the way. Won't take us long to catch up again at the rate they'll be moving."

Alex went to his bedroll and picked up his tin cup. He poured himself coffee and sat down near the fire with Joe. Early and Nevada hauled their boots off and arranged their blankets on the ground a little distance away.

Hoofbeats approaching brought Alex to his feet. He had his hand on the butt of his revolver by the time Joe heard it and jumped up.

"Ho the camp," a deep voice called.

Alex squinted into the darkness. "That you, Bronc Tracey?"

"The same." The dark-skinned cowboy rode up until his horse was barely within the circle of firelight.

"Heard there was a few of you out here. Got room for one more?"

"Sure," Alex said. Bronc was a good, dependable man, though he was quiet and kept his distance from the others most of the time. His skin color didn't make a whit of difference on the range. If a man could ride, rope, and shoot, he was welcome on most any outfit.

"Took me a while to find ya." Bronc dismounted. "My Rhonda's on the drive with Miss Maggie." He waited, holding his horse's reins, as if he thought that information might make a difference.

"Thought she might be," Nevada said.

"Does that bother you boys?" Bronc looked at Alex.

"I don't mind," Alex said. "Someone in the family's got to earn some money."

"That's the way we look at it," Bronc said, "and we figure we's helping Leo and Sela, too."

"Sela filling in for Rhonda at the doctor's again?" Nevada asked.

"That's right."

Nevada looked at Alex and shrugged. "I don't think we've got much chance of making this strike work for us, so I guess wives and sweethearts might as well work."

Alex wasn't sure whose sweetheart he was referring to, though he thought he recalled that Tommy Drescher had taken to calling on Sarah Bradley last spring. He sure hoped Nevada didn't mean Maggie. She was a far cry from being his sweetheart.

"Want some coffee?" Joe asked.

"Don't mind it. Got my cup." Bronc took it from his saddlebag and gave it to Joe, then went back and slipped his horse's bridle off. He came back to the fire and took the full cup from Joe.

"I reckon some of the fellas are pretty upset about what those women are doing," Joe said as they settled down around the fire.

Bronc took a deep sip of coffee. "I seen Tommy in town today."

That remark had to be connected to Joe's observation. Alex eyed Bronc sharply. "What did he say?"

"He's mad at Miss Sarah."

"Not surprised." Alex lifted the coffeepot to see if there was any left. "You want more?" he asked Joe and Early.

They shook their heads, and Alex poured himself the last half cup.

"Bill an' Stewie are hiring on with the Lazy S."

"Really?" Early said, and Bronc nodded.

"Tommy said they was right glad to get new jobs. They don't figure Porter will ever take us back."

"I'm afraid he won't," Nevada said. "This thing set him off pretty bad."

Bronc grimaced. "So, what you fellas goin' to do?"

"Not sure yet," Joe said. "You think the Lazy S will hire more of us?"

"I been out there and they said no, they got plenty of help now." Bronc sipped his coffee.

"Why you all followin' the herd?"

Joe glanced at Alex.

"I'm not sure we know the answer to that, Bronc." Alex set his cup down and kicked the end of a burnt stick into the fire.

"I thought maybe you was going to ask Miss Maggie for jobs."

"We can't do that." Nevada looked around at the others. "We pledged to stick together for the strike."

"Yeah," Early said. "Can't undercut the other men."

"I s'pose not," Bronc said. "Tommy, he wanted to make trouble for the ladies, but maybe he'll get that out of his head if nobody else goes with him."

"What kind of trouble?" Alex asked, shooting a quick glance at Nevada. "I thought we set him straight on that at the roundup."

"He thinks we all should try to stop the drive. I didn't like the way he was talkin', what with my Rhonda out there."

"You think he'll actually do somethin'?" Early asked.

"I dunno."

"I hope not," Alex said.

"Well, I'm going to get some sleep. You fellas do what you want." Nevada stood and ambled to his bedroll.

"Reckon I'd best put my hoss up," Bronc said. He went over to where his horse had begun to browse and removed his saddle.

Alex got up and walked to the edge of their campsite. They couldn't actually see the herd, but he could still hear it. And he thought, when he listened hard, that he could hear sweet voices. The women riding herd, no doubt. He wondered if Maggie was singing lullabies to the cattle. He sent up a quick prayer for her and her new employees. He wasn't quite sure what to ask for, but he didn't wish her ill. Quite the opposite, even if it meant he could never work in this county again.

Bronc's words about Tommy rankled with him. The women would have enough to think about without sabotage. And it didn't take much to cause a cattle drive to go wrong.

he second day out, the herd covered almost ten miles—near enough so that Maggie recorded it as such. They camped in a place her father had recommended, a narrow valley with high bluffs on each side and a shallow creek in the bottom. The natural boundaries gave her confidence in posting fewer people on night watch. After supper, enough light still shone to allow them to write, and several of the women sat down to pen letters. Maggie wrote a brief note to Dolores.

> *Dear Dolores,*
>
> *We're doing fine so far. We're far enough out that the cattle have settled down. Tell Papa we're camped for the night in that valley he said to use if we were moving slow. It's a good place to stop—plenty of grass, and peaceful. I wish we'd made more ground, but so long as things go well, I'm not complaining. Do send word to me at Brownwood if you need me to come back.*
>
> *Lots of love, Maggie*

She almost scratched out the last sentence, but let it stand. She signed off and slipped it into an envelope.

"How are you doing?"

She looked up into Carlotta's lovely face.

"I'm fine. How about you?"

Carlotta chuckled and sat down on the ground beside her. "I miss the comforts of home, but this is going to be something we'll brag about for the rest of our lives."

"I expect you're right." Maggie held up the note she'd written. "I'm telling Dolores to let me know right away if Papa has a medical crisis. She could send me word at Brownwood or Comanche."

"Sure," Carlotta said. "You'd want to be home if he needs you."

"Yes. I'm glad we're doing this for him, but if he gets worse, I can't stay away. Can you take over if that happens?" Her voice choked, and tears slid down her cheeks. "It could happen any time."

Carlotta put her arm around Maggie and hugged her. "Of course, *querida*. With Sarah's ability and Shep's wisdom, we would be able to get the job done."

Maggie nodded. "Thanks. I figure the stock buyers would listen to you on principle—your father is one of their valued clients."

"And so is yours. This will be a good business deal for the Rocking P."

Maggie sniffed. "Thanks."

"But I have confidence you will be there with us," Carlotta said. "He is not going to get worse."

Maggie didn't bother to debate that. Her father *would* get worse. But dwelling on the prospect wouldn't help. "Now help me work out the assignments for tomorrow. Do you think we can make it to the sheep ranch?"

"Maybe not. Best to allow another day. The rancher won't let you stop on his land."

"That's what Papa and Shep said. So I guess it's another fairly easy day tomorrow. I make it to be nine miles." Maggie frowned. "We'll have to pick up the pace once we cross it, or we'll be all summer getting to Fort Worth."

"Do not worry," Carlotta said. "The cattle, they stay fat when they move slow. And the fatter they are at the stockyards, the more money you get for your papa."

←——— ★ ———→

Alex and his four companions trotted their horses along the road to Brownwood, paralleling the route of the cattle drive.

"How long you thinking to follow them?" Early asked as his bay gelding jogged alongside Red.

"Got nothing better to do," Alex said. His careless words belied his inner resolution. He wouldn't let those women—Maggie—come to grief if he could prevent it.

"I'm thinking I should start looking for work. I'm not as young as you are. Might be hard to get a job now."

Alex had never thought of Early as old—older, sure, but not so old he wouldn't be considered an experienced, able-bodied cowpuncher. Probably he'd seen the back of forty, but still . . .

"I know Bronc's concerned about Rhonda."

Early eyed him keenly for a moment then winked. "I reckon you've got concerns of your own."

"I'd like to see them succeed," Alex said.

"You know that's contrary to what we're doing."

"I do. But you don't want to see them fail, do you? Lose the herd, or meet up with calamity?"

"No, I s'pose not. If it was men out there, I might feel different. But ladies . . . nope, I don't wish 'em ill. But don't forget, they'll be taking home our pay, and we're not earnin' nothin' out here."

Alex sighed. "If you want to light out and look for work, you should go."

Early rode on for a few more minutes in silence. "They should pass Milburn tomorrow."

Alex nodded. "Maybe three days from there to Brownwood." It was the first good-sized town along the route to Fort Worth, though Milburn was big enough to boast a post office, general store, hotel, and three churches.

"I might hear about work around Brownwood," Early said.

Alex took that for consent to stay with them until Brownwood. He'd be sorry when Early left them. Already his ties to the Rocking P were few and tenuous.

The five halted their horses at a crossroads. "You want to stop and eat pretty soon?" Joe asked. "We'll get way ahead of them if we don't."

"All right by me," Alex said, looking back. They'd outdistanced the dust cloud the cattle stirred up.

"We were just discussing how long we should trail this outfit," Early said. "I reckon I'll stick around a few more days, but then I'd better be looking for some work if I want to keep eatin'."

"What do you boys think?" Alex asked.

Bronc frowned. "I'd like to keep an eye on them."

"Worried about Rhonda?" Nevada asked.

"Well, yeah. She's not used to being in the saddle all day, or to working cattle."

Joe laughed. "I still can't believe those girls are getting by. Some of 'em can ride, I know that."

"Maggie's got what it takes." Alex wished he'd kept quiet when the others laughed.

"You're just cheering on your sweetheart, aren't you?" Joe said.

"Well now, Señorita Herrera can ride and rope both,"

Early said. "I'd wager Sarah Bradley can too."

"Yes, and the Key girl." Nevada looked down the road. "But sooner or later, those women are going to need help. I figure if we're handy when that happens, we might be able to use it as leverage to get our jobs back—at the pay we want."

"That'd be great," Joe said, "but I'm not countin' on it."

They all dismounted.

Nevada took the bridle off his horse and turned him loose to graze. "Hey, that sheep ranch is up ahead. They ought to be coming to it today."

Alex shook his head. "Doubtful. Tomorrow morning, maybe."

"I remember when we crossed their land last year," Early said. "Stinking sheep."

Joe grimaced. "Yeah, the cattle won't eat there."

"No, but that's all right," Alex said. "It gets them across quicker if they don't want to stop and get a belly full. And it's only four or five miles, but it will save them a day if they don't have to go around."

They made a small campfire and heated some canned stew that Nevada produced from his pack. Joe still had a few rolls left, and Bronc contributed a can of peaches.

"Enough for a taste each," he said.

As they waited for the coffee and stew to heat, Alex thought about the road ahead, and how it would affect Maggie and the women with her. He'd be surprised if they completed the demanding feat without a mishap.

After they'd eaten, Joe rose and stretched. "Guess maybe I'll ride into Milburn."

"Could be some jobs there," Early said.

"You want to go? Come on." Joe picked up his saddle.

In the end, Nevada went with Joe and Early. Bronc opted to stay with Alex, within sight of the Porter herd.

Near sunset, the others found them setting up camp over a rise from the Rocking P camp, about half a mile away from Shep's chuck wagon.

Joe rode in laughing. "We sure are giving those gals a lesson."

"What do you mean?" Alex asked. "I thought we agreed not to do any harm."

"Oh, we wouldn't *harm* them," Joe said. "Just give them a hard time."

"You don't think they have it hard enough?" Bronc asked. Joe laughed.

"What did you do?" Alex eyed Joe and then Nevada, whom he expected to behave honorably.

"Now, don't get mad, Alex. It's just a little joke." Nevada began to strip his horse's tack off.

"Remember that sheepherder?" Joe said. "How fussy he was about where the cattle could walk? We had to keep them bunched up tight and make sure they moved along across his range."

"I remember. He's not such a bad fellow. Carter's his name, isn't it?"

Early nodded, but he looked a little sheepish. "We paid Mr. Carter a little visit on our way into town."

"What for?" Alex didn't like their talk—or their joviality.

"We told Carter the ladies are coming and they'll take the herd through his land," Joe said. "He doesn't much like letting cattle through. It's a headache for him. Even if they stay in the path he chooses and don't spread out—which is mighty hard to prevent with that many head—they do some harm to the land."

"Not as much as sheep do," Alex said. "Besides, he gets paid. He charges a toll for all those cattle. We paid him ten dollars last year."

"Did we?" Joe shrugged.

"We sort of suggested he boost up the price for Maggie," Early said.

"You what?" Alex asked. Bronc watched in silence.

Nevada scowled at him. "Quit acting like a fussy old hen. We just told him to ask more. Say, fifty dollars, not ten."

"You start him doing something like that, he'll do it all the time," Alex said. "That will hurt all the ranchmen."

"Nah," Joe said. "We told him about the ladies and let on it was a joke."

Early pulled his saddle and blanket off his horse. "We don't want him to make too big a stink. If he did, they'd head around the long way. But it ought to hurt old Porter in the pocketbook."

"Yeah," Joe said. "If we don't get the extra money we should, make him give it to somebody else."

"It could end up pretty funny." Nevada looked at Alex.

"Or pretty mean and stupid." Alex shook his head. "I can't believe you did that."

Nevada's jaw clenched. "Alex, you seem to forget what we're trying to accomplish. This might lend a little credence to the strike. We men would be able to deal with Carter, but I'll bet these women won't know how to handle it."

Alex's stomach knotted. "I don't know."

"You're just soft because of Maggie," Early said. "I don't see why we shouldn't do something like that. It'll cost Porter, but it won't hurt the women any. Just slow 'em down a little."

Later, when the others were laying out their bedrolls, Alex paced by the fire. He didn't like this. If the prank went over well, next time they'd want to do something more outrageous.

Nevada came over and stood beside him. "Got no stomach for it?"

Alex shook his head.

"You don't want to get on the wrong side of these boys,"

Nevada said. "We may be your last friends. If you go over to Porter's side, no telling what will happen."

"You all would do something to me?"

"I wouldn't, but if it got back to Tommy and the others—well, you never know, do ya?"

Alex shook his head.

Nevada nodded. "I'm just saying, don't get any ideas about riding over to Carter's tonight."

Alex looked into his friend's eyes. "I don't like it."

"So you said."

"You promise you won't hurt the girls or stampede the cattle?"

Nevada held up both hands. "Not me. And Bronc's wife is out there. Nobody wants any of them to get hurt. Just stay out of it. For your own good."

"You're threatening me."

"No. I'm giving you the facts, as your friend. Let the boys do this. You take a kid like Joe and you don't let him *do* something, he feels like he's got no control over his life. I won't let him hurt anybody. Not Maggie and the other women, and not you. But you need to let him feel like he's got some leeway right now."

Alex let out a long breath. His stomach was still tied in knots, and he knew he wouldn't sleep. "All right. But I still don't like it."

———— ★ ————

Right after breakfast, Maggie rode ahead of the herd, taking Celine with her. They quickly left the cattle behind with the other women to get them moving. Shep was packing up the chuck wagon and would head out as soon as he was ready.

They came to the homestead and cantered into the barn-yard. They both dismounted, and Maggie handed her horse's reins to Celine and went to the door.

A middle-aged woman in a drab brown calico dress responded to her knock. She blinked at Maggie and looked her up and down.

"Hello. I'm Maggie Porter, Martin Porter's daughter." Maggie pulled out the brightest smile she could find. "Is Mr. Carter here?"

The woman pointed behind her, toward the long pole barn. Maggie looked at it. "In the barn? Thank you."

The woman closed the door. Maggie and Celine walked their horses toward the barn.

"I wonder if she can talk," Celine said.

Maggie chuckled. "I guess she doesn't get many women dressed like us coming to her door."

She left Celine outside and followed the sound of hammering into the barn. She found the farmer inside, building an enclosure. A boy of about fourteen was helping him, holding boards in place for him while he drove nails.

"Mr. Carter?"

He glanced up at her then quickly straightened.

Maggie repeated her introduction. "My father's cow-punchers are going to be bringing his herd along this morning. We'd like to cross your range, if you've no objection."

Carter scratched his chin through his bushy beard. "Well, now, I don't know. A lot of cattle have come through here already this spring. Kinda late, ain't ya?"

"A little." Maggie smiled. "We have a good crew, and we'll make sure the herd stays within the boundaries you give us. May we pass?"

He shook his head as though in doubt. "I reckon you ought to go around, missy."

"I—" Maggie swallowed hard. "Please, sir, we'll take extra care with the cattle."

"Who's your foreman?"

"Well, sir, I am."

He laughed and looked her over again. Even his son was smirking. Maggie straightened her spine.

"Mr. Carter, I'm perfectly capable of driving my father's cattle to Fort Worth. If we go around your range, it will add twelve miles to our trip. That's at least a whole day."

"Well, I'm not too thrilled with the idea. What happened to Bright—that man you had last year?"

"Uh . . . he . . ."

"He knew what he was doin'."

Maggie felt her face go red. Maybe she ought to have brought Shep along with her to talk to the farmer.

"Look, Mr. Carter, please. I assure you that I have my father's full confidence and authority."

"I heard your cowboys was strikin'. That true?"

"Yes, sir." She held his gaze, wondering what affect her admission would have on him.

"I usually collect a toll. Them longhorns like to get loose and tear up the grass."

Maggie smiled. "Yes, sir, I'm prepared to pay your usual fee."

"It's fifty this year."

She stared at him for a moment. "I beg your pardon."

"Fifty dollars."

"But that's—"

He stared back, not relenting. She knew the foreman had paid Carter ten dollars each time he'd crossed his land for several years.

After a long moment, she said, "Is that what all the herds are paying this year?"

"It's what I'm asking now."

Maggie hesitated. Her supply of cash was limited, and no doubt she'd need more farther down the trail.

"I'll give you twenty."

"Guess you'll have to go around, then."

She clenched her teeth. "Thirty, then. My father won't be happy, though."

Carter scratched his chin. "I reckon I can take thirty this once."

"I'll get it."

She went out to where Celine held the horses. Without saying anything she took the extra money from her saddlebag and added it to the ten-dollar bill she'd had in her pocket.

When she entered the barn again, Carter gave her detailed instructions on where to take the cattle. "My boy will ride along with you to make sure you stay where you should."

"Fine." She reached into her pocket for the money and noted a smirk on the boy's face. Fury exploded in her heart. She tried to keep her voice steady as she asked, "Did the strikers come talk to you and put you up to this?"

Carter only shrugged, but the boy's smile grew, and he turned his face away.

"My father told me you were an honest man."

"Well, now, there's honest and there's honorable. We agreed on thirty dollars. Take it or leave it, missy."

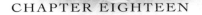

CHAPTER EIGHTEEN

aggie's legs and back ached that night when they bedded down the cattle on the other side of Carter's land. She stood in line with the others at the chuck wagon and accepted her tin plate from Shep.

"How are you doing, Miss Maggie?"

"I'm all right, Shep. I'm a little tired."

"I brought this for your biscuits, 'cause I know you're partial to it." He reached into the cupboard on the back of the wagon and brought out a small honey pot.

Maggie smiled. "Thank you, Shep. That's sweet of you. Of course, all the other ladies will want some when they see what I have."

"Up to you if you want to share."

"Of course I do. If anyone asks you for it, let them have some, won't you?" She took a step then turned back. "Oh, I thought I'd ride into town tonight. Carlotta says we can send a telegram from the hotel in Milburn."

"Going to send one to your pa?" Shep asked.

"Yes. I hate to spend the money, but I want him to know we got this far."

"I heard about the trick Carter pulled on you."

"Trick? I call it highway robbery. I was so angry at that man! And if I ever get hold of those cowboys again—"

"You really think Alex and the boys done it?"

"I think they talked him into it, yes. It was mean and spiteful."

Shep shook his head. "High spirit, them boys got."

"Boys! They're grown men, and they ought to be past doing such juvenile things. You just wait until the next time I see them. They'll regret it." Maggie's face flushed.

Shep only smiled and turned to Sarah, who had patiently waited for her beans and biscuits.

After supper, Maggie picked out a fresh horse. Sarah had offered to ride with her. As they saddled up, Rhonda came to the place where they had the remuda horses picketed.

"Maggie, would you care if I rode to town with you?"

"Not at all," Maggie said. Most of the women were too tired to do any more riding that evening, and she was surprised that Rhonda volunteered. Maggie judged they had an hour of daylight left. She hoped they could complete their errand and return quickly.

They'd gone about halfway when a horseman rode toward them from the town. They said nothing, but continued on until Sarah cried, "Tommy!" and spurred her mount toward him.

Maggie pulled up and looked at Rhonda. "What do you suppose he's doing out here?"

"I don't know, unless Sarah told him where we were headed and he wanted to see her."

Maggie frowned. She didn't want any man trouble on this

drive. She nudged her horse forward. As they approached the couple, Tommy didn't look happy. He said something to Sarah, and her smile drooped. By the time Maggie was close enough to catch her words, Sarah's mood change was complete.

"You can't tell me what to do, Tommy Drescher!"

"Oh yeah?" the handsome young cowboy said. "I guess I know whose side you're on then."

"I'm not on a side. I'm helping my friend and earning a little pocket money."

"Ha! As if your pa won't give you pocket money whenever you ask him. Some of the men need their wages. Ever think of that? You're taking a man's job for the fun of it. How do you think Leo Eagleton's kids feel about that when they go to bed hungry?"

Sarah's face colored. "Stop your nonsense. Those children are not hungry. I happen to know their mother found a temporary position to support them until their father's well again. And I can do whatever I please, so stay out of it."

"Stay out of it? Oh, no." Tommy's laugh had a sinister ring. "I'm the one fighting for a fair wage. I can't stay out of it. But I suggest you go home where you belong."

Maggie stopped her horse a few yards away, and Rhonda halted beside her. Sarah seemed to be holding her own. She rounded on Tommy now, her fist clenched around the reins. "Home where I belong? You insufferable man! Don't bother coming around to call on me ever again."

"Ha! Who said I wanted to?" Tommy kicked his horse and steered around Maggie and Rhonda, avoiding their curious stares. He loped away from the town, back toward Brady.

Maggie walked her horse over to Sarah's. "Are you all right?"

"Mad as can be, but yes. That man is despicable. Don't know what I thought was so terrific about him."

Rhonda moved in on Sarah's other side. "Well, he is rather dashing, I have to admit. Of course, he's not as handsome as my Bronc."

Maggie laughed, and Sarah swiped at the tears on her face, giving a rueful chuckle. "Papa never liked Tommy. I guess he was right, but I'll never admit that to him."

"Come on," Maggie said. "If we don't get a move on, we'll be riding back in the dark."

They loped the last mile into town. When they rode up before the hotel, they brushed the dust off their skirts and hats.

"We're a sight," Sarah said.

"That can't be helped. But I do look forward to a long, hot bath when we get to Fort Worth." Maggie straightened her clothing and headed up the steps.

No one was behind the desk in the hotel lobby. The three young women stood in the cramped, narrow room for a moment. The noise of conversation and the clink of silverware on dishes came from behind a closed door.

"The clerk must be in the dining room." Maggie walked over and pulled the door open. About a dozen people were seated at two long tables inside, eating their supper. A thin man with a large mustache glanced over at her and rose, pulling his napkin from his collar. He tossed it on his chair and hurried toward her.

"May I help you ladies?"

Maggie stepped aside and he squeezed out into the lobby.

"I'd like to send a telegram," Maggie said.

"I'm sorry. Our telegraph office closed at five. Could you come back in the morning?"

Maggie's shoulders slumped as she considered how complicated that would make their morning start with the herd. "No, it's all right. Thanks just the same."

"Wait," Sarah said. "Is your operator nearby? Is it possible he could open up for us? Miss Porter wants to get a message to her father, and it would be extremely inconvenient for her to come back tomorrow."

"Porter?" The man eyed Maggie sharply. "Are you related to Martin Porter?"

Maggie raised her chin and smiled. "Yes, he's my father."

"Well, it's irregular, but you could ask. Our operator's a female, and she lives down the street. It's a plain house just beyond the mercantile. Lives with her aunt and uncle, and they've got flowers along the path out front."

"Thank you," Maggie said.

"She doesn't like to come back to work once she's gone home," he called after them.

"Maybe we shouldn't disturb her," Maggie said as they reached the street.

"It's too bad to come all this way and not get to send your telegram," Rhonda said.

"All right, we'll walk down there and see if we see the house."

"Let's leave the horses here," Sarah suggested. "It can't be too far."

"I wonder if that mercantile is open." Rhonda peered down the street, squinting.

Dusk was falling, and Maggie looked around uneasily. A little ways ahead, a couple of men were sitting on a bench outside a house. "Maybe we should just go back."

"Oh, come on," Rhonda said. "It won't take long to ask if she'll do it for you."

One of the men stood and strode toward them. Maggie hung back. He was very tall, and though she didn't like to admit it, his dark skin and confident manner frightened her. She was about to speak when the man called gleefully, "Well, lookee here!"

"Hey!" Rhonda laughed and ran to meet him.

"Is that her husband?" Sarah asked.

Maggie peered at the grinning man, who was now lifting Rhonda in an exuberant bear hug.

"Let's hope so." Now that she thought about it, Maggie decided she'd seen him at the roundup camp the day she went out to talk to Alex and again the day the men picked up their wages. "I think it is—Bronc Tracey is his name."

"Well, come on then." Sarah strode toward the couple, and Maggie followed more slowly.

"Miss Maggie, Miss Sarah, have you met my husband?" Rhonda asked, turning to them with a big smile.

"I believe I have." Maggie held out her hand. "Hello, Mr. Tracey. This is Sarah Bradley."

"Oh, Mr. Bradley's big girl?"

Sarah's face screwed up as though she'd just bitten into a sour pickle. "That would be me. Nice to meet you."

"What are you doing out here?" Maggie asked him. The smirk on Rhonda's face told her enough—and it was no wonder she'd been so eager to ride into Milburn tonight.

"Well, I met up with Alex and a few of the boys, and we come up here together," Bronc said, almost apologetically.

"Alex?" Maggie gasped.

"Hello, ladies."

Maggie's gaze slid past Rhonda's extra-large husband and landed on Alex, who had approached quietly from the bench.

"Well, Alex Bright!" Sarah grinned at him. "How've you been? I haven't seen you since the dance at the Lazy S in February."

"Other than being unemployed, I guess I'm all right, Miss Bradley."

"Good. Why are you in Milburn, though?"

Maggie kept quiet and let Sarah do the talking, since she

was willing and, unlike Maggie, didn't seem tongue-tied.

"Oh, Bronc and I decided to see if we could get some home cooking," Alex said.

"That's right, sugar." Bronc grinned down at Rhonda. "I missed your cookin', so we come to this here boardin' house and got some supper."

"That's a long ways to ride for supper," Sarah said. "Couldn't you get anything in Brady?"

"Oh, we been out lookin' for work," Bronc said.

"Find anything?" Rhonda asked, keeping her arm around his middle.

"Not yet."

Alex shook his head. "We've asked at a few ranches. Early thinks maybe we'd have better luck up around Brownwood, so we're headed that way."

Maggie started to speak then clamped her lips together. So, they just happened to be drifting northeast at the same time as the cattle drive. Sounded fishy to her.

"Is Early Shaw with you?" Sarah asked.

"He sure is," Bronc said. "He's a good man to have with you when you're campin'."

"I always liked him." Rhonda looked around. "Where is he?"

"Oh, he and Nevada and Joe stepped down to the saloon." Bronc stopped and cast a glance at Maggie. "I beg your pardon if that's not proper to tell ladies."

Sarah laughed. "Don't be silly."

"We could get you ladies a glass of lemonade from the boardinghouse," Alex said.

"That's right." Bronc grinned at him. "That Miz Kruger, she makes fine lemonade. I'll bet she's got more of it, too."

Sarah smiled at him. "Why don't you go ask her, Mr. Tracey? We'll wait here."

"Oh, I'm Bronc," he said. "Just Bronc—no mister."

"I'll go with you." Rhonda clung to his arm, and the two started toward the side door of the boardinghouse.

"She really is an accommodating lady," Alex said. "She serves meals to lots of travelers who pass this way." He glanced cautiously in Maggie's direction. "Maybe you'd like to sit down for a minute?"

"We were going to see if we could rout out the telegraph operator for Maggie," Sarah said.

"It's getting so late." Maggie looked down the street, feeling much less inclined now to seek out the woman. "I think we'd best let her be."

Alex frowned at her. "You want to send a telegram? Nothing wrong, I hope."

She glared at him, unable to hold back her resentment. "Oh, nothing thirty dollars didn't cure. I don't suppose you know anything about the outrageous toll that sheepherder charged me?"

Alex winced. "I, uh . . . That was not my idea. I tried to talk them out of doing anything like that."

"I guess you didn't try hard enough." Maggie whirled and stalked down the street.

"Wait, Maggie!"

She heard his quick footsteps behind her. A woman poked her head out the window of a nearby house and stared at her.

"Maggie . . ."

She stopped walking and faced him. "Leave me alone, Alex. I don't want to talk to you, and I don't want to drink lemonade with you."

"I'm really sorry."

"Do you know how hard it was for me to scrape up enough cash to finance this drive? To pay off the women who helped finish the roundup?"

"Well, I . . ." He couldn't look at her.

Sarah came down the street behind Alex, looking anxiously from him to Maggie.

"How many more surprises have you set up for us?" Maggie glared at him.

"None. I promise. And if the boys suggest something, I'll put my foot down, even if it means we split up."

"That's such a comfort." She tried to wither him with one disdainful look, but he still stood there, rugged and handsome, with eyes like chocolate. She turned on her heel and hurried to the horses.

Sarah caught up with her, panting.

"What about Rhonda?"

Maggie swung into the saddle and turned toward the camp. "I'm sure Rhonda's brawny husband will see her safely home. Come on."

Sarah scrambled onto her horse and kept pace. Maggie fought to control herself. Tears threatened, and she went over and over the short interchange with Alex in her mind.

A half mile out of town, Sarah said, "You were pretty rough on Alex."

Maggie's tears broke and streamed down her face. Angry with herself, she pulled off her neckerchief and used it to wipe them away.

Sarah reached over and pulled Maggie's reins. "Whoa," she said in a low, firm voice, and both horses stopped. "Are you all right?"

Maggie sniffed and nodded. "I will be. Oh, Sarah, why did he have to side with them? If he'd just stayed on, I could have gotten through this. I'd be home with Papa right now, and he could be handling the cattle for us. How could he abandon us when we needed him most?"

Sarah hauled in a deep breath. "You haven't been exactly

open about your father's situation, have you? We girls all figure it's worse than you've let on. That day we met at your house and the doctor came—that's what decided a lot of us to do this. Maggie, Alex isn't a bad man. If he knew how deeply this would hurt you, don't you think he'd have acted differently?"

"I have no reason to think that."

Sarah looked down at her hands. "I guess we've both been disappointed in our menfolk today. I'm sorry."

"Oh, Sarah!" Maggie sobbed and leaned over to give her a hug. The horses shifted, and they drew apart. "Thanks for being so good to me."

"You're in love with Alex, aren't you?"

Maggie bit her lip. "I'm afraid I am."

Sarah gave a little laugh. "Why afraid?"

"Because I'll never have a chance with him now. Papa started to drive him away, and I've finished the job." She wiped her eyes again. "What about you and Tommy?"

"Oh, I think Tommy and I are through. I should have known from the start he wasn't the kind of man I want to marry. He was interesting, you know? Exciting. Maybe a little dangerous."

Maggie studied her friend's face. "That kind of danger we can do without."

CHAPTER NINETEEN

aggie couldn't rest after they returned to camp. Sarah made a funny tale from their encounter with Bronc and Alex, but she didn't mention seeing Tommy. Maggie took Carlotta into her confidence and revealed everything to her, including her heartbreak.

"I was crushed. He admitted it was the strikers who got Carter to cheat us. And who knows what Rhonda's telling that husband of hers! She might be giving them ideas to plague us even worse without meaning to. I shouldn't have left her there." Maggie paced back and forth near their bedrolls.

"Well, everything was quiet here," Carlotta said. "I'm sorry you didn't get to send a message home."

"Who did you put on night herd?" Maggie asked.

"Celine, Bitty, Mariah, and Helen are out there now. I figured one of us would take the midnight watch and the other the 3 a.m."

Maggie nodded, still distracted. "That's fine. I want to be

in camp when Rhonda gets back though."

Carlotta laid a hand on her sleeve. "Don't take out your anger with Alex on her."

"But she's been sending messages to Bronc somehow. Those two knew we'd be there tonight."

"That's silly. You only decided this afternoon to go into town."

"I know but . . ." Maggie frowned. "All right, but I still think she let Bronc know we'd be near Milburn. Maybe they arranged to meet, maybe not, but he wasn't more than half surprised to see her."

"I guess I can picture that. But you don't want to lose her. If you rail at Rhonda now, she might pack up and leave with Bronc. She's already crossing the picket line that her husband's a part of, so to speak. I doubt it would take much to put her squarely in their camp, cooking for those men. I mean, she's free now, and she doesn't want to—"

"What do you mean?" Maggie asked.

Carlotta's lovely dark eyes narrowed. "You mean you don't know she was born a slave?"

"Rhonda?"

"Yes. Her folks were on a cotton plantation down Victoria way."

Maggie let out a slow breath. She'd always felt rather remote from the days of slavery. The War Between the States, emancipation—it all happened so long ago. She was born the year the proclamation was written, freeing the southern slaves. Her father had hired cowboys indiscriminately, and she'd grown up with white men, blacks, and Mexicans working on the ranch as a matter of course. They'd even had a half-Kiowa for a couple of years. But she'd never thought about any of them having been enslaved in their youth.

"What about Bronc?"

Carlotta shook her head. "I don't think so. His mama came to Brady after the war with him and his two brothers. I don't know what happened to his papa. But Bronc went back and got Rhonda when they'd got a cabin and he had a job. I guess they could have been slaves before that."

Shadowy memories came to Maggie. "I met his mother once. She's dead now, isn't she?"

"Yes. One of Bronc's brothers worked for us for a long time, but he left last year. Said he was going to Utah to try his hand at prospecting. I don't know if he found anything."

"We'll have to ask Rhonda if they've heard from him." Maggie looked up at the moon, peeking from behind a wispy gray cloud. She couldn't harbor anger on such a beautiful night. "Do you want some coffee?"

"No thank you," Carlotta said. "I think I'll go and get some sleep now that you're back. I can take the midnight watch."

Maggie sat by the fireside sipping her coffee. Everyone else was either out with the herd or rolled up in their blankets. Nearly an hour passed before she heard horses approaching. They stopped near the remuda line, and she got up and walked over.

"Rhonda?" she called softly.

"It's me, Miss Maggie. Bronc brought me home."

Maggie smiled at her designation of their one-night camp as "home." She walked closer and found Rhonda holding Bronc's horse while he unsaddled hers.

"How are you communicating with your husband? I want you to tell me now."

Rhonda caught her breath. "We didn't mean any harm. The men are following the herd. When I'm on night watch, I ride out to the edge, and Bronc finds me. Well, the last two nights, that is. I'm sorry, Miss Maggie. We won't do it anymore if you don't like it."

"I *don't* like it. Maybe you should leave with Bronc, Rhonda. After what the men did today—"

"I'm sorry we made trouble for you, Miss Maggie," Bronc said.

Maggie eyed him in the moonlight. The large man looking down at her pleaded as well with his face as if he'd knelt and grasped her hand. "I didn't suppose it was your idea," she said at last.

"Nope, t'warn't mine, and t'warn't Alex's neither."

Rhonda said, "Alex wants you to know it wasn't his intention to hurt you none."

"That's right. He asked us to tell you."

"Why didn't he come himself, if he wanted to apologize?" Maggie asked.

Bronc shook his head. "I don't expect he thinks you'd listen to him, ma'am—no offense intended."

Maggie felt tears brewing and scrunched up her face. "I don't expect I would." Not being able to trust Alex hurt more than anything else right now—so long as she didn't think about her father's condition.

Bronc opened his mouth and closed it, then blurted, "The truth is, Alex and I didn't know anything about it until it was done. The other fellas went to the sheep ranch and talked Carter into doin' that, and we wasn't even there."

Maggie stared at him. "Why didn't Alex tell me that?"

"Because he's a man who sticks by his friends, that's why."

"Funny, I thought he was *my* friend." Maggie turned away so he wouldn't see the tears in her eyes.

"Please forgive me, Miss Maggie," Rhonda said. "I surely didn't know anything about what they were doing with that sheep rancher, and I believe my husband, that he didn't have any part in it. I didn't even know Bronc was going to come out here. When I left home, he said he'd be out looking for a new job."

"And so I did," Bronc put in. "But most of the ranches around Brady aren't hiring. I heard where a few of the boys were, and I caught up to them. But those fellas ain't mean-spirited. We were near to your herd, so I rode out the other night, just to see if I'd have a chance to speak to Rhonda. I found her riding night herd, and we had a nice visit, so I came back last night. Me an' the boys thought we'd look for work farther north when we get there. We truly didn't mean you no harm."

"Joe and Early said it was all in fun." Rhonda eyed her with expectation.

"Well, it wasn't fun for me having to pay so much to that sheepherder." Maggie looked at them, not sure what to say. "Look, my family's well-being depends on this drive's success. If I don't get the cattle to the buyers and sell them for a good price, the Rocking P will be in no position to hire anyone for the rest of the season." Horrified that she'd revealed information that might be used against her and her father, she said quickly, "But you mustn't tell anyone that."

Rhonda nodded soberly. "Don't you worry about us. We won't tell anybody. Will we?" She looked up at Bronc.

"No, ma'am."

Maggie nodded, her throat tight and teary. "Thank you. You mustn't tell Alex especially."

"I won't." Bronc pulled the saddle off Rhonda's horse's back. "Where you want me to put this, darlin'?"

"Just set it down. I'll take it over to the camp when I go." She turned back to Maggie. "I did tell Bronc about when we met Tommy on the road."

Maggie snapped her gaze to Bronc again. "Is Tommy riding with you?"

"No, ma'am. I didn't know he was anywhere hereabouts. There's just me and Alex and three other fellas—Early Shaw, Joe Moore, and Nevada Hatch."

Maggie nodded. She knew all of them, and a month ago she'd have said all were trustworthy employees.

"All right. Do you think you can influence them not to pull any more so-called pranks on us?"

"I'll do my best, ma'am, but I'm low man in the camp. I come in late, and I was just glad they took me in. But if Joe or any of 'em wants to cross you, I'll stand with Alex. I'm sorry I didn't before. Didn't know where the chips was going to fall."

"Alex wanted to go against them?" Maggie asked.

"Well, not sure I should say that. I mean, they *are* treating me good. I don't want no trouble with them fellas."

"Do you want me and Bronc not to see each other anymore?" Rhonda asked. "I'll do whatever you tell me."

"I don't expect we'll go all the way to Fort Worth," Bronc said. "I'm hoping to find a job."

Maggie hesitated. Now that she knew of their rendezvous, it might work to her advantage. Bronc didn't seem to mind sharing with his wife, and even with Maggie, what the other men were up to.

"I guess it's all right, so long as the men aren't using anything Bronc learns to cause us trouble."

"Oh, no, ma'am." He grinned. "I'll make sure that don't happen."

———— ★ ————

Alex paced back and forth under the cottonwoods. What kind of idiot was he to go along with these men? He'd known talking to the sheepherder was a bad idea from the moment he heard it. Yet he'd let the others convince him it was "all in good fun" so that he wouldn't interfere with their plot. It didn't seem right to throw all the blame on Joe and Nevada, though. He should have gone and tried to straighten things out with Carter before Maggie got there, no matter what the other men did to him. He'd failed Maggie, and he'd failed himself.

No "fun" that hurt Maggie was worth it. He didn't care how badly her father had treated them, this came back directly on her.

Nevada approached, lounging slowly toward him through the shadows, carrying two tin cups.

"What's got you frettin' now?"

Alex stopped walking. "Same old thing. I think maybe it's time for me to cut loose from you fellas."

"Oh? Hate to see you go." Nevada held out one of the cups and Alex realized it was his, with the blue enamel.

"Thanks."

Nevada shrugged. "Saw it by the fire and figured you wouldn't say no."

Alex held the cup to his lower lip and tested the temperature. The coffee must have been boiling when his friend poured it. He blew on it and took a cautious sip.

"Early's saying the same thing. Wants to go on up to Brownwood and put his name out there for work." Nevada sipped his coffee and turned to look back toward the fire where Joe and Early were sitting.

"What about Joe?"

"He's at loose ends, doesn't know what he wants to do."

"That kind of mood is what gets us in trouble," Alex said.

"I'm sorry what happened with Maggie, but she's a big girl. She can take it."

Alex frowned. "She shouldn't have to."

"You still thinking to go back to the Rocking P? Because I don't see that happening, for any of us."

"No, I don't either. Especially now. I'll probably keep going once we hit Brownwood. Ride up to Abilene and over to my father's place."

"Thought you hated freighting."

"I do." Alex took another swallow of coffee. "Maybe he'll let me run a few cattle on his land. There's not enough range to build a very big herd, though."

"You might be able to hire on with a ranch around Abilene."

"Maybe. When I first came to the Rocking P seven years ago, I was heading for Mason County, where I've got a cousin with a small spread. I hoped he could give me some work, but I didn't expect much, so I was glad to get on with Porter. But maybe Buck Morgan could help me now. Or I've got an uncle down near Victoria. He has a horse ranch. I could write to him and ask if he'd have a spot for me."

They stood in silence for a moment. "Mind if I ride along? If we don't find anything right off, I might hang around Abilene."

Alex hesitated only a fraction of a second, but it was too long.

"I won't make trouble for you," Nevada said. "We've been friends. If you want to go different trails now, it's all right."

"Actually, it'd be nice to keep riding with you. I just can't promise you a job or anything."

"I know that."

Alex nodded. He'd always liked Nevada, and they'd gotten along well, until the friction over the strike. Nevada occasionally went overboard at the saloon—but that wasn't likely to happen with their current financial straits. Nevada could be very charming, and he was always a solid companion in a fight.

"Let's do it then. If the others want to head out tomorrow for Brownwood and leave Maggie's herd behind—"

"You don't feel you need to see her to Fort Worth, then?" Nevada asked.

"You said it. She's a big girl. So far, she'd have been better off if we weren't here. And it's not helping us get work."

Hoofbeats approached, and Nevada jerked his head toward the trail. "Likely that's Bronc."

They walked over to where their horses grazed and met Bronc as he rode in.

"Everything all right with the missus?" Nevada asked.

Bronc swung down from the saddle. "Oh, she's right fine. Miss Maggie's none too happy with us."

Nevada let out a deep chuckle. "Can't imagine why."

"You saw her?" Alex asked.

"Sure did. She'd liked to have Rhonda leave at first."

"Really?" Alex eyed him closely. "I'm sorry about that."

"I hoped for a minute she would. Then she could come over here and tend to our vittles." Bronc chuckled, but quickly sobered. "Course, then we'd both be out of work. We'd have to go back to Brady, and she'd have to take her job back from Sela."

"We don't want that," Nevada said.

"Nope. Not if we can help it. So I was glad when Rhonda patched things up with Miss Maggie."

"We should have left them alone," Alex said. "Driving cattle's hard enough without any hijinks."

"Well, I have to agree with you, knowin' what I know now," Bronc said.

Nevada stepped closer to him. "What do you know? Something we don't?"

"I reckon. Rhonda said she learned it at the doctor's office, but she ain't supposed to tell anybody what she hears there, not even me."

"But she did anyway, on account of you being her big, handsome lout of a husband?" Nevada said.

Bronc barked out a short laugh. "Mebbe so."

Alex had heard enough shilly-shallying. "So what is it?"

"Mr. Porter," Bronc said. "He's dyin'."

CHAPTER TWENTY

*A*lex rode up a hill with Early, Nevada, Bronc, and Joe. They were nearly to Brownwood, the point where he and Nevada had tentatively agreed to leave the others. If they split up, today would be their last day to trail Maggie and the herd.

Alex tried to think of a good reason why he should stay close to her, but he couldn't. She seemed to be handling the everyday headaches that a trail boss faced, and they'd moved twelve miles or more the last two days. Maggie didn't need him to help her survive the dust and fatigue. Might as well admit it and move on.

Nevada was out in front on his big sorrel gelding, and as they broke from the trees for the last stretch to the top of the hill, where they'd be able to look down on the Rocking P herd, he held up a hand and stopped. Alex reined in Red and looked around at the others. All of them paused, waiting for a signal from Nevada. He turned and trotted back to them.

"There's three men up there on the ridge."

"What are they doing?" Alex asked.

"Watching the herd, I reckon."

"No law agin' that." Joe spat a stream of tobacco juice off into the grass.

Nevada met Alex's gaze. "I think it's Tommy Drescher. I don't know who else."

"What do you suppose he wants?" Alex frowned and looked toward the hilltop, but he couldn't see the men Nevada mentioned.

"Rhonda told me Tommy gave Miss Bradley some grief the day we saw the ladies in Milburn," Bronc said.

Alex looked over at him. "Didn't know that."

Bronc shrugged. "Slipped my mind. But he was alone when she saw him. Said he and Miss Bradley had some unpleasantness."

"Hmm." Nevada glanced behind him. "How about if you all wait here, and I walk up a little closer and see what I see?"

"All right." Alex reached to take his horse's reins.

Nevada slid down and walked stealthily up the grade to where some brush blocked their view of the top. Joe walked his horse a few yards up the trail, but Alex called him back.

"We don't want them to see us until we know what's up."

Joe shrugged and spat again.

"That Tommy always was a hothead," Early said. He fished in his shirt pocket and came out with a twist of tobacco.

They waited in silence. Alex let Red and Nevada's horse put their heads down and grab a few mouthfuls of grass.

"Gonna be hot today," Bronc said.

Alex nodded his agreement and looked up as Nevada jogged down the trail toward them.

He reached Alex and scooped up his reins. "It's Tommy and Diego and one other I'm not sure of. I think he's from the Star B." Nevada swung up into the saddle.

"Diego?" Early scratched his chin. None of them had shaved for a week or more, and Early's beard was coming in nearly all gray, in contrast to his flowing brown mustache. "How'd he hitch up with Tommy?"

"I don't know," Alex said. "He was always pretty quiet."

"Them's the ones you gotta watch," Joe said.

His logic didn't make a lot of sense to Alex, since over the last couple of years, Tommy had seemed far more volatile than the *vaquero* from Chihuahua.

"That fella from the Star B," Nevada said. "What's his name? Harris? The skinny puncher with the red hair."

"Harris?" Early snorted. "Didn't Bradley fire him a month or so ago?"

"Yeah, right before their roundup," Bronc said. "I recollect that. Said he was all the time drinkin'."

Alex considered that and looked at Nevada. "So what do you think they're up to?"

"Maybe they want to make trouble for Sarah and her pa."

"And for the Porters at the same time," Early added.

They all looked at each other.

"We've got 'em outnumbered." Immediately Alex wondered if he'd live to regret those words.

"Come on." Nevada gathered his reins. "Let's at least show ourselves. Let 'em know they're not the only ones out here."

Alex took the lead, riding quietly up the hill. The others came behind him without talking. He glimpsed the horses and ducked a little lower in the saddle. As soon as he could clearly see the three riders, he stopped Red. Tommy was drawing a rifle from his scabbard, and Diego was holding up a revolver, pointing skyward.

Nevada's horse edged up beside him.

"I believe they're fixin' to stampede the herd." Alex could scarcely believe it, but as soon as he said it, he knew it was true.

They had to stop the three men before they barreled down off the hill toward the cattle, guns drawn. He pulled his revolver and urged Red to leap forward and sensed Nevada's mount close beside them.

"Tommy!"

At Alex's shout, the three horsemen turned. Tommy Drescher's face screwed into a scowl. Alex and the four men with him loped up the slope and encircled them.

"You all best not be bothering Porter's herd," Alex said.

"And why not? Porter owes us."

"He paid you everything you agreed to work for. Do you want your job back?"

"Not at his wages."

"Then I suggest you start looking elsewhere." As he spoke, Alex kept an eye on the rifle Tommy still held against his thigh. He didn't spare a look for the others, but he knew Nevada at least would be keeping a sharp lookout on Diego and Harris.

"Did you know they got women running the drive?" Tommy's contempt hit Alex like a bucket of slop.

"What's wrong with that? We walked off the job and the boss needed punchers. Well, he found them."

Tommy laughed and shook his head. "I don't know when folks started calling gals in corsets punchers."

His friends laughed, but Alex's men remained stony-faced.

"Whyn't you put those guns away?" Nevada said quietly.

"Whyn't you put yours away?" the Star B man countered. "You're Harris, ain't you?"

The man's eyes narrowed as he looked Nevada up and down. Alex's friend made an imposing figure on his big sorrel gelding. The man was tall, muscular, and darkly handsome. Cowboys in his outfit considered him a good man to ride with, while women at the ranch socials seemed to find him fascinating.

"So?"

Alex almost laughed at Harris's response.

"So, if you three have ideas about getting something back on Jim Bradley or his daughter, think again."

The air between them almost crackled.

Diego looked to Alex. "Hey, we not gonna do nothin' to them."

"Oh?" Alex looked pointedly at his revolver. "What do you need that for?"

"Folks ride up behind you on the trail, you need to be prepared," Tommy said, not moving a muscle.

Alex lifted his hat with his left hand, swiped his brow with his cuff, and put his hat back. "Two things, Tommy. One, you're off the trail. Two, you had those guns out before you knew we were here. Now put 'em away and get out of here. If I catch you near the Porters' herd again, I'll turn you over to the law."

"We ain't doin' anything wrong," Tommy said.

"The sheriff might think otherwise when I tell him we found you watching that herd and drawing your weapons."

"That's your word against ours," Harris said.

Nevada barked out a laugh. "Whose word do you think the sheriff would take? Yours or Alex Bright's?"

Tommy gritted his teeth. "Seems to me you fellas are awfully protective of Porter's property. Is he payin' you to watch out for his little darlin'?"

"No more'n he's payin' you," Early growled.

Harris shook his head. "I warn't there, but it sounds to me like you all were too nice to Porter when you left."

"That's right." Tommy eyed Alex as if he was a manure heap. "Thanks to you, we tied everything up in a ribbon for him. We should have run those cattle off and taken all the remuda horses."

"He paid us all because we kept working," Alex said.

"Ha! Fifteen bucks don't go far." Tommy spat in the grass.

Nevada nodded toward the trail but kept his revolver steady. "You'd best be on your way now."

"Put your guns away first," Alex said.

"Hey, we don't mean any harm," Diego said, sliding his revolver into his holster.

Tommy glared at Alex but dropped the rifle into his scabbard.

"You boys had better go look for work someplace else," Nevada said.

"Me, I think I'll head down to Laredo," Diego said with a smile. "I know somebody there. Maybe I can get on with a ranch down that way."

"I hope you find something," Alex said. "I don't think any of us can plan on going back to the Rocking P."

He moved Red aside, and the three men rode between him and Bronc, toward the trail. Alex and his men sat in silence, watching them go.

"Think they'll stay away?" Joe asked as they disappeared into the trees below.

"I sure hope so." Alex put his revolver away.

"You gonna tell Maggie about this?" Nevada asked.

Alex thought about that for a minute. "If I rode into her camp to tell her to watch her back, she'd probably dress me down right fine."

"I could tell Rhonda," Bronc said. "I told her I'd see her tomorrow night, in Brownwood."

Alex came to a decision. "No, don't tell her. They've got enough to worry about."

"You stickin' with them?" Nevada asked.

Alex looked into his friend's eyes. "I know I said I'd go to Abilene with you . . ."

Nevada shook his head and holstered his gun. "No need to

explain. If you want to keep an eye on them all the way to Fort Worth, I'm with you."

"Me too," Early said.

Joe hesitated. "I really ought to be looking for work."

"Yes, you should," Alex said. "You, too, Bronc. You're married, and you'll need it."

Bronc sighed. "That woman'll probably send me packin' tomorrow, after I see her. It's s'posed to be the last time, and then I go back and look for work around Brady again. She wants to keep her job with the doctor, so I got to find somethin' close by."

"You do that. And Bronc?"

The cowboy looked at him expectantly.

"If you don't get a job by next month," Alex said, "don't be too proud to go to Maggie Porter with your hat in your hand. She knows you're a good man."

"Miss Maggie? What about her pa?" Early asked. "You just told Tommy and Diego they can't go back there. Doesn't that apply to us, too?"

Alex glanced at Bronc. He'd learned of Mr. Porter's condition in confidence, and he didn't think it was up to him to spill it. Bronc said nothing, but watched him with a wary expression.

"I just think things may be changing at the Rocking P in the future," Alex said. "You see Maggie in charge of the herd now. Well, it could be she'll take over more responsibility for the home ranch, too. I'm saying that if you don't find something else—and I hope you all do—that she might take another look at you down the road a ways."

"What about you, Alex?" Early asked.

"I dunno. I'll probably wind up with my father again, or at my uncle, Jud Morgan's ranch. But you just don't know, do you?"

Nevada smiled. "No, you never know. Boys, let's keep our

heads down and circle back behind the herd, just to make sure nobody else is tracking them. And if things look quiet, we can ride into town tonight for a drink."

"You payin'?" Bronc asked.

Nevada just laughed, and they all followed his sorrel gelding along their back trail.

———— ★ ————

The next day the men watched from a distance to see that the herd moved out in good time. Once the cattle were plodding along, Joe and Early rode into Brownwood to scout the job prospects.

An hour later, Joe came galloping back to where Alex, Bronc, and Nevada had stopped to graze their horses. Without frequent pauses, they would soon outrun the cattle drive, so they lounged in the shade of a big cottonwood. Alex had been feeling useless again, and was glad to see Joe coming, though his breakneck speed signaled that he bore news.

"What happened?" he called as Joe rode in close. Nevada stood and joined them.

"Early and me got work for the day. If you want to, you can too." Joe stopped to catch his breath.

"What kinda work?" Nevada asked.

"It's unloading freight at the feed store. It might not take all day if you three come, but he'll pay us a dollar apiece. Four wagons to unload. Big ones."

Nevada looked at Alex. "You want to?"

"I expect we'd better," Alex said. "We're all pretty nearly broke." They'd spent a bit on supplies for the trip, and Alex had contributed more than was perhaps wise toward Leo's doctor bill. "Might as well, I guess."

"Think the cowgirl brigade will be all right without us?" Nevada asked.

Alex hesitated then gave a shrug. They hadn't spotted any trouble for the last day, and even if it came along, Maggie was the most capable woman he knew.

He looked at Bronc. "You want to work?"

"Rhonda'd prob'ly like it if I did. Sure."

Remembering Tommy's actions, Alex was still reluctant to ride off out of reach of the Porters' herd.

"Tell you what," Nevada said. "I'll go work with these fellas, and you tail the herd. And I'll share the coffee I buy with my dollar with you."

"Well, I—"

"No buts. At least one of us should be close by, just in case. Joe, where's the job?"

"Right on the main street in town. Logan's feed store."

Nevada nodded. "If you need us, Alex, that's where we'll be." He and Bronc went to saddle up.

"Oh, and I saw three men from the Lazy S," Joe said. "They're headed home from their drive."

"They give you any news?" Alex asked.

"One of their old-timers said the trail was easy, compared to the old days. No Injuns, and they had decent weather. He did say they lost some cattle near Granbury. A gang cut out a hundred or so from the herd at night."

"Tell Bronc to pass that on to Rhonda tonight," Alex said. "Or if you see any of the Rocking P gals, tell them yourself."

Joe nodded. "You want us to watch for 'em in town, or would you rather we stayed out of sight?"

"Well, if Rhonda sees Bronc, she'll know we're still around. But I think Maggie would feel better if she didn't know. I mean, we promised not to interfere with their operation anymore."

Joe nodded. "Got it."

Nevada and Bronc trotted their horses over.

"Ready to ride?" Joe asked.

"Sure are," Nevada said. "Alex, we'll see you tonight."

"I'll set up camp nearer to town and have your supper ready."

"You just watch yourself."

Alex eyed Nevada soberly. His friend might not be the most cheerful companion, but he was smart. "You think Tommy will come back?"

"He might. And he's as mad at us now as he is at Porter."

CHAPTER TWENTY-ONE

*S*hep was building up his cook fire to make breakfast as Maggie and the other three women who had ridden the last night-herd shift rode into camp. Maggie unsaddled her horse and turned it out in the rope corral they'd improvised. She took her small New Testament from her saddlebag and stashed her gear outside the corral. She'd need it again in an hour.

As she ambled toward the chuck wagon, Shep waved and grinned at her. Maggie returned his salute but didn't call out to him, as some of the women still slept nearby. She found a quiet place to read for a few minutes behind the wagon and sank to the grass with her back against the front wheel. She couldn't always find time to read Scripture during her long, arduous days, but she felt more settled and confident when she could. For the past three days, she'd struggled to get through Psalm 119—the longest chapter in the Bible. If she could read one or two of the short sections this morning, she'd be satisfied.

The words of the 111th verse struck her as odd: *Thy testimonies have I taken as an heritage forever; for they are the rejoicing of my heart. I have inclined mine heart to perform thy statutes always, even unto the end.* She hadn't felt much inward rejoicing lately. With her father's health problems, their financial worries, her grief over her mother, and the grueling work of the cattle drive, she was thankful if she got through each day in one piece. Chronically short on sleep and aching from her labor, she could barely recall what joy felt like.

She leaned back against the spokes of the wheel and closed her eyes. Her father had given up hope. He'd said that if not for her . . . what? Was he desperate enough to end his life to avoid the pain ahead and the shame of debt? How could she feel anything akin to joy while she wondered if he was still alive?

Lord, this says Your testimonies are my rejoicing. I guess I always thought our families and just plain living were what brought us joy. But right now, living's worn me down. Show me how to perform Your statutes to the end. She sat still for a moment, thinking about that, and not completely sure what it meant. She supposed when David wrote it, he was expressing the hope that he would keep God's commandments all his life. Was there more to it than that?

Lord, show me what to do. Help me to pay down the bills so Papa won't be worried, and so he won't feel ashamed of being in debt. And please, could You let Papa feel better? If it's not part of Your plan for him to recover, Lord, at least let him not suffer. Please.

She lingered another minute in prayer, then rose and dusted off her skirt. As she rounded the end of the wagon, Carlotta was rolling up her blankets.

"Good morning."

Her smile lifted Maggie's heart, and she sent up another

quick prayer of thanks for the friends who gave so much to help her.

"Are you going in to Brownwood tonight?"

"I'd like to," Maggie said. "Let's see if we make a good distance today."

"If you go, I will go with you," Carlotta said. "I think my mama would like it if I sent word that we are doing so well."

"Yes, and I'd like to send Papa a telegram, too. I didn't get to do that in Milburn."

Maggie hated to spend the money, as her funds for the trip were now lower than planned, thanks to the steep toll she'd paid.

The day was as hot, dusty, and demanding as any, but they moved the cattle nearly fifteen miles and camped on a stretch of range not far from Brownwood. After a quick cleanup, Maggie, Carlotta, and Rhonda saddled fresh mounts, leaving Sarah in charge.

They rode into town and found the telegraph office still open. Maggie struggled to save words and therefore money. Finally she settled on ARRIVED BROWNWOOD ALL WELL. Not very personal but adequate.

Carlotta also sent a message to her parents. She didn't divulge what she said, but her telegram was considerably longer than Maggie's, and she paid three times as much without apparent qualms. But then, her father's ranch was not failing, and his men had probably just returned from their roundup with a huge profit in hand.

They strolled along the street, keeping an eye out for Bronc Tracey—Rhonda's tall, strapping husband would be easy to spot. When they didn't see him along the length of the main street, Carlotta said, "Come into this restaurant. I will buy supper for all."

"We can't let you do that," Maggie said.

"Why not? I would like to. Besides, I want some pie, and Shep doesn't make pies in his chuck wagon."

Rhonda laughed and eyed Carlotta cautiously. "Miss Carlotta, if you won't be hurtin' for money . . ."

"That is not a problem," Carlotta said. Maggie was very familiar with the Herrera home, and she was sure her friend made no exaggeration. "And you may call me Carlotta. 'Miss' seems very formal for trail mates."

Rhonda smiled. "All right. Thank you." She looked expectantly at Maggie.

Maggie gave a chuckle. "I give in. But you mustn't make a habit of treating us, Carlotta. We'll become quite spoiled, and I'm very thankful we have Shep."

"Oh, yes, Shep is wonderful, and he cooks fine for a cattle drive. But now and then I get this—you know—longing—for something sweeter than his flapjacks with sorghum."

"A craving," Maggie said.

"Oh, yes ma'am." Rhonda closed her eyes for a second. "Give me a slice of berry pie and I'm happy. Of course, Bronc likes it too. Feeding that man is a chore, and I tend to eat too much of it myself." She patted her stomach, which was thicker than Maggie's or Carlotta's.

Maggie just smiled, but Carlotta put an arm around Rhonda's shoulders. "My dear, you look lovely, and if it is any comfort to you, I believe you are slimming on this adventure."

"That's true," Maggie said. "I think we've all lost weight on trail rations and all-day exercise."

As they talked, Carlotta herded them toward the restaurant.

"I do hope you're right," Rhonda said. "If I can earn a few dollars and come home thinner too, Bronc will be tickled."

"Well, if Poppy Wilson gets any thinner, she'll be too light to throw a calf," Maggie said, and they all laughed.

"That girl." Carlotta shook her head. "She looks frail, but she's anything but."

They entered the dim dining room, where several long tables were set up for customers. More than half the seats were taken, but they managed to position themselves so that Rhonda had a view out one of the windows and could watch for Bronc. Maggie looked around at the other patrons. While the majority were men, a sprinkling of respectable-looking women had also come in for supper, most with male escorts. All seemed to enjoy their meal.

"The food must be good here," Carlotta said.

They ordered the fried chicken dinner and mashed potatoes all around, with plenty of wheat bread and fresh tomatoes on the side. The dishes they didn't get in camp tasted heavenly to Maggie and made her a little homesick for Dolores's kitchen.

The waitress had just brought their blackberry pie when Rhonda cried, "There's Bronc and Alex." She pushed back her chair and rose, her eyes aglitter and her dark cheeks flushed.

"Do you want to see Alex?" Carlotta asked Maggie softly.

"I most certainly do not." Maggie hated the way her heart had leaped and ricocheted when Rhonda spoke his name. "I told him to go away and stay out of our business."

Carlotta stood and said to Rhonda, "Why don't you go out and tell Bronc we're in here. If he wants to come in for some pie, that's fine—I'll buy him a piece and a cup of coffee. But we'd rather not see the rest of their bunch."

"I understand." Rhonda threw Maggie an apologetic smile and wove her way between the tables to the door.

"That man infuriates me," Maggie said as Carlotta resumed her seat.

"Bronc?"

"No, not Bronc. You know who I mean."

Carlotta smiled. "Yes, I know."

"You think it's funny. Well, I'm starting to get downright aggravated with him."

"Settle down, *chica*. Enjoy your pie."

Maggie managed to keep silent and not spew her anger, but the blackberry pie's flavor wasn't nearly as good as she'd anticipated.

A couple of minutes later, Rhonda bustled in with Bronc in tow.

Carlotta stood. "Hello, Bronc. I'll go ask the waitress to bring you some pie and coffee."

"Thank you, señorita." Bronc sat down beside Rhonda and shot Maggie a shy glance. "Evenin', Miss Maggie."

"Hello, Bronc. I do hope you and your friends aren't trying to interfere with our drive again."

He blinked at her directness. "Oh, no, ma'am. We come into town lookin' for work. I was tellin' Rhonda, Joe Moore's goin' to stay here and work for the freighter down the street, and I can stay too, if I want. We all worked for him today."

"That sounds good," Maggie said. "I'm glad you all found a way to earn some money."

"Well, I don't really want to stay here long iffen Rhonda's going back to her old job."

"I'd be crazy not to," his wife said.

Bronc nodded, but his dark eyes flicked a troubled glance her way.

Carlotta returned with the waitress close behind her, bearing a coffeepot and a plate that held a generous slice of pie.

"Mm, mm, that looks good." Bronc grinned at Carlotta. "Thank you kindly."

While they all finished their pie, Maggie thought about the Traceys' situation. She certainly didn't want the couple to separate in order to earn a living. Still, they'd never had children, so their needs were not as great as some families'.

"Bronc," she said when they were all sipping second cups of coffee, "if you want to stay here and work for two or three weeks, we could pick you up on our way back from Fort Worth."

Rhonda and Bronc both stared at her across the table.

"You'd do that?" Rhonda asked.

Maggie shrugged. "I don't blame your husband for what happened at the sheep ranch."

"Oh, no, ma'am," Bronc said quickly. "It warn't my idea."

"So you said. I'm not sure who came up with that plan," Maggie said, "but I can't release the leaders of your group from blame."

"That's not really fair of you, my dear," Carlotta said gently. "I don't suppose Alex is *that* angry with you."

"Oh, no, Alex didn't do that," Bronc said. "He was against it. But the others said it was all in fun, and they sorta talked him out of trying to do anything about it."

"That sounds more like Alex," Carlotta said, "though I might have thought he'd shame them out of such a childish stunt."

"That's why they didn't tell him until it was done, ma'am." Bronc's dark eyes met Carlotta's in a plea for understanding.

Maggie pressed her lips together and shook her head. "It still wasn't right."

"No, ma'am." Bronc lowered his chin and looked down at his coffee mug.

"But anyway," Maggie went on, "I've been thinking about the ranch. When I get back from Fort Worth, I'm going to have to hire a new crew. You're a hard worker, Bronc. If you came around the Rocking P in a month or so, there might be work for you there."

Bronc stared at her for a moment, his eyes huge, then his face split in a big grin. "Why, thank you, ma'am."

"What about Mr. Porter?" Rhonda asked.

Bronc sobered. "Yes'm. Will the boss want to take me on?"

Maggie's lip trembled, and she raised her coffee and took a sip, giving herself time to regain control. "Come around then if you still need a job, and we'll see, all right?"

"Oh, yes, ma'am." Bronc grinned at Rhonda. "See, sugar? Maybe we can keep the house after all."

"You were going to move?" Carlotta asked in surprise.

Rhonda shrugged. "Well, if he wasn't workin', we didn't know if we could pay the rent."

"You could stay in one of the cabins on the ranch," Maggie said. "It would be farther for you to go to work, though."

"If we both got jobs, it won't be no problem," Bronc said. "But we'll keep it in mind. Thank you, Miss Maggie."

She nodded, hoping she could make good on the offer. So much depended on her father's condition. More than anything, she wanted him to get well, but Dr. Vargas held out no hope of that. If her father did recover enough to run the ranch for a while, he might not want any of his former employees back. But Maggie didn't expect that to happen. If the doctor was right, she had better plan for her future without her father's guidance.

"So, where are the other men, if I may ask?" Carlotta smiled at Bronc. "Are you all in town tonight?"

"Yes'm. They're all over to the saloon. Early and Nevada said they'd stand Joe a drink, since he's leavin' 'em tomorra."

"Maybe you should be over there too," Maggie said, "if you're staying to work for the freighter with Joe."

"This here pie's better than what they got." Bronc reached for Rhonda's hand. "But if you ladies don't mind, I'd like to show Rhonda the town. They got some bigger stores than Brady, and I thought she'd like to see 'em. Of course, if you ladies want to come along, you're welcome."

Maggie smiled. "You two go ahead. I'm going to head back to camp, since I have the early shift on night herd."

"I'll go with you, Maggie." Carlotta folded her napkin and laid it on the table. "It was good to see you, Bronc."

As Maggie rose and reached for her hat, Bronc stood on the other side of the table. "Miss Maggie?"

"Yes?" She looked over at him.

His big, handsome face had a wistful air. "Ma'am, do you think you'd hire other fellas too, or was you only speakin' about me?"

Maggie hesitated. Was he asking for Joe and Alex and the others who were with him now? She was still angry at them—angry for leaving her father when he was sick and in trouble. Angry with them for making her difficult job on the drive even harder. Perhaps she was most angry because they'd found that funny. She'd thought better of Alex. Nevada and Early, too, though she'd had no expectations for Joe. Some of the other cowboys she would never hire back, with Tommy at the top of that list. On the other hand, men like Stewie and Leo and Harry had been the backbone of her father's operation. She needed men like that.

Carlotta said softly, "Sometimes it is better to have friends you know near you, even if they aren't *perfect*."

Maggie pulled in a deep breath. All she had to do to drive Alex away forever was to say it now. If she told Bronc she wouldn't hire Alex back, he would never come around the Rocking P again.

To her discomfiture, tears flooded her eyes.

"I'll consider any man for a job if he'll pledge his loyalty to the ranch—except Tommy Drescher. If you know of any more like him—troublemakers—I don't want them. But the rest, if they haven't scattered, you can tell them this: The Rocking P is going to come back. It's going to be as strong as it was five years ago. And we're going to need a good, solid bunch of cowboys."

Bronc grinned. "Yes, ma'am. I'll surely tell 'em."

Maggie nodded. "Well, give me some time first. There'll be things I'll need to take care of when I get home. But I'll expect to see you next month."

Maggie walked outside. Carlotta stopped to pay for an extra piece of pie for Bronc and hurried out to join her.

"You did fine, *querida*."

"Did I?" Maggie choked. Maybe she'd made a big mistake, opening the door to Alex and the others. "I hope I don't regret this."

"You won't." Carlotta gave her a squeeze. "Come on. You need some rest before you go on watch."

←—— ★ ——→

The men headed back to their camp later than Alex liked. What if Tommy and his friends had taken advantage of the quiet evening to make trouble for the women on the cattle drive? With three of the women in town, they could have wreaked havoc.

Before approaching their campsite in a secluded hollow, they rode to the high point they'd scouted earlier. Maggie's herd had spread out some, and they couldn't see all of it, but things looked calm. There wasn't much of a moon tonight, but a multitude of stars shone overhead, and after he'd sat for a while surveying the scene, Alex could pick out a couple of nightriders.

"Looks like they're doing fine," Early said.

"Them gals are always fine." Joe's speech was a little slurred from all the celebrating.

"Let's get you into your bedroll," Nevada told him. "Come on."

Alex let Nevada and Early take Joe down to the camp. They'd roll him up in his blankets and tend to his horse. They'd left Bronc in town with Rhonda. Alex hoped the big cowboy wouldn't stay away too late. He'd need sleep too, since he'd decided to throw in his lot with Joe and go back to work for the freighter in the morning.

Alex hated to see the small band break up, but it was probably for the best. They couldn't drift forever, and they all needed an income. The more he thought about it, the more eager he was to see his parents and his younger siblings. He'd at least go home for a visit. Pa and his partner, Tree Garza, would have a good idea of the job situation in that area. If it didn't look too promising, Alex could write to his uncle, Judson Morgan, and see if things looked better down Victoria way.

It seemed like a good plan, and Alex relaxed a little in the saddle. Maybe his family could help Nevada find a place, too. He wouldn't mind staying in touch with his friend. As to Maggie, he'd see her safely to Fort Worth, and then he'd be off.

He lifted his eyes skyward once more. *Lord, show me where You want me. I don't want to just drift.*

———— ★ ————

Beyond Granbury, Maggie's spirits buoyed. They were within reach of their goal—the stockyard. Another three or four days, and this trial would be over.

Poppy Wilson rode up beside her on the afternoon of June tenth. "We're close to Benbrook. I'd like to ride into town and send my father a telegram if you don't mind."

Maggie nodded. She'd like to send one, too, but her funds were so low, she knew she couldn't afford it until the cattle buyers paid her.

"Would you go now, so you can get there before the post office closes?"

"Sure," Poppy said. "Do you want me to ask for your mail?"

"Yes, Benbrook is one of the towns I told Papa I'd check in at."

Poppy eyed her gravely. "I can ask my folks to let your pa know we got here."

Maggie's heart leaped. "Thank you, but I wouldn't want you to spend extra money to do that."

Poppy brought her horse in closer and touched her shoulder gently. "We're all praying for your father, Maggie. You don't talk about it much, but we know you're worried about him. He kept to his bed the day we got back from the roundup, and I figured he was pretty sick. I do hope he's feeling better now."

"Thank you," Maggie choked out again. A tear slid down her cheek, and she rubbed it away. "It would be a relief to know he'd get word about us. In a few more days, I'll send him a wire myself, but right now I just can't."

Poppy nodded. "Consider it done."

Maggie supposed spending an extra dollar or two wouldn't matter as much to the banker's family as it would to most of those represented in her outfit.

"Take Mariah and Helen," Maggie said. "I don't think they've been in town this whole drive."

"Well, I thought I'd take Shep."

"Does he want to go?"

"I don't know," Poppy said with a rueful smile. "I just thought he deserved to."

"He's gone ahead to fix supper. You can ride up there and ask him if you want. If everything's ready, he could go, and we'll serve ourselves."

In the end, Shep stayed in camp.

"Tell Miss Maggie I'll cut loose when we get to Fort Worth" was the message Poppy brought her.

Poppy took Mariah Key and her cousin, Helen Branch, and headed into town. The other women pushed on for two more hours and settled the cattle for the night a mile beyond the cutoff to Benbrook.

Twilight had fallen and Maggie was riding herd, watching the stars pop out, when the three women returned to camp. Poppy rode out to her with a letter in Dolores's handwriting, but nothing from Maggie's father.

"I sent my telegram, and I decided to send another to your pa," Poppy said.

"Oh, my dear, you shouldn't have done that." Maggie was astounded at the gesture, but Poppy just laughed.

"I'm afraid I let it look like you'd sent it. Do you mind awfully? I just said, *Safe at Benbrook. Love, Maggie*."

An onslaught of tears prevented Maggie from answering. She gasped and put a hand to her mouth.

"Dear Maggie! I'm sorry, did I do wrong?" Poppy drew her horse closer to Maggie's and reached for her.

Maggie shook her head. "No. Thank you so much."

Poppy nodded, watching her closely. "Do you need to rest for a while? I'm not scheduled until midnight, but I could come on now."

"No, I'm fine." Maggie pulled off her bandanna and wiped her cheeks. "Bless you."

Poppy smiled and reached in her pocket. "Brought you this."

Puzzled, Maggie reached out for the little bag she held.

"Horehound drops," Poppy said. "I'll see you later."

She trotted away in the darkness. Maggie took two deep breaths. Poppy was a dear girl she'd need to get to know better. She opened the little bag of candy and took out one hard, sugary nugget and tucked it into her mouth. She tore open Dolores's letter and squinted in the darkness. She made out the first lines—"Your papa's holding his own, and his appetite is better." That was enough for now.

Thankful for the reassuring news, Maggie bent over, fussed with the buckle on her saddlebag, and dropped the bag of candy and her letter inside. She'd read the rest in the morning, when she didn't have tear-fogged eyes. She quickly assessed the herd's attitude—all seemed quiet. Bitty was riding the edge of the herd some distance away. All was well. Maggie urged her horse into a slow, steady walk around the grazing cattle.

A couple of hours had passed, and Maggie, Bitty, and Rhonda were due for relief on their watch. The wind blew gently but persistently across the plains, and Maggie wished she'd tied her jacket to the back of her saddle.

She met Rhonda on the edge of the herd, close to the base of a low hill. A few of the cattle had ventured up the slope, pulling grass, and she hated to drive them back down, but she'd have to soon, or they'd be over the top.

"Nice and peaceful," Rhonda called from a few yards away.

Maggie walked her horse closer. "Have you heard from Bronc?"

"No. That man better be workin' hard back in Brownwood."

"I hope he's putting some money by for you." Maggie cocked her head. She'd caught the sound of hoofbeats. "Must be the midnight watch coming."

Rhonda turned toward the increasing sound. "They're comin' awful fast."

Maggie caught her breath. She kneed her horse into a trot and rode toward the newcomers. "Slow down," she called, low but urgent.

The horses came on—four of them. They rumbled past her, and one of the riders let out a shriek. Another fired a pistol into the air, and Maggie's heart all but stopped.

It took her less than a second to collect her wits and her

horse. She whirled him back toward the herd, but the inter-lopers were already in their midst, yelling and shooting. The cattle lowed and snorted, jostling one another as they sought room to bolt.

Most of the herd headed north, but small bunches tore off and lit out for parts unknown. Maggie looked around for Bitty and Rhonda. She thought she glimpsed Rhonda, fifty yards ahead, but she wasn't sure. It might be one of the men. She brought her horse up beside a steer running on the edge of the herd and galloped past him. Their only hope was to turn the leaders and make the cattle run in a circle until they tired and slowed down. Otherwise, they'd scatter from here to Canada.

More horsemen galloped past her. How many of them were there? They'd heard rumors down the trail about rustlers, but she'd thought they were past the danger corridor.

"Yeehaw!" Another rider thundered by her, and Maggie stared after him.

She would never—even by starlight—mistake Alex Bright.

lex charged along the edge of the stampeding herd, trying to get past the bulk of the animals to the leaders. Red galloped past the terrified long-horns, eager to do the job he'd trained for.

Up ahead, a couple of riders moved along with the cattle, silhouetted in the moonlight, but Alex couldn't tell if they were trying to turn the herd or to make matters worse. Another gunshot split the air, and he knew the marauders weren't finished yet. He gritted his teeth and put his spurs to Red's ribs. If not for his anxiety, Nevada and Early would have been asleep and not available to charge down the hill to help when the Rocking P herd erupted in panic. They'd ribbed him about mother-henning Maggie, but they'd followed his lead of sleeping away the afternoon and then sitting up there with him after dark, watching the peaceful cattle below and listening to the ladies' sweet singing as they tended the herd.

As near as he could tell, three or four riders had galloped out from a stand of cottonwoods farther along the valley and wreaked this havoc. He and his friends had jumped into the saddle without a thought and zipped down the hill to aid the women. Alex had two missions clear in his mind: stop the herd from running to destruction, and then hunt down those riders.

Red poured on the speed, and they surged past the cattle. The steers only wanted to get out of there, away from the noise. In their panic, they knocked each other down, trampling those that moved too slowly.

So long as Alex stayed out of their way, he could move up on the outside of the writhing mass, but small bunches of cattle broke from the main herd and veered off to run their own course.

Red dodged among them, making progress. Alex passed one rider. He was pretty sure it was a girl, but he had no time to speak to her, or even to be sure she was safe. He squeezed Red's sides and kept moving forward.

Finally he neared the front of the herd. A few rogue animals charged ahead, and the rest strung out behind them. Alex pushed Red, asking for more effort than he'd demanded for weeks. The roan bounded forward, sensing the urgency of the task. As he did so, Alex eased off his jacket.

He thundered alongside the lead steers and flapped his jacket at them. The frightened cattle snorted and veered away from him. Alex kept at it, letting the first few run past him in a crooked path and rode in toward the next few.

"Get, you! Haw!" He waved the jacket practically under the nose of a wild-eyed longhorn. Red pivoted just in time to avoid being gored by a horn.

They weren't turning fast enough. Up ahead was a small town—less than half a mile away now, unless Alex was mistaken. If they couldn't turn the herd, it would plow through the town leaving chaos behind. Martin Porter could ill afford to pay for the damages.

Alex pushed Red up with the front-runners again and pulled his pistol. Yelling and flapping the jacket wasn't enough. He fired a shot and ran his horse toward the leaders. They turned ninety degrees. Alex looked back. Two more riders were barely visible in the darkness, on his side of the herd. If they worked with him, they might be able to push the cattle aside and turn them back toward the camp.

Lord, let those riders be on our side!

He didn't spare another thought to the identity of the other riders. Whether they were his friends, Maggie's cowgirls, or the outlaws who had started this mayhem, he had no idea. Alex held his ground, pushing the oncoming cattle around to follow the few that led them on their raucous run.

Within minutes he knew his hopes had been realized. A couple of other riders supported his efforts, turning the cattle as they came on. The stock lumbered off in a right turn toward a steep hillside. When they neared that natural barrier, they swung around more, so that the entire herd was now moving in the shape of a giant U, with the leaders pointing back toward their night camp, nearly two miles behind them.

In the distance he heard a few more gunshots. Alex hoped those were fired by cowpokes turning cattle, not by the marauders, but he couldn't leave his post to investigate.

He stayed near the farthest point they'd come, trotting Red back and forth and waving his jacket, giving any doubtful critters an incentive to turn and run the other way. By the time half the cattle had reached that point, they were trotting and lowing, instead of tearing at a flat-out run. Other riders must be guiding them farther down the valley, making them mill around, slower and slower.

The whole herd might be manageable now, though they'd probably be jumpy for the rest of the night. Alex rode in closer to start actively driving them back toward the camp.

A horse trotted up to him. "Alex!"

He turned to greet Nevada. "You all right?"

"Yup. Good job."

"Thanks. Where's Early?" Alex asked.

"He's hit."

"What do you mean?"

Nevada took his hat off and wiped his brow. "We saw those riders lightin' out for the trees, and we took after 'em."

"The ones who started the stampede?"

"The same. We think it was Tommy and his bunch."

Alex let out a deep breath and shook his head. "What happened?"

"They turned around and shot at us. As soon's I saw they'd hit Early, I left off. But I shot one of 'em out of the saddle."

Bile rose in Alex's throat. "Is Early dead?"

"Nope. Winged him. He told me to go on and help you. I left him lying by a big rock, with his six-shooter and my rifle, just in case they came around him again."

"Let's get these cattle settled and go get him."

It took them nearly an hour to help guide the herd back to the starting point. Alex saw a couple of the cowgirls and waved to them. Mariah Key, rancher John Key's sister, rode up to him and squinted at him in the moonlight.

"That you, Alex Bright?"

"Yup. We saw that you ladies were in trouble and thought we'd help."

"You didn't 'help' start this thing, did you?"

"No, but we saw it happen. Do you know where Miss Maggie is? I'd like to talk to her about it once we get the herd bedded down."

"She'll be in the thick of it," Mariah said. "If I see her, I'll tell her to speak first and shoot later, at least as far as you're concerned." She wheeled her pony and loped away.

Maggie wove her horse among the cattle, keeping her neckerchief over her face to filter out some of the dust the herd churned up. She wasn't sure how to get the animals to bed down—she didn't think she could sing right now if her life depended on it. Several bunches of cattle had charged off away from the main herd in the confusion. When daylight came, they'd have to look for them.

Carlotta trotted her horse over.

"Hey, you all right?"

"Yes." Maggie's voice croaked, and her throat felt raw. "We need to get a head count. I saw Bitty a while ago, and I think Rhonda."

"Mariah and Poppy are fine."

"Well, see who else is out here."

"We all ran for horses when we heard the gunshots," Carlotta said.

Maggie nodded grimly. "We need to make sure nobody got caught in the stampede."

"Right." Carlotta wheeled her horse away.

Most of the cattle were grazing now, but the least noise or sudden movement could send them off in a panic again. Maggie rode out to where a few had separated from the rest and gently nudged them back toward the herd.

Mariah found her a half hour later.

"Maggie, have you seen Alex?"

Maggie jerked her chin up. "He's in this?"

"Well, he's out here somewhere. I saw him an hour ago at the head of the herd, when they were still stampeding. I don't know if we could have turned them without him."

Maggie's chest tightened. Had Alex started the maelstrom so he could ride in and be the hero?

"Who else have you seen?" she asked.

"Helen, Poppy, Celine, Rhonda . . . oh, and Carlotta."

Maggie nodded, cataloguing in her head all the women. "Have you seen Sarah?"

"Not for quite a while." Mariah rode in closer. "Are you sure you're all right? You sound awful."

Maggie coughed. "It's the dust."

"Well, Alex said he wanted to talk to you after the herd calmed down."

"Oh, I'll just bet he did."

———— ★ ————

Alex rode slowly behind Nevada. They didn't dare go faster than a jog, for fear of agitating the cattle again. They came to a large boulder near the tree line, and Nevada dismounted. Alex grabbed his canteen, jumped down, and followed him to the base of the rock, where Early lay sprawled on the ground.

"How are you doing?" Alex crouched on one side of the old cowboy and Nevada knelt on the other.

"Thought you boys fergot about me."

"We'd never do that." Alex pulled the stopper from his canteen. "Here—drink some of this."

"What's in it? Warm water?"

"Well, yeah. It's all we've got."

Early took it, but he fumbled using only one hand. Alex reached to steady the canteen, and Nevada slipped an arm behind Early's neck and held him up while he drank.

"Thanks." Early pushed the canteen away and wiped his mouth with his sleeve. "I tried to get up a while ago, but everything spun around, so I stayed put."

Alex peered at his left arm. A bandanna was tied around it just below the shoulder. He couldn't tell in the darkness how much it was bleeding. "Maybe the gals have something medicinal at the chuck wagon."

Nevada leaned over Early. "Can you ride to their camp if we hoist you onto your horse?"

"Maybe."

Two horses trotted up, and Maggie and Carlotta hit the ground within yards of them.

"Who's hurt?" Maggie asked, striding closer.

Alex stood and pulled his hat off. "It's Early Shaw. One of the outlaws shot him."

"Outlaws?"

"Yes'm."

Maggie glared at him. "You expect me to believe you didn't have a hand in this?"

Alex's heart raced like a freight train. "I do."

"I told you weeks ago to leave us alone, but you followed us all this way."

Alex swallowed hard. As he'd thought, she'd set her mind and her heart against him. "It was only to make sure you'd get to the stockyards all right."

"Oh, because I'm an incompetent female?"

"No. Because we heard there were rustlers working this area earlier, and because we knew Tommy Drescher was having thoughts of harming you and your enterprise."

Maggie stood scowling at him for several seconds. "I'm not sure you're telling the truth."

"Why would he lie to you?" Nevada Hatch towered over Maggie. "You're acting like a spoiled brat. We caught Tommy and his bunch once near Brownwood, about to stampede your cattle, and we ran them off. Tonight we risked our lives to try and help you. Early got hurt defending your property. Now, if you want to treat him the way your pa treated Leo, just get on your horse and ride away. We'll take care of our own."

Alex pulled on Nevada's arm. "Take it easy."

"What, and let her wipe her feet on you?"

Alex kept one hand firmly on Nevada's arm and raised the other as a signal for him to pull back. He turned to face Maggie and squared his shoulders.

"First things first, and then we'll leave if you want us to. Did all your drovers make it?"

Carlotta stepped up beside Maggie. Silver conchos on her hatband glinted in the moonlight. "I just took a head count. We've got a few bruises, but all of our women are accounted for."

"Good. Glad to hear it. The women I saw working the herd did a good job." Alex focused his attention on Maggie again. "Now, second: We think Nevada hit one of the outlaws. We'd like to go to the next town and see if they've got a lawman. If you'd be kind enough to lend your wagon, we'd take Early and see if he can get some medical help."

Maggie cleared her throat. "I . . . Yes, of course. But Rhonda could look at him right away if you want. She's very good with nursing."

"That'd be fine. If he needs a doctor, we'll take him afterward." Alex held her gaze. "Third thing."

"Yes?"

"When it's daylight, we'll look for the man Nevada shot, and we'd be pleased to help you round up any cattle that strayed off during the stampede."

Maggie looked down. "We haven't got a count of the herd yet, but I think we're missing a couple of hundred head."

Alex nodded. "It'll take a while to find them. If you can use Nevada and me, we're at your disposal for the day." He flicked a glance at Nevada.

"That's right," his friend said. "But if you still want us out of here, we'll be gone as soon as we get Early tended to."

Alex nodded and waited for Maggie to speak. Carlotta

leaned over and whispered something in her ear.

Maggie hauled in a deep breath. "Do you swear you weren't involved in causing this trouble?"

Alex's throat tightened, and his eyes burned. He wasn't sure he could speak. "Maggie, I would never do something like that. *Never.*"

Nevada shifted, but Alex shot him a warning glance, and he remained still.

"Hey, boys," Early said plaintively, "if you all are done yammerin', how about askin' Bronc's wife if she's got any whiskey in camp? I'm feeling kinda peaked."

"I'll get her," Carlotta said and hurried to her horse.

Maggie went to Early's side and crouched down. "Early, I want to thank you, and to say I'm truly sorry this happened to you. When you get better, if you need a job, you come and find me, all right?"

"Yes, ma'am. Much obliged."

She stood and looked toward Alex and Nevada, her face white as milk and her eyes heavy. "I owe you an apology as well. Thank you very much. And we'll accept your offer to help round up the strays in the morning. Now I'll go check in with Shep and see if he can bring the buckboard up here and help you with Early."

Alex watched her mount and ride off, her head high.

"Well, now," Nevada said. "She's still got a ways to go, but that's an improvement."

"I don't blame her for thinking ill of us," Alex said. "We did plague her back at the sheep ranch, and we followed her after she said to stop."

"You *would* think that way." Nevada shook his head. "Well, you can have her, so far as I'm concerned—she's not to my taste. But that Herrera girl, now she might interest me. She's spunky. I can see myself ridin' the range with her."

By sunup, Maggie's fatigue had her slumping in the saddle. Carlotta tried to persuade her to sleep, but she couldn't do that yet. The cattle had begun to graze and seemed fairly well settled, but she wanted to keep them where they were for the day, while she and her outfit rounded up strays.

"Let's eat breakfast, and then we'll count the herd," she said.

Alex and Nevada returned an hour after dawn with a third man. Maggie and eight other women met them on horseback near the herd, where they'd just finished their tally. The others had gone to their bedrolls so they could relieve Maggie's team after noon.

Maggie rode toward Alex with her stomach fluttering. She still wasn't sure where she stood with him, or if she ought to love him as fiercely as she did. She'd acted with inexcusable rudeness last night.

"How's Early?" she asked.

"Not too bad." Alex looked tired. His new beard was coated with dust, and his eyes creased at the corners. "It's a flesh wound, like Rhonda thought. The doctor's keeping him today. We'll pick him up tomorrow, if he's able to ride."

"I'm glad."

"Oh, and Shep's bringing your wagon in. We rode on ahead." Alex looked to his left, past Nevada, to the other man. "We brought along a Ranger. He's going to look at where Nevada and Early had the dust-up with that bunch last night."

The Texas Ranger touched his hat brim. "Ma'am."

"Thanks for coming out here," Maggie said. "I asked my drovers not to go near that area."

"Did you get a count on your cattle?" Nevada asked.

"Yes. As near as I can tell, we're out about two hundred and fifty. We're heading out now to look for them." Maggie pressed her lips together. She hoped the cattle hadn't caused any damage in their rampage. All she needed was some irate landowner demanding money.

"We'll help you, as soon as we show the Ranger where it happened," Alex said. His brown eyes held her gaze for a moment, steady and true.

Maggie's tiny flame of hope flared. Maybe when she was rested she could think about Alex and what he meant to her. Right now she had to keep moving, or she'd collapse from fatigue.

He gave her a quick smile and touched his hat brim, then loped with the other men toward the rock where Early had been shot.

"All right, ladies, let's split into two groups," Maggie said. The other women clustered their horses around hers for directions.

Maggie took Sarah, Bitty, and Helen with her and put Carlotta in charge of the second group. They rode northwest, where they'd earlier found tracks leading away from the herd. They trotted along, checking in copses, behind scattered buildings, and over knolls. They'd just spotted a bunch of about forty cattle bearing the Rocking P brand when Alex loped up behind them on his red roan.

The women stopped and waited for him. "Did you find anything?" Maggie asked as he brought Red closer.

"Yeah, we did." Alex glanced at Sarah and then back at Maggie. "Tommy Drescher was lying just a few yards inside the woods. He's dead."

Sarah gasped and covered her mouth with one hand.

Maggie nudged her horse over next to Sarah's and touched her shoulder. "Why don't you go back to camp and lie down? We can get these cattle."

Sarah shook her head. "No . . . I'm . . . I'm all right."

"Sweetheart, you've been up all night, and this is a shock," Maggie said softly.

Tears streaked Sarah's dirty face. "Oh, Maggie, this is all my fault."

"Don't be silly. How could it be?"

"Tommy was furious with me. You heard him."

Maggie shook her head. "Tommy was angry with my father. It's Papa he wanted revenge on, not you."

"But he was so upset when he saw me riding with you!"

Maggie patted her shoulder. "Sarah, whatever sorrows you're having may be your fault, but my troubles are not. God put us in this situation. And do you know what He says?"

Sarah blinked through her tears and shook her head.

"He says to do our best for Him. You've been doing that. But you won't answer for Tommy's actions. He will."

Sarah drew in a shaky breath. "I know you're right, but it hurts." Her voice broke.

"Of course it does." Maggie leaned over and managed to give her a hug before their horses shifted apart. "Look, Sarah, I want you to go back to camp. Helen, will you go with her?"

Helen nodded. "Sure. Come on, Sarah. They've got a big, strong cowpuncher to help them now. Let's you and me go back."

Alex smiled without humor. "I'd be happy to assist with the cattle."

Sarah allowed Helen to guide her back toward camp. Maggie looked at Alex from beneath the brim of her Stetson. Her heart ached for Sarah, but her love for Alex was building, even when she'd neglected it. She couldn't turn him away again to prove she didn't need him. She didn't want to.

"Thank you."

Alex's eyes brightened. "No problem. Let's get these critters moving."

CHAPTER TWENTY-THREE

With Alex and Nevada helping, they were able to bring back most of the strays by midafternoon. Maggie had dark circles under her eyes, but Alex feared she wouldn't rest until they'd found every one.

"Look, you're only thirty short of your count," he told her as they left their horses on the remuda's picket line. "I think you should rest up and go on in the morning."

"Thirty head," she said bleakly, looking off toward the south. "We've looked everywhere."

"Not really. It's impossible to look everywhere. That bunch could have kept running for a long time. Cut your losses, Maggie, and be thankful it's not worse."

She sighed. "I suppose that's good advice."

Alex hesitated, but decided there wouldn't be a better moment, so he cleared his throat. "Nevada and I talked last night. If you'll let us, we'd like to go on with you and help you get them to the stockyards. You don't have to pay us."

"You'd do that?"

"Yes."

He thought she wavered, but after a moment she set her jaw firmly. "Thank you, but I can't accept."

His heart sank. "Why not? Because of the strike? I think we can officially say the strike is at an end now."

"Not because of that. These women have earned the right to bring the herd in on their own. I'd like them to be able to go back to Brady and tell their friends we did it without men." Her eyes flickered. "That's not to disparage your help last night and today. We appreciate that more than I can say, but up until now we've had a successful, all-woman drive."

Alex gave her a grudging smile. "I understand. If we come into it now, we'll ruin your reputation."

"Well, not exactly."

"What about Shep?"

"Yes, well, he's been a big help, but he hasn't driven the cattle."

"So he doesn't count."

She huffed out a breath. "Of course he counts, as far as work goes, but not as a drover. I think my girls can claim the distinction of being part of the first all-female cattle drive."

Alex laughed. She was a stubborn thing, and even with a dirt-streaked face and matted hair, she was the most attractive woman he'd ever seen.

"Have it your way. Would it upset you if we tag along—at a distance, of course? Just until we know you're safely there?"

"No, that wouldn't upset me. It might even be a comfort."

Her smile was a bit wan, but Alex felt more encouraged than he had since leaving the Porter Ranch.

"Thanks. I promise we won't interfere unless you have a crisis. But I'll be praying that doesn't happen."

Tears glistened in Maggie's eyes, but she smiled. "Tell you

what: if all goes well, we'll treat you boys to dinner in Fort Worth."

Alex's pulse picked up. She hadn't said she liked him, but at least she didn't hate him.

"Sounds good. Now why don't you get some rest? I'll take one more look around for those thirty head."

———— ★ ————→

Four nights later, Maggie's cowgirls dressed for dinner at the hotel's dining room—one of the finest restaurants in Fort Worth. They'd delivered the cattle to the stockyards the day before, and Maggie had negotiated with the hotel manager to let the women have rooms and baths while she sold the herd. Now that they'd all cleaned up and had a good night's sleep followed by a day of shopping, they were ready to head home tomorrow.

"So, your papa will be happy, you think?" Carlotta asked as she brushed Maggie's hair. They shared a room, and Maggie would have enjoyed it tremendously if she could have quit fretting about the money it cost.

"Well, the income is a little lower than we hoped for, but I think Papa and I will breathe a little easier. It will cover all the accounts we have for the ranch in Brady, and it should get us through the year, if we're careful."

Carlotta nodded. "Good. And what about the hospital?"

Maggie grimaced. "I'm going to send the sanatorium a substantial payment. But it won't wipe out the debt. It'll take at least another year to do that."

Carlotta hugged her. "I'm sorry about that, but you have done well. Did you hear back from your papa or Dolores?"

"Not yet. I sent the telegram this morning, as soon as I got paid, but I suppose it might be a while before someone takes it to the ranch."

"They'll get it."

"I'm just glad we didn't have one waiting for us here with bad news."

"Yes," Carlotta said. "Dolores would have sent one if she needed you to come home."

"Thank you. That's comforting." Maggie smiled. "And I feel a lot better since I paid you girls off."

"It was fun shopping today." Carlotta grinned. "Now help me decide—which dress should I wear? The one from home, or the new one?"

Maggie laughed. "The new one, of course. And we'd better hurry. I told Alex we'd meet him and Nevada at six."

———— ★ ————

Alex caught his breath as Maggie and Carlotta appeared on the stairway landing. This was the first time he'd seen them up close since the day after the stampede. Maggie's golden halo of hair was the perfect contrast to Carlotta's dark mane. Carlotta wore a flamboyant dress of green shiny stuff shot through with silver. Maggie's gown was much less dazzling, but the soft blue folds set off her coloring and accented her trim figure.

"Well now," Nevada murmured.

Alex chuckled. "Told you this was worth hanging around for."

They'd spent their last coins on food and hot baths, and had camped outside of town. It felt good to have shaved, but they hadn't been able to do much about their worn clothing.

"Well, don't the gals look fine?" Early said. He'd insisted on going with them, and though his arm was sore and stiff, he'd kept up with them on the trail, wearing a sling and stopping frequently to rest. Alex was glad they hadn't left him behind.

Maggie smiled broadly and descended on Early first.

"I'm so glad you're up and about. You look wonderful."

Early blushed and ducked his head. "Thank you, ma'am. You look right fine yourself."

She turned to Nevada and held out her hand. "Thank you so much for your help. I'm glad you could come tonight."

"Thanks for inviting us." Nevada looked past her to Carlotta. The darkly handsome cowboy appeared to be on his best behavior tonight, and Alex was sure Carlotta's presence had a taming effect.

"Alex." Maggie extended her hand.

He shook it, marveling at how soft her skin was after all these weeks on the trail. "That dress suits you," he said, and when her eyes flared in response, he flushed as badly as Early had.

More of the transformed cowgirls floated down the stairs in their dresses, and soon the entire party had assembled, with Shep ambling in last to join them. Maggie had apparently warned someone connected to the restaurant of the size of their group, and they were shown to two long tables pushed together. A little shuffling ensued, and Alex wound up next to Maggie, with Carlotta between him and Nevada. Early sat farther down the table, between Sarah and Mariah, who appeared to be fawning over him outrageously. To Alex's surprise, the old cowboy seemed delighted with the attention.

The roast beef dinner spoke to Alex's soul—he hadn't eaten this well in months. As the waiter brought around chocolate cake and coffee, he leaned back in his chair and grinned at Maggie.

"This is fine eating."

"Isn't it? I thought the ranch owed everyone here a celebration. And I'll bet Shep's glad he didn't have to cook it."

Alex laughed. "You know . . ." He hesitated, then reached for her hand and gave it a quick squeeze. "I'm proud as I can be of you, Maggie. And you were right—this is a momentous feat. I'm glad you ladies stuck it out."

She gave him the smile that had haunted his dreams for the last month. "Thank you. I'm not sure we'd have made it without you and your friends, but, well, we are quite a bunch, aren't we?"

"You sure are." Alex sipped his coffee and watched Maggie take a big bite of her cake. "Listen, if you can stand it, we'd like to ride home with you. Now, I'll understand if you don't want us to, but we can go along with you and maybe make the trip a little easier for you."

"Well . . ."

"Or, if you'd rather, I could ride ahead—go to the ranch to help your father until you get back. If he'll let me on the place, that is."

"Alex, thank you so much. I don't know as Papa would want you around, though."

"Maggie."

"Yes?" She looked into his eyes.

"I know about your pa." He glanced down the table to make sure no one else was listening and then leaned toward her. "I sort of accidentally found out, and I'm sorry."

"You mean—"

"I mean how bad off he is."

She laid her fork down. "Well."

"I'm very sorry. But if you wanted me to ride back there ahead of you, I could tend the stock. Shep told me there were some calves in the pasture to be taken care of. And there's the filly—"

"The palomino filly?" Maggie's eyes widened in excitement. "I've wondered about her. Who does she belong to?"

"Well, your father, I guess. Or maybe to you. He asked me last fall to train her for you to ride when you came home."

"Really? He didn't tell me. Guess I should have asked."

"Well, don't you go trying to ride her before I give her a few more lessons. She hasn't been touched for quite a while now."

Maggie smiled, and he wondered if he'd underestimated her ability. If so, she was too polite to say so. "I guess we'll have to go slowly, because of the wagons."

Alex considered that. "Well, you know, Early might drive one of them for you, if you thought you could pay him for his time. That might be easier on his arm than riding. He and Shep could take their time going home, and the rest of us could go a lot faster. We could be back in a week or less."

"Oh, I'd like that."

Alex nodded. "I'll talk to Nevada about it later and let you know."

←——— ★ ———→

Six days later, Maggie and Alex rode into the yard at the home ranch. Dolores ran out the kitchen door and had Maggie in her arms the moment she hit the ground.

"Dear little Maggie! I missed you so much!"

Maggie kissed her, laughing. "Oh, I missed you, too. It's good to be home."

Dolores stepped back and looked Alex over from head to toe. "I see you've brought a fine cowhand with you."

"Yes. Alex will be staying in the bunkhouse with Shep."

Dolores arched her eyebrows. "Well there. Welcome back, Alex."

Alex grinned. "Thanks. I'll put the horses up."

Maggie put her arm around Dolores and walked with her toward the house. "How is Papa doing?"

Dolores let out a deep sigh. "Not good. I almost sent for you three days ago, but I knew you were coming as quick as you could. The doctor was here yesterday. He doesn't think it will be long now. I'm glad you came today."

Maggie's eyes misted, and her throat tightened so badly she wasn't sure she could speak. Once they were in the kitchen, she squeezed Dolores's hand. "I'll go to him now."

"All right. He wouldn't take his medicine this morning because he wanted to be awake if you came. So you'd better give him a dose. After he sees you, he'll need to rest."

Maggie took off her hat and walked through the parlor. Maybe she ought to clean up first. The thought of her father waiting in pain pushed her to his bedroom door. Whether she was dusty or not, he'd be glad to see her. She knocked gently on his door and opened it.

Her father's form seemed longer and thinner than usual beneath the quilt. He'd lost more weight, and his face looked bony and sharp. His eyes turned toward her, and his lips twitched in a brief smile.

"Hello, sugar."

She could barely hear him. She sat on the edge of the bed and leaned down to kiss him. "I'm so glad to be home, Papa."

"How did it go?"

"Fine." She smiled. "You can stop worrying about me for a while. I'm home for good."

"How many head did you lose?" he wheezed out.

"About fifty, all told." She held her breath.

"That's not bad." He grimaced then said, "Once Jim Bradley and I lost a third of the herd going to Kansas."

"You've told me that story. Now I'm going to go clean up, but I'll give you your medicine first."

"You'll have to hire some men," he said.

"Yes, I've been thinking about that. Don't worry, Papa. We'll be fine."

His eyes flickered for a moment, but he nodded.

"I love you," Maggie said.

In the kitchen once more, she found that Dolores had heated plenty of water for her bath. "I told Alex I'd give him a couple of pots of hot water too, if he wants to bathe out in the bunkhouse. No sense putting fuel in two stoves."

"Thanks," Maggie said. "Oh, and I think we'll all eat in the kitchen tonight, if Papa can't get up."

"You, me, and Alex?" Dolores asked. "Or will Shep be here too?"

"Shep probably won't get back until late tomorrow—or maybe even the day after. We rode on ahead."

"I'm glad you did, but I miss that man. I had to put the filly out in the pasture, so I didn't have to water and feed her every day."

"I'm sorry you had to do that. We should have thought of it before we left." Maggie lifted a large kettle of hot water carefully off the stove. "Did you know that Papa picked that horse out for me?"

"I had a suspicion."

"Alex told me."

Dolores's smile went deep. "Did he, now? Bless that boy. He surely will be a good addition to this place."

———— ★ ————

After supper, Dolores shooed Maggie and Alex from the kitchen.

"Are you sure you want to talk to Papa?" Maggie stopped in the parlor and looked up at him. "I'll hire you back without telling him."

"Is that what you really want?"

"No, but . . ."

Alex lifted her chin and gazed into her blue eyes. "I'd like his approval, even though you don't need it. And he's still got a lot of wisdom when it comes to ranching. It'd be nice for both of us if we could talk things over in the evening, so long as he's able."

She nodded. "Thank you. But if he throws you out again—"

"I won't go far."

Maggie smiled.

They walked softly down the hallway, and she looked in at her father's room. Gazing over her head, Alex thought Mr. Porter was sleeping, but he turned his head toward them.

Maggie quickly stepped forward. "Papa, are you up to seeing someone?"

He frowned. "Who?"

"Alex. He brought me home, and he'd like to speak to you."

"Alex Bright?"

Maggie nodded. "I plan to hire him back, Papa. Him and some of the other men."

"They went on strike—" Her father craned his neck to look toward the doorway, where Alex stood. "Why are you here?"

Alex stepped into the room and came around where her father could see him easily. "Sir, I'd like to work for you again. I'll work hard, and I promise you I'll do what's best for Maggie."

Mr. Porter's eyelids flickered. "How do I know you won't go off and leave her when things get tough?"

"I won't, sir. I give you my word."

After a long moment, her father nodded.

"Thank you, sir." A huge weight lifted from Alex's heart, and he sent a prayer of thanks upward.

Mr. Porter lifted his hand a couple of inches from the coverlet. "Shake on it."

Alex took his hand firmly, but careful not to squeeze too hard.

Maggie bent and kissed her father's forehead. "Thank you so much, Papa. You rest now."

"Blow out the lamp," her father said.

Alex and Maggie went outside. The sun was setting over the hills to the west.

"I brought the filly up to the corral," Alex said and turned his steps that way.

"Can I ride her tomorrow?" Maggie asked.

"Maybe. Let me try her out first, all right? I know you're a good rider, but we don't know how much she's forgotten."

Maggie made a face at him. "I suppose so, but I want to be there when you saddle up."

They reached the corral and leaned on the fence. The golden filly whickered and trotted over. Maggie stroked her nose.

"You gorgeous thing. I can't wait to ride you."

Alex watched her, smiling. Much of the care she'd borne on the trail had lifted, and she looked peaceful now. He was sure she'd be even lovelier once she'd had a few days of rest. He longed to open his heart to her, and yet he wasn't sure she'd welcome that. Could he stand it if she kept him at arm's length? His timing might not be the best—he recognized that. Some folks might think he was taking advantage of her situation, seeing as her father lay on his deathbed. But Maggie shouldn't have to go through what the future held by herself. He took a deep breath. There might not be an ideal moment for quite some time.

"Maggie, if I'm not speaking out of turn, I'd like to say something."

She looked over at him, still patting the horse. "Go ahead."

"I've come to admire you greatly. You're a capable grownup woman now, and—I think you've turned out well, and you'll run the ranch well."

"Thank you, Alex." Her smile held a measure of sadness, and he turned to lean on the fence next to her, looking at the filly, his shoulder nearly touching Maggie's.

"I know it's hard times for you now. You told me most of it, I think, in Fort Worth."

"I did. And I trust you."

"Oh, I won't discuss your affairs with anybody else."

"Thanks. I still may end up having to sell the ranch." She shrugged. "I don't want to, but I have to face facts. The money we got for the cattle will get us by for a while, but, well, if I can't do the same thing next year and again the next . . ."

"All you can do is your best."

She nodded. Alex turned and put his hand up to her cheek. She hadn't put on her hat, and her hair fluttered in the breeze. He caught a lock for a moment, then let the wind take it.

"Maggie, I want to take care of you, no matter what happens. If you have to give up the ranch, I'll still be here for you."

Her eyes flared. "That's a pretty brave thing to say. You know I'm all but broke."

He chuckled. "Said to a man who hasn't got two dimes to rub together in his pocket. I expect some would say I'm after your property, but it's not like that, Maggie. I love you. I want to be with you."

She started to speak, but he cupped her chin before she could raise an objection.

"If I have to hire out as a cowpuncher on another ranch, I will, but we'll make it somehow. Just let me be with you, Maggie."

She brought her hand up to cover his for a moment, then pulled his hand down, clasping it. She turned toward the fence. The filly had lost interest and trotted to the far side of the corral.

"My dream is to keep the ranch going and rebuild what my father had," she said softly. "But I'll need a good foreman for that. Someone who can advise me on all aspects of running the ranch."

Alex's heart sank. She didn't want him as a mate, just as a workman. He released her hand and leaned heavily on the rail. "I'm sorry you feel that way, and I hope I didn't offend you."

"Not at all."

He nodded and swallowed. "Look, I'm not sure I could . . . I mean, I'd rather be your husband and live in a little cowboy's cabin than to be foreman of the biggest, finest ranch in Texas."

"So why can't you do both? Not that this is the biggest or the finest, but I think we could make a go of it here together."

Slowly he raised his gaze to meet hers. "You mean . . . "

"I mean I love you, too, Alex. I have ever since you came here. I'm sorry I didn't speak plainly. I didn't intend to make you think I don't want to marry you. I only meant I'd need a business partner as well as a husband."

He pulled her to him and kissed her. Before he could wonder if he'd overstepped the bounds, she raised her arms and hugged him around his neck, warm and comfortable, but at the same time exhilarating.

"Don't you dare leave again," she whispered.

He kissed her again, and she clung to him. The filly trotted over and nudged his elbow. Alex swatted her nose and went back to kissing Maggie.

aggie tucked the log cabin quilt her mother had stitched around her father in his armchair. "There now. If you get tired, Papa, you let me know."

"Come on, Maggie," Carlotta whispered urgently. "You need to get dressed. The guests are arriving."

"All right, I'm coming." They'd filled the parlor with every chair and bench they could find, so that the wedding guests would have ample seating. Alex had carried Maggie's father from his bedroom to the overstuffed chair so that he could take part in the ceremony.

A month had passed since the end of the cattle drive, and Maggie felt she'd aged ten years. Her father's illness had progressed until he was no longer able to get out of bed, and she or Dolores fed him his meals, if they could get him to take anything.

They'd planned a fall wedding, but it had become obvious that Papa probably wouldn't last that long, and so on July twelfth, their friends from Brady and the nearby ranches, as well as a contingent of Alex's relatives from Mason County and the Fort Chadbourne area, made their way to the Rocking P.

In her room, Maggie's bridesmaids laughed and chattered as they helped her don her wedding dress, gloves, and a new hat with a short veil. Maggie had refused to spend money on a new dress when she had several perfectly good ones, so the bride donned the blue gown she'd worn to dinner in Fort Worth at the end of the drive. It was one her cousin Iris had helped her pick out in San Francisco, and both Maggie's father and Alex were partial to it.

"Now your bouquet," Carlotta said. "Poppy, bring it here."

Maggie was a little embarrassed at having such a large wedding party. For a small wedding at home, four bridesmaids seemed excessive. But Alex had asked if the four men who'd ridden the trail with him could stand up with him, and Maggie hadn't the heart to say no to Nevada, Early, Bronc, and Joe. So there were four groomsmen to find seats for everyone in the crowded parlor, and Maggie had four doting attendants in Carlotta, Poppy, Sarah, and Mariah.

"I think Alex's cousin must be here," Mariah reported from her post near the window. "A man and woman just drove up in a buggy, and Alex's mother is out there hugging them."

Maggie smiled. "We expect his cousin Buck Morgan and his wife from Mason County. Any children in the buggy?"

"I see a boy getting out." Mariah turned away from the window. "Alex's mother is beautiful. Isn't she the one who lived with the Comanche?"

"That's right," Maggie said. She'd only met Ned and Billie Bright two days ago, when they'd come bringing Alex's youngest sister. Billie's nephew, Buck, was Alex's nearest kin geographically, and he and his family, with Billie, would represent the entire Morgan clan.

Someone knocked on the door, and Sarah hurried to open it.

"Hello," Rhonda said. "May we see Maggie?"

Sarah let her and Celine squeeze into the bedroom.

"I'm so glad you're here." Maggie gave them each a hug.

"Thank you," Rhonda said. "We thought you'd want to know that all the cowgirl outfit is here."

"All of them?" Maggie's heart swelled.

"Every last one," Celine assured her. "Hannah and Bitty and Lottie—everyone from the roundup and the drive."

"That's perfect," Maggie said, unable to stop grinning.

"Oh, and not a one of them's wearing a split skirt," Celine added, and everyone laughed.

"Leo and Sela and the children just came in," Rhonda said. "Leo's using the crutches the doctor gave him."

"Good," Maggie said. "Leo probably won't be able to go back to work for a few more months, but Alex and I decided to let them stay in their cabin. The men put a new roof on it and added two small rooms on the back. I think they're comfortable."

"That's a good thing you did," Celine said.

"Well, it was the right thing." Maggie smiled up at her. "And Celine has a very good head for figures. I may have her keep the ranch books for us. Is Dr. Vargas here yet?"

"Yes, he's sitting by your papa."

Maggie nodded in bittersweet satisfaction.

"Hold still." Carlotta reached to adjust Maggie's veil. "Are you and Alex going to make a wedding trip?"

"No, we had enough traveling during the drive. We want to stay here with Papa as long as he holds up." She blinked and looked down at her posy of wild roses. "Dr. Vargas thinks he won't live much longer."

Carlotta touched her shoulder. "I'm so sorry. It's good that you're getting married now."

Maggie nodded and cleared her throat. "We thought we might take a trip up in the hills this fall. And no tagalongs this time."

The others laughed, and Sarah said, "Carlotta, you'll have to make sure Nevada stays put and doesn't chase after them to pull pranks on them."

Carlotta smiled. "I'll see if I can keep him at our ranch for a few hours when you go away, so he can't follow."

"He spends enough time at your house now," Maggie said. "I'm afraid I'm going to lose him to the Herrera ranch."

"Well, you never know, do you?"

"Ooh, Carlotta," Poppy said. "Is there something we should know?"

Carlotta smiled but said nothing.

Another knock came, and Mariah opened the door. "Time to start." Dolores looked in at the crowded room. "What are all you ladies doing in here? Shoo, Rhonda! You too, Celine! There's a house full of handsome cowboys. Get on outa here."

A few minutes later, Maggie walked down the hallway on Carlotta's father's arm. Papa had asked his friend to take his role while he watched, since he was too weak to escort Maggie. She proudly held Señor Herrera's arm. He looked resplendent in his short black jacket with silver buttons and a silver-trimmed sash.

Her father sat where she'd left him, shrunken low in his chair, but he smiled at her. Maggie's heart lifted with the knowledge that he accepted her choice of husbands. He'd had several long talks with Alex and seemed content that Maggie and Alex could handle the ranch competently, and that Alex would take care of his daughter.

Besides the four dashing cowboys who stood in a line

beside Alex wearing their best clothes, half a dozen other men they'd hired back had cleaned up and come in for the wedding. With Alex and Shep, Maggie had a dozen solid, hardworking men to help her as she began to rebuild the ranch.

They had no organ, but Alex's mother had brought her flute. When she saw Maggie and Señor Herrera appear at the corner of the room, she began to play a lilting melody. Maggie turned toward the spot where Alex stood beside the preacher and walked slowly toward him. Alex's eyes shone with promise. When she reached him, he held out his hands to her. A quiet settled on Maggie that she hadn't known for a long time. She was ready to begin her new life with Alex at her side.

PROLOGUE

WACO, TEXAS, 1886

*Y*ou're a good son, Brooks, but your father is right."
Brooks stared at his mother, halfway stunned
that she'd sided with his pa against him. "You don't
feel I do my share of the work around here either?"

Annie Morgan winced and gazed out the parlor
window, not looking at him. She might not admit in words that
she agreed, but that tiny grimace told Brooks she did. He
ducked his head, hating the feeling of disappointing his mother.
He'd always been her favorite—her first son. He craved her
warm smile, but that was hard to be found just now. Still, he
pushed aside disturbing feelings and retrieved his charming
smile—the one his ma said could make a die-hard Texas cattle
rancher invest all his money in a herd of sheep—and squeezed
between his ma and the window.

She flicked a glance up at him, then it swerved away. "Don't try to charm me. This is all my fault. I shouldn't have coddled you so much."

His grin faltered. Now she sounded like his father talking. "You didn't coddle me."

"Yes, she did. She still does." Melissa's voice sounded from upstairs, followed by quick footsteps on the stairs.

He spun around, glaring at his bossy older sister. "Nobody asked you."

"I'm getting married soon. That means you'll be the oldest child at home." She reached the bottom of the stairs and shifted the basket of dirty clothes to her other hip, cocking her mouth up on one side. "It's time you start acting like you're sixteen instead of six."

Brooks clenched his fist. As much as he might like knocking that know-it-all look off Melissa's face, he would never hit a female.

"That's enough, Missy. Get the laundry started and then check on Phillip. I'll be out in a few minutes." Ma turned her gaze on him as Melissa—smirking—slipped out the door. Ma's brown eyes were laced with pain and something he couldn't quite decipher. "Your sister is right, but she shouldn't have said what she did. After you nearly died in that fall from the hayloft when you were four, I kept you close. Too close. Wouldn't let you out with your father to do chores anymore. I blamed him for not watching you. He warned me not to be so overprotective, but I was stubborn and wouldn't listen."

"No, Ma—"

"Let me finish." She held up one hand, palm out. "You know how much I love you, but my coddling you has made you soft. Spoiled."

Brooks winced. Never had his ma said such a thing to him, and he didn't like the uncomfortable emotions swirling around inside him because of it. She really thought he was spoiled?

"You're nearly a man now, and you need to start acting like one. Quit taunting your brother and help your father more."

"But I do—"

She closed her eyes and shook her head. "Not nearly enough." She looked deep into his eyes. "What if something happened to your father? Would you know enough to take over running the ranch?"

"Of course I could." He stated the words with vibrato, but inside, he felt less sure. Not sure at all, in fact.

"Well, I've said what needed to be said, now it's up to you. It's time you grow up, son."

Brooks stared at his mother. She'd never talked to him so firmly. So harshly. He felt betrayed by the person who loved him the most. He stomped outside, slamming the door behind him. If he'd been eleven, like Phillip, he'd probably have cried, but like his ma said, he was a man now—or almost one.

He did his share of work. Hadn't he just filled the wood box in the kitchen and hauled in a bucket of water? She had no call to lay into him like she did.

Just because he and his pa had argued after breakfast.

Because he didn't want to mend fences and shovel horse flops. He glanced at the barn, then back at the house. Maybe it would be worth cleaning the stalls to get back on his ma's good side—and maybe then she'd make some more of those oatmeal cookies with raisins and nuts that she'd baked for the first time last week. His mouth watered just thinking about them.

Blowing out a breath, he moseyed to the barn. What he'd really like to be doing right now was fishing or swimming in the pond with Sammy or visiting pretty Sally Baxter. He ambled into the barn, dragging his boots and wrinkling his nose at the smelly hay in the floor of the stalls. His pa had left the muck there just like he'd said he would.

Jester lifted his head over the side of one stall and nickered. Brooks strode over to the black gelding and stroked his nose. "Nobody understands me, boy. I'm not like Pa. He likes working hard, getting sweaty and smelly, but I don't."

The horse nodded his head, as if agreeing with him.

"Hey, you want to go for a ride?" Casting aside thoughts of work, he bridled and saddled Jester and led him out of the barn. A long, hard gallop would do them both some good.

"Just where do you think you're going?"

Brooks jerked to a halt at his pa's deep voice. "Uh . . . riding."

Pa shook his head. "No, you're not. There's work to be done. Get back in there and muck out those stalls."

Hiking his chin, Brooks glared at his pa. "Maybe I already did."

Riley Morgan stared at him with those penetrating blue eyes. "I wish you had, but I can tell by your reaction that you haven't." He shook his head, his disappointment obvious.

Brooks gritted his back teeth together. It wouldn't matter if he had cleaned the stalls, his pa wouldn't be pleased. Nothing he did made Pa happy. "I'm sorry to be such a disappointment to you."

Phillip trotted around the side of the barn. "Pa, Pa, look at the frog I caught."

Brooks glared at his little brother. How come he couldn't do stall duty? He sure had to do it when he was Phillip's age.

His pa's harsh expression softened, and he tousled Phillip's light brown hair. "That's a mighty fine frog, son. Did you finish weeding the corn like I told you?"

Nodding like a little cherub, his brother smiled. "Sure did, and I got some of the beans weeded too."

"Good job, son. Go in and show that nice frog to your ma."

"Look at my frog, Brooks." Phillip held up the common-place critter.

"Ain't nothin' special about it. Just a dumb ol' toad."

Phillip's happy expression faltered.

"Go into the house, Phillip."

The boy nodded and shuffled to the house.

Brooks's ire mounted. When was the last time his pa had told him he'd done a good job?

The smile on Pa's face faded as he spun back around. "That was a cruel thing to do. Just 'cause you're upset doesn't give you the right to talk to Phillip that way."

Brooks shrugged, feeling only a tad bit guilty.

His pa reached for Jester's reins but Brooks yanked them away and scowled, matching his father's expression.

"I want that barn cleaned out, or you can go without dinner. The Good Book says if a man doesn't work, he shouldn't eat."

"Fine. I'd rather not eat than mess with that muck."

"I guess I was wrong in giving you that gelding. A man who can't clean up after his horse doesn't deserve to have one. Give me the reins."

"Why?" Brooks backed up another step, tugging Jester along with him. The horse was his best friend.

"You stuffed yourself full of your ma's cooking this morning, but did you even give a thought to feeding your horse?"

Brooks hung his head at that comment. He'd forgotten again to feed Jester.

"Harley Jefferson came by earlier asking if I had a good riding horse for sale. I've just about decided to sell him Jester."

Brooks's eyes widened, and he felt as if he'd been gut shot. "You wouldn't."

"I don't want to, but obviously it will take something drastic to get your attention. You've got to learn to pull your weight and tend this place. It will be yours one day."

"I don't want it. Give it to Phillip since you love him so much." Brooks's frown deepened.

Pain creased his father's face, but Brooks hardened his heart against it. He was sick of being told he was no good. And he wasn't about to let his father sell his horse.

"I love you too, son, and that's why I'm working so hard to teach you to become a man. I just hope it's not too late." He shoved his hands to his hips and stared out toward the plowed field. "I joined the war when I wasn't much older than you. It's time you grow up, son."

Tears stung Brooks's eyes in spite of his resolve to not allow such sissy behavior. He was so sick of hearing how his pa had fought in the war. It wasn't his fault there was no war for him to fight in. He was sick of being bossed around. Sick of his whole family.

He threw the reins over Jester's neck and leaped into the saddle. He kicked the horse hard, causing him to lunge away from his pa's frantic attempt to grab the reins.

"Get off the horse, boy. You hear me?"

"I'm no boy. And since no one here realizes that, I'm going somewhere else where I'll be appreciated." He kicked Jester hard in the side again, and the horse squealed at the unusually harsh treatment, but he leapt forward.

"Brooks. You come back here right now. Stop!" Fast footsteps chased after him.

Sitting straighter in the saddle, Brooks ignored his pa's ranting and squeezed away the moisture in his eyes. He'd stay away a few days—maybe a week—and when he returned, everyone would be happy to see him again. And Ma would bake those oatmeal cookies to celebrate his return.

At least he hoped they would.

But he knew the truth—they would all be happier without him. All he'd ever done was cause them trouble.

He turned Jester to the west. Maybe by the time he visited every town in Texas his family would forget how much trouble he'd been and welcome him home.

And maybe Houston would get a foot of snow this winter.

A Morgan Family Series

CAPTIVE TRAIL

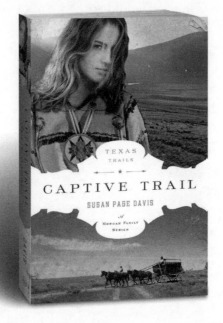

paperback 978-0-8024-0584-5   e-book 978-0-8024-7852-8

Taabe Waipu has stolen a horse meant for a dowry and is fleeing her Comanche village in Texas. While fleeing on horseback she has an accident and must complete her flight on foot. Injured and exhausted, Taabe staggers onto a road near Fort Chadbourne and collapses.

On one of his first runs through Texas, Butterfield Overland Mail Company driver Ned Bright is escorting two nuns to their mission station. They come across Taabe who is nearly dead from exposure to the sun and exhaustion. Ned carries her back with them and begins to investigate Taabe Waipu's identity.

MOODY
PUBLISHERS

MoodyPublishers.com   TexasTrailsFiction.com

A MORGAN FAMILY SERIES

THE LONG TRAIL HOME

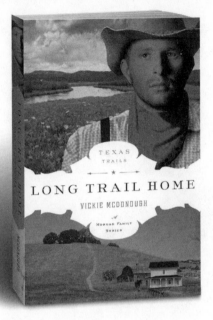

paperback 978-0-8024-0585-2   e-book 978-0-8024-7876-4

Riley Morgan returns home after fighting in the War Between the States and there is nothing he wants more than to see his parents and fiancée again. He soon learns that his parents are dead and the woman he loved is married. To get by, Riley takes a job at the Wilcox School for the blind.

At the school Riley meets a pretty blind woman named Annie, who threatens to steal his heart even as he fights to keep it hidden away. When a greedy man attempts to close the school, Riley and Annie band together to stop him and start falling in love. But Annie has kept a secret from Riley. When he learns the unwelcome truth, Riley packs his belongings and prepares to leave the school that has become his home.

MOODY
PUBLISHERS

MoodyPublishers.com   TexasTrailsFiction.com

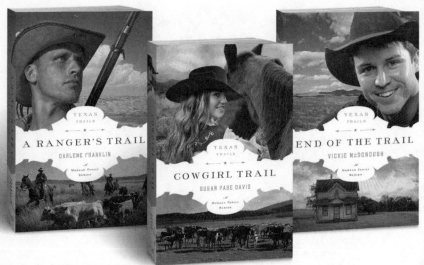